D1050120

CHEYENNE
RAIDERS

By Robert Jordan from Tom Doherty Associates

THE WHEEL OF TIME

The Eye of the World
The Great Hunt
The Dragon Reborn
The Shadow Rising
The Fires of Heaven
Lord of Chaos
A Crown of Swords
The Path of Daggers
Winter's Heart

The World of Robert Jordan's The Wheel of Time

The Conan Chronicles
The Further Chronicles of Conan

WRITING AS REAGAN O'NEAL

The Fallon Blood
The Fallon Pride
The Fallon Legacy

WRITING AS JACKSON O'REILLY

Cheyenne Raiders

A Tom Doherty Associates Book
New York

CHEYENNE RAIDERS

◇

Robert Jordan
writing as Jackson O'Reilly

This is a work of fiction. All the characters and events portrayed in this novel are either fictitious or are used fictitiously.

CHEYENNE RAIDERS

This book is printed on acid-free paper.

A Forge Book
Published by Tom Doherty Associates, LLC
175 Fifth Avenue
New York, NY 10010

www.tor.com

Forge® is a registered trademark of Tom Doherty Associates, LLC.

Book design by Amanda Dewey

Map by Ellisa Mitchell

Library of Congress Cataloging-in-Publication Data

O'Reilly, Jackson.
    Cheyenne raiders / Robert Jordan writing as Jackson O'Reilly.
        p.   cm.
    "A Tom Doherty Associates book."
    ISBN 0-312-86486-8 (hc)
    ISBN 0-312-87607-6 (pbk)
    1. Frontier and pioneer life—Missouri—Fiction. 2. Cheyenne Indians—
Fiction. 3. Missouri—Fiction. I. Title.
PS3560.O7617 C48 2000
813'.54—dc21   99-089971
                                                                    CIP

First Hardcover Edition: February 2000
First Trade Paperback Edition: June 2001

Printed in the United States of America

0 9 8 7 6 5 4 3 2 1

CHEYENNE
RAIDERS

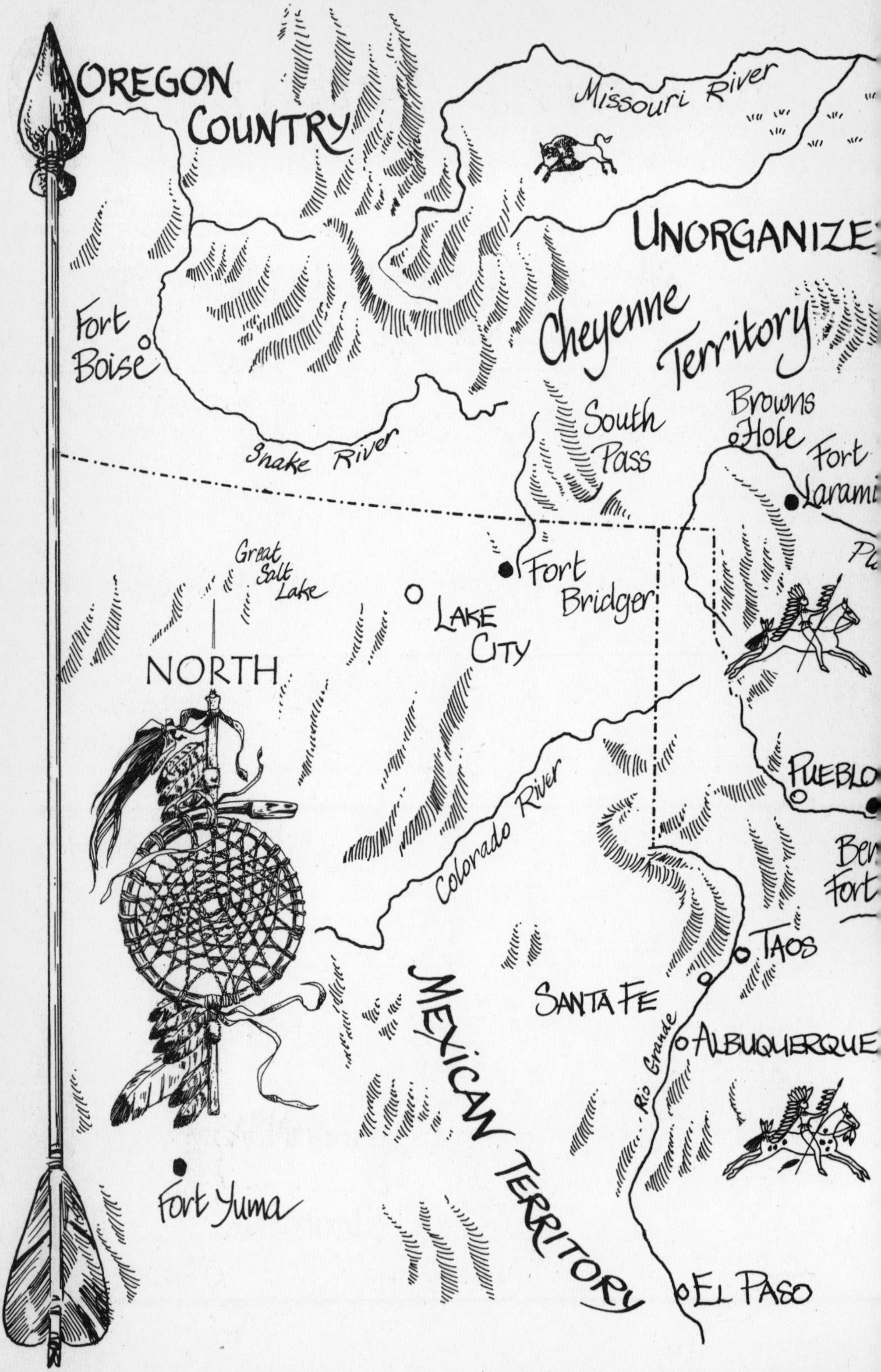
OREGON COUNTRY
Missouri River
UNORGANIZE
Cheyenne Territory
Fort Boise
South Pass
Browns Hole
Fort Larami
Snake River
Great Salt Lake
Fort Bridger
LAKE CITY
NORTH
Colorado River
PUEBLO
TAOS
SANTA FE
MEXICAN TERRITORY
Rio Grande
ALBUQUERQUE
Fort Yuma
EL PASO

1

M r. Russell," the tall, dark-haired young man called out as he turned in his saddle. "You said we'd reach the Arkansas yesterday. When will we get there?"

"Soon, pilgrim," the lean, buckskin-clad guide replied laconically.

The two riders were eight days out of Independence, Missouri, and far into the Unorganized Territory. It was nearly April of 1837, and the last remnant of the winter's winds raised swirls of yellow dust from the Great Western Desert, but tufts of grass and clumps of tiny yellow and blue flowers had already begun to dot the vast, arid expanse of flatland.

Thomas Benton McCabe turned back to the trail ahead and subsided into uncomfortable silence. Phillips Russell had the knack of making him feel foolish, as did many Westerners, despite McCabe's degree from Yale and his four years of reading law in Boston. Hunting and fishing in New England had not prepared him for the hardships of life on the Western frontier—no matter what they believed back at the Office of Indian Affairs.

He turned in the saddle to look back. His ruddy, boyish face twisted in a frown, as it did almost every time he looked at his pack mules plodding along to the tug of the lead tied to his saddle. Russell, who was going farther, had brought along only one mule, and that was another matter for frustration. Every trader in Independence had sold him something 'nobody tried the plains without,' and now he was weighted down with twice the gear he needed.

"You'll find out which stuff is worth carrying," Russell said suddenly. McCabe jerked around, but the trapper wasn't even looking at him. "You won't really believe the rest ain't any good till you see it don't work. Then you'll just toss it away. Or trade it. There's always some damned fool ready to buy anything." McCabe colored, but Russell still didn't look at him. "Things you hang on to are your Hawken, your horse, your knife, and them Paterson Colts, in that order. I don't know how good those newfangled revolving pistols will work out here in the heat and the dust and the snow and the rain, but the others will keep you alive." He grinned suddenly and looked over his shoulder at McCabe. "Most important thing to hang on to, of course, is your hair. Won't need any guns if you lose that."

"I don't expect to need them anyway. I'm coming peacefully, and you said the Cheyenne would accept me if I showed peaceful intent."

"There's others, boy," Russell snorted, pulling his fur cap farther down over his forehead. "You spend much time with the Cheyenne and you'll most likely run into Osage, Kansa, Iowa, Omaha, Pawnee, Ponca, maybe some Sioux, Crow, Blackfoot, Shoshone, Utes, Apache, Kiowa and Comanche. Quite a list, ain't it? And they'll all want to lift your hair. Especially the Kiowa and Comanche."

"But I'm just here to write a report for the government. Like dozens of other men. I have no part in Indian conflicts."

Russell laughed drily. "If Sitting Bear brings the Kiowa calling, you try telling him that. I'd be right interested to hear what he has to say."

McCabe hadn't considered that the Cheyenne's allowing him to stay might put him in danger. The wind suddenly seemed colder, and he tugged his heavy wool coat tighter.

Russell suddenly stopped and swung his horse around to face McCabe. "A man back in Independence told me you've got over a hundred pounds of seed corn on those mules," he said. "Is that true? You bringing seed corn out here? To the Cheyenne?"

"A gift," McCabe replied awkwardly. "I also brought beads, mirrors and hatchets, but I thought seed would be a more useful offering."

Russell put back his head and brayed a laugh. "McCabe, I'll be double damned if you ain't going to have a right interesting time with the Cheyenne."

McCabe's ears burned, but he kept a rein on his anger. "Mr. Russell, what I do or don't do among the Cheyenne is no concern of yours. You agreed, for forty dollars in gold, that I could accompany you as far as the Arkansas River, and that you would then put me on a trail that would lead to the Cheyenne lands. I'm getting no closer with you sitting here making noises like a jackass."

Russell became serious. "You're right where you ought to be. River's about a mile over to the south, but this is the place you want to start from." He pointed to a six-foot-high pile of rocks, on top of which a cow skull had been placed.

McCabe squinted. Near the rocks was a stand of cottonwood trees, and the glint of the sun on water.

"I haven't seen anything like that out here before," he remarked. "There seem to be some sacks pushed into the rocks." He walked his horse closer and bent down out of the saddle to reach for a leather bag.

"I wouldn't do that, McCabe."

"Why not? Is it an Indian shrine? Some religious place?"

"It ain't Indian. It's sort of like a post office. You got a letter you want mailed back East, you leave it here with a pelt or two. Anybody going from Bent's Fort to Independence or St. Louis has to pass this spot. They stop regular and pick up anything waiting here."

McCabe shook his head. "What an undependable way of doing things. Don't the letters and pelts ever get stolen?"

"I ain't never heard of anyone stealing from this cairn, McCabe. Not even the Indians. They figure it for some kind of white man's shrine. A holy place." Russell spat and licked his dry lips. "I thought you were eager to get on your way, McCabe."

"You still haven't shown me the trail."

"Well, it ain't exactly a trail the way you likely think of one. You begin at this cairn and head off that way," Russell explained, pointing.

McCabe quickly pulled out his compass and checked the direction. West-northwest.

"Well, I suppose you can use that fancy compass, but all you need to do is to keep the sun over your right shoulder in the morning and in front of your left shoulder in the afternoon. That'll fetch you up among the Cheyenne."

"Thank you, Mr. Russell." He stuffed the compass back in his pocket and shook Russell's hand.

"You take care of yourself, McCabe, and try to hang on to your hair." As he started off at a slow walk, trailing his pack mule, he called back over his shoulder, "You're going to have a right interesting time, McCabe, you and your corn."

As the trapper rode away, McCabe was struck by the chill realization that, except for Russell, there was no one else for two hundred and fifty miles but Indians. "Well," he muttered, "that's who I came to see."

The contour of the land didn't change much for the next two days, and as McCabe rode through the prairies, he wondered why the Indians there didn't farm. The fertile, black loam was better than most farm soil in New England.

Late on the second day, he was sunk deep in his thoughts about farming as he rode along when suddenly his horse shied.

He clucked at his mount, then looked around to discover the cause of the animal's alarm. There could be wolves behind one of those dips, or even a grizzly bear, though Russell had said they weren't often seen this far out of the mountains. Swallowing hard, McCabe thumbed back the hammer on his heavy Hawken rifle. It might even be some of those unfriendly Indians the trapper had spoken of, the ones who might want his scalp, he thought.

He considered what to do. If he simply rode as fast as he could, he might get away, but he would have to leave the pack mules behind. There'd be no fast riding with them, and despite Russell's admonition, he wasn't yet eager to abandon them.

Whatever the horse had shied from seemed to be in front of him and to the left. Keeping the muzzle-loading rifle pointed in that direction, Mc-Cabe rode slowly to his right and down into a shallow ground depression.

Slowly he worked his way around to his left. Every time the ground rose enough to make him visible, he kicked his horse into a trot, risking the extra noise to make his way into the next draw quickly. There were no sounds except his own, but his eyes darted warily over every bush.

Suddenly his mount started again, and he had to saw at the reins to keep it from breaking into a run. The mules stamped their feet and blew nervously. Quickly his eyes probed the low bushes clinging to the sides of the gully, his rifle following his gaze. Nothing moved, but the animals still wanted to be out of there.

Abruptly he let out an exclamation. Under a bush, where his gaze had already passed twice, was a man's hand. He climbed down and ran to pull the bush aside.

"I'll be damned," he muttered.

Underneath lay an unconscious Indian, huddled up as if he had crawled there to hide before passing out. He was easily as tall as Tom, and he wore three feathers fastened in his hair. A necklace of beads and claws hung across his bare chest. His left leg was bent unnaturally below the knee, and its leather covering was stained dark.

Quickly he picketed his animals, hacked a pit in the side of the draw with his knife, and built a small fire. Putting water on to boil, he returned to the Indian.

The man stirred slightly as McCabe cut away the bottom of the legging. A sharp point of white bone stuck through the Indian's swollen flesh. Tom was no doctor, but to him the wound looked at least a day old. He took the boiling water off the fire to cool, then cut two straight branches and dug a spare shirt out of his pack to tear up for bandages. The man groaned as Tom washed the puffed, purple flesh, but there was no use in waiting. He swiftly set the leg, pulling until the bone disappeared and gently probing the distended limb to align the broken ends. When the leg was finally splinted and bandaged, he got the man down to the fire and covered him with a blanket.

An hour later, over a plate of beans and dried beef, McCabe suddenly became aware of being watched. He filled another tin plate and held it out to the Indian, but the man's dark, unblinking eyes stayed on Tom's face.

After a minute Tom set the plate where the other could reach it if he chose.

"How is your name called?" the man said in a hoarse voice.

"You speak English!" McCabe exclaimed. "McCabe. My name is Thomas Benton McCabe.

"Mack Cabe," the other said slowly, shaking his head at the strangeness of the sound. "I am called Spotted Fox. I am a stranger to you. Maybe an enemy. Why have you helped me?"

"Your leg looked pretty bad, and there was nobody else around but me." He shifted awkwardly under the injured man's unwavering stare and wondered angrily why he should feel as if he had done something wrong.

After a minute Spotted Fox picked up the plate and began to push beans and meat into his mouth with his fingers. He talked between swallows. "Two days ago a snake frightened my pony. We fell into a draw. My leg was broken, and the pony ran away. I have crawled far, but today I could crawl no more. I sang my spirit-song and hid myself in the bush to await what would come. Then you came to help me, Mack Cabe, though you are not of my tribe. Our legends tell us that men with white skins will come and bring destruction to my people. But you helped me."

"I don't bring anyone destruction, Spotted Fox. In fact, I don't even know the name of your tribe."

"I am of the *Tsis-tsis-tas*," Spotted Fox answered proudly. "The Real People. White men call us the Cheyenne."

"This is a piece of luck," McCabe said eagerly. "I'm looking for the Cheyenne. My government wants to know about your people. My chiefs in Washington wish to befriend the chiefs of your tribe."

"Your chiefs wish to learn of us," Spotted Fox stated, "because we avoid the white man. Perhaps you wish to learn of us as the mountain lion does the deer."

"I bring no threat of harm to your people, Spotted Fox. I come in peace."

"Peace," the Indian grunted. "All white men say they come in peace. The hair-faces come and take all our beaver. They think because women of other tribes will take any man to their blankets, our women will also. They do not speak our language, not even the sign-talk, but they call us ignorant because we do not speak their tongue. They give firewater to rob a man of his brains, then trade trinkets for all of his furs. Is this your peace, Mack Cabe?"

"I don't want any furs, and I don't have any whiskey." He was uncomfortably aware of Spotted Fox's gaze on him. "I'm afraid I don't speak your language either. What's this sign-talk you mentioned?"

"It is way that men who do not speak each other's tongue may talk." He pointed at McCabe. "You." He touched his chest with his thumb. "Me. I." An index finger straight up in front of the chin. "Man." He made a sweeping motion beside his head as if to comb long hair. "Woman."

After showing McCabe a few more signs, Spotted Fox lay back with a sigh. "I am tired. Tomorrow I will show you more as we ride."

Long after the other man had fallen asleep, McCabe sat watching him. Spotted Fox had shown him the sign for lie, too: forked fingers moved in front of the mouth to represent the tongue of a snake. His lie was a small one. He did mean no harm to the Cheyenne, but he had the uncomfortable feeling Spotted Fox wouldn't understand if the whole story were told to him.

He thought back to the day when this adventure had all begun.

Washington was crowded. McCabe had just arrived from Boston. He took a room in a hotel and hurried up Pennsylvania Avenue to the grey stone building that housed the Department of War.

"I'm looking for the Office of Indian Affairs," he told a bored clerk at the reception desk. "I have an appointment with Mr. Charles Madden."

"Second floor," the man said, barely giving him a glance. "First right at the top of the stairs. You'll see the plaque on the door."

The clerk's indifference couldn't dampen McCabe's enthusiasm. He climbed the stairs and found a door with a brass plate. Inside sat a thin, bald man, his sharp nose almost touching a ledger as he wrote in crabbed handwriting.

"Mr. Madden?"

"Mr. Madden isn't here today." The bald man didn't even stop writing as he spoke."

"But I have an appointment for ten o'clock today, and it's five minutes of."

The man stopped writing with a heavy sigh. "You can't see Mr. Madden if he isn't here, now can you? Why don't you come back and try again tomorrow?"

"Will Mr. Madden be here then?"

"I don't know. Mr. Madden is a very busy man."

"But . . ."

"See here. Among other matters, there is, at present, a war being fought with the Seminole, the Republic of Texas is objecting to our resettlement of Indians west of the Mississippi, and the Utes are raising havoc on the western frontier. There are a great many problems in this office, beside which your appointment counts for very little.

"If you'll just let me explain," he persisted, taking a letter from his pocket. "This is an acceptance of my application to work for the Office of Indian Affairs. It says I am to be here at ten o'clock today to receive an assignment from Mr. Charles Madden. If Mr. Madden isn't here, perhaps someone else can help me."

The other man took the letter and perused it sourly. "Thomas Benton McCabe. That's you, eh? Yale, class of 1832. That won't do you much good with the savages. I see you're one of the special appointees. That means you'll be making a report on a Western tribe."

"That's what I was told." McCabe forced a polite smile. "Excuse me, but I didn't catch your name."

"Hart."

"I was led to believe I might be of some help in educating the primitives in the ways of the white man."

The other man had paused in the act of thumbing through a drawer of folders in his desk to stare at McCabe. "Hart," he repeated. "Mr. McCabe, you are not being sent to help or to educate anyone. You are to make a report. We need to know a great deal about these Western Indians before we deal with them."

"I understand that," McCabe said eagerly, "but they'll be much better able to live with us if they know something of our ways, something of the benefits of civilization. Agriculture, for instance. Medicine. Books. Newspapers. Look at how well the Cherokee did. They even established their own seminary for young ladies."

"The Cherokee," Hart said levelly, "have been resettled."

"You mean their lands were stolen," McCabe retorted. "It's a miscarriage of justice that I hope President Van Buren will correct."

"President-elect Van Buren will no doubt continue the policies of President Jackson. Mr. McCabe, are you certain you're, ah, cut out for the Office of Indian Affairs? You don't seem to have much of an idea about what we do here."

"I worked very hard for this appointment. I've dreamed about going among the Indians since I was a small boy."

Hart stared dourly at McCabe for a long moment, then he snorted and bent back to the files. "I think I have just the assignment for you, Mr. McCabe. What is that tribe called? Chien. No, that's French for dog. Ah, here it is." He pulled out a slim folder. "The Cheyenne, Mr. McCabe. Small tribe in the Unorganized Territory. We'll want to know their customs, their strength in numbers, and anything else you can find out. Pay is ten dollars a month, half now, half when I get the report."

"I'm sure I can send you regular reports on my progress, if you like. . . ."

"Don't bother me with mail, Mr. McCabe. I have enough clutter around this office. Just send me the whole report when it's finished."

After copying the information in the folder—there was little more than that the Cheyenne were nomadic hunters who lived between the Mississippi and the Rocky Mountains—McCabe returned to the hotel. The desk clerk gave him a sly wink as he handed him his key.

"There's a lady waiting to see you, Mr. McCabe. In that small waiting room to the left, there."

McCabe took his key with a frown and walked across the lobby. Who could it be? He wondered. As he entered the room, a diminutive brunette arose with a grim look.

"Isobel!" he exclaimed. "What are you doing in Washington?"

"I came after you," she replied shrilly. Isobel Grantham was a pretty woman, but for the first time he saw how quickly a shrewish look could mar her delicate features. "What do you mean with this nonsense?"

"It's not nonsense, Isobel. And you still haven't told me what you're doing here."

"When I heard about this insane thing you've done, I managed to invent an invitation from Helen Armstrong. I arrived this morning. It wasn't hard to find where you were staying. Your father told me. He also told me he's promised to disinherit you if you go through with this.

He looked down and sighed heavily.

Isobel's face tightened angrily. "Thomas McCabe, what you're doing is an insult to me and to yourself. We've been betrothed since we were practically children. Now I find you're about to run off to some godforsaken wilderness with only a note to tell me you were going."

"There was no time for more," he drawled lamely. "I tried to find you before I left, but . . . for heaven's sake, Isobel. You know how much I want to do this, how much I've always wanted to. And you knew I was waiting to hear from the Office of Indian Affairs. I would have come back to say good-bye. . . ."

"I know only that you've always been a fool over these Indians. I remember when you were a little boy, you talked about becoming a missionary, just so you could go out among those savages. Then it was an army officer, and then an explorer. You're almost twenty-five, Thomas. In another year you'll enter the bar, and we can get married."

"This won't stop me from entering the bar. It just means putting it off for a year or two. Listen to me. I'm going among a people called the Cheyenne, nomads who have no written language and no agriculture. I'll take seed corn with me and I'll show them how to plant it. I'll show them how to build houses so they can stop their life of wandering. By the time government finally reaches them, they'll be farmers, settled farmers, and they won't end up like the Cherokee—chased off their land because people think they're savages. If I can give them only that much, it'll be enough."

"Be damned to the Cheyenne," she spat.

"Isobel," he gasped.

"And be damned to you and your corn!" Her face twisted in rage, and an edge of hysteria rose in her voice as she spoke. "How long do you expect me to wait? I've passed up other offers, you know. Henry Campbell asked me to marry him, and I turned him down, even though he's going to be a doctor. I'm twenty-two, Thomas. Twenty-two. I've waited four years for you to finish all this silly reading in your father's office. In another year you'd have been a lawyer. Instead you go scurrying off to God knows where. Damn all Indians!"

"You seem to have spent a lot of time thinking about my profession," he noted coolly. "I begin to wonder if it's me you want to marry, or just any lawyer."

"How dare you!" she shrieked. He glanced worriedly at the door. "I thought you'd settle down, Thomas, but now I see you're little better than a light-footed wanderer."

"Perhaps you'd better marry Henry Campbell, then."

"I will," she hissed. "And if the Indians don't scalp you, you can attend the wedding."

As soon as she stalked out, he was filled with a wonderful sense of freedom. She had always been so soft and sweet. Discovering how shrewish she could be had loosed him from the last bond that might have held him back.

The next day he left for St. Louis and the West, feeling for the first time in his life completely unfettered. There was nothing and no one back East left to worry about.

2

The Cheyenne camp was a circle of lodge-tepees set over a mile and a half around. Some were painted with animals; many were left plain white. Smoke rose all around from breakfast fires. The wind carried the acrid smell of smoke, leather, horses and cooking food. By every lodge a horse was tethered. A score of women, blankets wrapped around their shoulders, plodded toward the camp, carrying bundles of firewood on their backs. Others scraped stretched hides staked in the center of the camp. Boys ran among them, wrestling and rolling hoops while a knot of squealing girls playfully kicked a ball in a circle around the workers.

McCabe rode toward the opening in the circle with Spotted Fox mounted behind him. He wiped his sweating palms on the front of his coat. He was certain they'd accept his peaceful intent. After all, Spotted Fox was there to vouch for him. But even the Indian wasn't certain his people would allow a white man to remain with them.

Well, even if they would make me go, they'd at least let me go in peace, McCabe thought. Wouldn't they? He wiped his hands again.

The children stopped their play to stare as McCabe rode into the camp, and even a few women became so curious that they looked up from their tasks. But all bent back to their work as soon as they had seen what was causing the disturbance—all except one.

McCabe found himself looking straight into her eyes. Large dark eyes, they were. A fawn's eyes. She was beautiful, with a delicate heart-shaped face, high cheekbones, deep copper skin, and long, lustrous black hair. For a moment she returned his gaze, then abruptly seemed to realize what she was doing and instantly began scraping at the hide stretched on the ground in front of her.

McCabe's mouth went dry as he suddenly realized other riders were cantering along beside him. A dozen mounted men had appeared, long-haired and bare-chested, and like Spotted Fox, all were over six feet tall. Each man rode easily on a saddle blanket, and each gripped a lance in his fist.

Abruptly, Spotted Fox touched McCabe's arm and hissed, "Stop."

A leathery-skinned man with grey-streaked hair and a commanding look came out of a lodge that stood ahead of them. He was tall, even when compared to the men McCabe had seen so far, and he wore a deerskin shirt, colorfully worked with porcupine quills, and had a red blanket wrapped around his shoulders. In the crook of his arm he carried a coup stick, lined along its length with feathers.

"This is High-backed Wolf," Spotted Fox murmured. "Do as I do, but do not speak unless I tell you." Before McCabe could speak, Spotted Fox slipped from the horse and hobbled forward, talking so quickly that Mc-Cabe couldn't pick out a word. There was nothing to do but to dismount and wait.

He caught the words "Mack Cabe" as he walked up, but he still couldn't understand the rest. Spotted Fox gesticulated broadly as he spoke. High-backed Wolf nodded as he listened, occasionally eyeing Mc-Cabe. Other men gathered around as well. McCabe swallowed and tried to look unconcerned.

"Sit, Mack Cabe," Spotted Fox said, dropping awkwardly to the ground. High-backed Wolf sat cross-legged, facing the newcomer.

McCabe hesitated before complying. The stares of the other warriors made him uneasy. Finally he sat next to Spotted Fox. He wished his Hawken were in his hands rather than in its buckskin sheath on his saddle. For a moment he had some comfort at the thought of the Paterson Colts in his belt, but that comfort evaporated as he realized that if they wanted him dead, they could kill him long before he had one of the pistols in his hand.

A plump woman darted up to hand High-backed Wolf a long pouch. He drew out a pipe with a stone bowl and filled it from another smaller pouch. Sprinkling a fine powder atop the tobacco, he took a burning splinter from the woman and lit the pipe. McCabe started as the powder flared and crackled.

"What was that?" he asked Spotted Fox softly. "The powder, I mean."

"Powdered buffalo dung. To ensure a good light."

McCabe grimaced as he watched the older Cheyenne draw smoke deep into his lungs. Buffalo dung, for God's sake.

High-backed Wolf lifted the pipe to the sky, then touched it to the ground. He took another puff and passed it to Spotted Fox, who repeated the gestures of presenting the pipe to the sky and the earth before taking a deep draw. Then he held the pipe out to McCabe.

McCabe simply stared at it. Buffalo dung, he thought again. He had to take it. His momentary hesitation had already raised murmurs behind him, so he accepted the pipe and slowly repeated the others' moves. Grimly, he clenched his teeth around the stem and drew. There was the taste of tobacco, and another taste, sweet, but mixed with an acrid bite. All he could think of was buffalo dung. Somehow he managed to keep from gagging, exhaled and passed the pipe back to High-backed Wolf. He hoped he didn't look as green around the edges as he felt.

Neither of the other two seemed to notice his shakiness. They fell to talking again, once more too rapidly for him to catch any more than an occasional "Mack Cabe."

Finally High-backed Wolf held up his hand. "Mack Cabe," he pronounced in clear English, "I am called High-backed Wolf. I am a principal chief of the Cheyenne. I speak your language."

"I am honored, sir," McCabe returned, managing a sitting bow, which brought amused murmurs and a few titters from the onlookers.

"Spotted Fox tells me that you have saved his life."

"I helped him," McCabe admitted. The chief seemed to be waiting for something else, as did Spotted Fox. When it didn't come, both looked disappointed.

"Spotted Fox says to me that you wish to learn the ways of the Cheyenne," the chief said finally.

"That's right, sir. President Martin Van Buren, the chief of my people has asked me to come and learn your ways so that I may teach them to him. At the same time, I'll be happy to tell you about my people and to show you some of our ways."

The watching braves had listened quietly, but now a tall, broad-shouldered warrior, whose clothes were almost as resplendent as the chief's, stepped out of the crowd and glowered at McCabe arrogantly. A scar ran from under his long black hair down the right side of his swarthy face to his chin. "I am Grey Bear," he growled. "We want no white man here. No white man's ways. Go away or die!"

High-backed Wolf barked angrily in Cheyenne, and Grey Bear replied in kind, shaking his fist toward McCabe. But the chief, gesturing forcefully, ordered Grey Bear to keep silent. With a wordless snarl Grey Bear turned and strode away. Then a slender, handsome young man, and another warrior so heavily muscled that he seemed to be squatting, stalked after him. They were followed by a large group of thirty or more warriors.

"What's happening?" McCabe asked Spotted Fox.

Spotted Fox shook his head and motioned for quiet. Then High-backed Wolf, spreading his arms wide, addressed the rest of the crowd. Several times he gestured angrily toward the retreating warriors, and twice he pointed at McCabe. Abruptly, without another word, he folded his blanket around himself and disappeared into his tall, buffalo-hide tepee. The onlookers began to break up. Spotted Fox pulled McCabe to his feet and began to lead him across the camp.

"Spotted Fox, may I stay, or not?"

"You stay, Mac Cabe," Spotted Fox replied gravely, and McCabe let out a whoop that pulled heads around once more. "High-backed Wolf has said that you are his guest among us. A lodge will be made for you next to mine. I will help you learn about my people."

"I'm grateful to you and your chief."

Spotted Fox shook his head. "Many do not wish you to stay."

McCabe realized that some of the men who had followed Grey Bear were still watching from the line of lodges. "Why did Grey Bear and those others get so angry about my staying?"

"He is a Bow String, Mack Cabe. So were many who followed him. The slender youth who followed first was Otter Belt, his friend. The warrior with the large arms was Three Hatchets, Grey Bear's brother. The Bow Strings, and many others, believe the ancient legend that the doom of our people will come from strangers with pale skins and pale eyes?"

"But I mean no harm to your people. I want only good for the Cheyenne."

Spotted Fox looked at him flatly, then nodded. "I know only that you saved my life."

"Who are these Bow Strings, Spotted Fox? Is it the name of another tribe?"

"It is one of the six societies. The Bow Strings, the Fox Soldiers, the Elk Soldiers, the Red Shields, the Dog Soldiers and the Crazy Dogs. Do not worry, though. They will not hurt you. You are High-backed Wolf's guest."

McCabe looked toward where the watchers had been, but they were gone. Once more, though he found himself staring into the eyes of the same girl. She stared back as if mesmerized. "Spotted Fox, who's that girl?"

Spotted Fox looked at him sharply. "That is Night Bird Woman, the daughter of Elk Antler. Mack Cabe, remember what I have said. Our women are not as those of the Dakota or the Blackfoot. Our women have no man before their husband."

"I mean no disrespect, Spotted Fox. But she is a beautiful woman."

"Yes, she is," Spotted Fox grinned. "But she will be Three Hatchets' woman. Come to my lodge, and we will eat."

The buffalo-hide lodge was some fifteen feet in diameter and about as high. The outside was painted with pictographs. McCabe pointed to a red handprint. Several were scattered around the tent.

"What's that mean?"

"It stands for an enemy killed in hand-to-hand fighting," Spotted Fox answered proudly. "That one was a Crow, near their camp above the Black Hills, along the River of the Greasy Grass. Mack Cabe, why did you not tell of saving my life? It was a thing of honor, like the killing of the Crow. High-backed Wolf waited to hear of it."

"But you'd already told him. Anything I said would just be bragging."

Spotted Fox stared at him incredulously. "Bragging is when the hair-faces tell big lies. To tell what you have done is simply to tell what you have done. It was your . . ." he searched for the right word, ". . . your privilege, your right to tell it."

McCabe was about to say something about proper modesty when a boy suddenly erupted from the tepee with a shout. When he saw McCabe, he skidded to a halt, wide-eyed. Spotted Fox spoke to him sharply in Cheyenne. Then the boy nodded and darted away at full speed.

"That is Short Bull," Spotted Fox told him. "I have sent him to bring me another horse to tether at my lodge."

"He's your son? Or younger brother?"

"He is an orphan, Mack Cabe. An orphan is sent to live in a lodge until he becomes a man. They tend horses or fetch water, and in return are given food, shelter, and teaching."

Thinking of the bleak orphans' homes in Boston, McCabe shook his head. "It's a better way than ours."

"Come into my lodge. We will eat."

Spotted Fox ducked through the low opening into the tepee, and McCabe followed. A bubbling pot of stew was suspended over a fire pit in the center of the lodge, and various bags and bundles were stored around the edges. A round leather shield hung from one of the lodgepoles. From another hung a bundle of what at first seemed to be furs, but McCabe's jaw dropped as he realized it was a bundle of scalps. Somehow he remembered that he had been told to move to the right of the entrance and to wait.

Spotted Fox, who had gone immediately to a place facing the door, smiled. "You remember well. Sit beside me, Mack Cabe. Eat, and we will talk."

Tearing his eyes away from the bundle of human hair, McCabe sat cross-legged at Spotted Fox's left. The heavy smell of buffalo hide mixed with the smell of grease. He swallowed heavily as he took the bowl of stew the other man handed him.

"Spotted Fox," he said, gesturing with the horn spoon, "have your people ever thought of *growing* some of their food?"

Spotted Fox dismissed the idea with a shake of his head. "We do not plant. Now you must listen to me, Mack Cabe. High-backed Wolf has said you may stay, so you may. But a chief of the Cheyenne, even a principal chief of the Council of Chiefs such as he, leads only because what he says is thought to be good. He can command no man who does not respect his word."

"But you said I didn't have to worry. I'm High-backed Wolf's guest."

"No one will try to kill you, or openly force you to go. But the Bow Strings, especially Grey Bear, may try to shame you into leaving of your own will, or try to catch you violating some custom so even the chief will not be able to protect you. High-backed Wolf is a great warrior. These men do not want to bring his anger down on themselves, but that does not mean they will accept you just because he has said they should."

"But what can I do?"

"Be careful. Always."

Before McCabe could question him further, a woman's voice called from outside, and Spotted Fox answered. A young woman with a blue blanket wrapped around her shoulders stepped into the lodge and stooped one pace to the left of the entrance—proper etiquette for a woman entering a man's lodge. Immediately she began talking to Spotted Fox in a soft voice.

She's pretty, McCabe thought, with her oval face and high cheekbones. Almost as pretty as Night Bird Woman. When she took her blanket from her shoulders, he shifted uncomfortably at the way her breasts thrust out boldly beneath her beaded buckskin dress. While she spoke to the other man, she kept her dark eyes on McCabe. They sparkled with a forwardness that disconcerted him.

Finally Spotted Fox nodded ceremoniously. Before McCabe's astounded eyes, she shed her dress and stood naked. Proudly she turned, showing off her long, slim legs, her curvaceous hips, her full rounded breasts. With an effort he pulled his gaze away.

"What is she doing?" he whispered anxiously to Spotted Fox.

"She is a gift from High-backed Wolf. She displays herself for your approval."

"A gift!" McCabe blurted, then immediately lowered his voice. "I can't take a woman as a gift."

"How else will you learn our tongue? A woman who shares your blankets is the best teacher of a language. If you refuse his gift, you will insult High-backed Wolf."

"But he's given me too much already," McCabe persisted. "He has given me a lodge. He's allowed me to stay. He's . . ."

"He is a chief. A chief's generosity is greater than other men's."

McCabe sighed. His eyes flickered to the girl and away again. "Can she put her clothes back on?" Immediately she picked up her dress and wriggled into it. "Does she understand English?"

Spotted Fox shrugged. "How else could she teach you the tongue of the Cheyenne?"

"Oh." McCabe felt foolish. "Of course. Just how many of your people *do* speak English?"

"Perhaps twenty men of this camp know some words. Six or seven women."

"Does Night Bird Woman?"

"You must take your mind away from that woman, Mack Cabe. This one will warm your blankets. She is a captive, so it is allowed. Only remember to beat her often."

"I'll neither beat nor take advantage of her," McCabe retorted indignantly. "She will teach me the Cheyenne language. No more."

"If you do not take her to your blankets," Spotted Fox cautioned, "it is very important that you beat her so that she will not begin to act like a wife. A captive who acts like a wife is worse than a wife. You will get no rest."

"Perhaps it is your custom to beat women," McCabe said in his loftiest tone, "but it is not mine."

Spotted Fox smiled indulgently. "You will learn, Mack Cabe. I will leave you with her."

After the other man had gone, McCabe found himself tongue-tied. What could he say to a woman whom he'd just watched casually strip herself naked? He glanced at her and saw she was studying him boldly.

"You want Night Bird Woman?" she asked suddenly.

"I saw her," McCabe said defensively. "She's very pretty, that's all. What's your name?"

"I am Looking Glass, Mack Cabe. I have seen nineteen snows, and I am captive from my people, the Dakota, for nine." She smiled boldly and softly grasped his arm. "I will make you forget Night Bird Woman."

He cleared his throat. "You're supposed to teach me the language. Why don't we have a lesson now." Her smile perturbed him. To cover his confusion, he began eating the stew.

"Very well," she sighed. "But let me get you some more dog. Yours is getting cold."

He swallowed convulsively. "Some more what!"

"Dog stew. Mack Cabe, what is the matter? Are you not well?"

He closed his eyes and took deep breaths to calm his churning stomach. Buffalo dung. Scalps. Dog stew. He wondered how he was going to survive at all among these people. "I'm all right," he managed, setting the bowl down. "Let's have that lesson."

She eyed him doubtfully, but nodded. "We will begin with the months. This is *Matsiomuishi*, the Spring Moon."

"*Matsiomuishi*," he repeated awkwardly. "The Spring Moon. April."

"Next month is *Oassiowahtut*, the Shiny Moon."

"*Oassiowahtut.* . . ."

3

McCabe paused in his shaving to watch Looking Glass carry a large pot of water into his new tepee. She refused to let him drink water that had stood overnight. Such water was dead, she said, and he must drink live water.

His shaving mirror was hung on a stick beside the lodge, and as he drew the razor's edge down his cheek, he heard girls giggling behind him. They had gathered to stare at him, as they did every morning when he shaved. He slipped into his shirt and buttoned it before going on.

"They do not look at your chest," Looking Glass said, coming out of the lodge. "It is the scraping of your face. You do not pluck the hairs, as is proper."

"I figured that out." He rubbed his cheeks to feel for missed stubble. "But I'm not used to being barechested while girls stare at me."

She suddenly reached out to rub his cheek. "Your skin is smooth," she murmured.

He caught her hand and pushed it down gently. "I'm going to sketch the camp today, for my report. Will you fetch me the broad flat box from the lodge?"

She nodded and ducked inside with a smile. When she came she carried not only the box, but a leather bundle. Quickly she laid the box at his feet and unfolded a deerskin shirt, which was decorated with bands of red and white quillwork intertwining on the sleeves and red and blue porcupine quill squares across the chest. "I made it for you," she said. "You need a proper shirt."

He nodded approvingly, and she broke into a smile. "All right," he beamed, and he took off the wool shirt, then slipped the other over his head. She immediately brought out a black beadwork belt, which she fastened around his waist. Into this she thrust his pistols and his knife.

"Well?" he laughed as he put on his broad-brimmed hat. "Are you satisfied?"

"The hat is not proper," she said critically. "And your moccasins are stiff and clumsy."

"My boots are just fine, Looking Glass. And so is my hat. But I thank you for the shirt and the belt. They're beautiful." He touched her face, and she smiled so radiantly that he dropped his hand as if it had been burned. "I'll get on with my sketching, now." He snatched up the sketch box and hurried away.

He used the broad, flat surface of the box as a table to draw on. Although he wasn't an accomplished artist, he could sketch well enough to give an idea of what the camp and the people looked like. He wandered among the tepees, stopping to sketch boys who were shooting at targets with half-sized bows, and girls who were seeing how many times they could kick an antelope-hide ball without letting it touch the ground. He tried to keep out of sight as he sketched. They would be more natural if they didn't know he was there. He drew old women scraping fat from animal hides, and straight-backed young women going out to dig prairie turnips. Grey Bear, Three Hatchets and others of the Bow Strings made a colorful tableau as they squatted in front of a lodge. With a stack of a dozen sketches, McCabe sat down to draw a diagram of the camp—a great circle with its opening always toward the rising sun. He drew another of an individual tepee.

"You draw?"

McCabe looked around in surprise to find Night Bird Woman and a half dozen other young women watching him. Some, who also watched him shave every morning, hid their faces in their hands and giggled when he glanced at them, but his gaze was mainly on Night Bird Woman.

"Yes." He handed her a picture of the woman scraping hides. She gasped, and immediately showed it to the rest. They responded with excited murmurs.

"That is Elk Woman," she noted. "And that is Blue Sky Woman. I can recognize them plainly. You draw well, Mack Cabe."

"And you speak English very well," he replied. "I didn't think any women did except for captives."

"For four years my father lived in the camp on the Arrowpoint, near the place you call Bent's Fort. I learned to speak your language then." She handed the drawing back almost regretfully. "Will you make my picture also?"

"Indeed I will." Eagerly he drew out a fresh sheet of paper. She stood very still, and the other girls watched in wonder. A few hesitantly began to leaf through his other drawings, but he concentrated on Night Bird Woman. As hard as he tried, though, he couldn't help feeling frustrated, for he couldn't catch the full beauty of her. He couldn't even come close. At last he was forced to give up and hand to her what he had.

She gasped, touching the colorful quill-and-beadwork on her dress. "This is what I see in a looking glass. Even my dress is as it is."

"The picture's not nearly as pretty as you are," he praised.

She smiled shyly and looked down. "You must draw the other girls, too, or they will think you are making me a favorite."

"I am," he replied, but she didn't seem to hear. She clapped her hands and gathered the other girls around her. Quickly she explained to them, and he found himself drawing a portrait of each as she sat giggling nervously.

Afterward, they darted away, clutching their pictures. Only Night Bird Woman paused. "Thank you, Mack Cabe," she said softly. And then she too was gone.

He thought about her for a long time after that, about her pretty eyes and her deep, throaty voice, about her innocent enthusiasm and open admiration of his artistic efforts. There was something about her, something open and true, that he somehow knew he would never find in any woman back home. . . .

When he returned to his lodge, he found Spotted Fox putting a padded buckskin saddle on his horse.

"Ho, Mack Cabe," the Indian called. "I go to hunt. Will you hunt with me?"

"I'd like that," McCabe allowed, but he paused at the entrance to his lodge as he remembered the dog stew. "What are we going to hunt?"

Spotted Fox shrugged and slung his bow over his shoulder. "Deer, antelope, whatever there is. Perhaps we will find no more than prairie dogs."

"*No* kind of dogs," McCabe laughed, ducking inside to fetch his Hawken.

From the encampment the two men rode north over flat, sparsely vegetated countryside. The sun shone high in the sky.

"It will be a good day," Spotted Fox observed. "No rain. Little wind."

McCabe looked at him in surprise. "You seem sure."

"The sky was grey this morning. If it had been red, there would be bad weather before night."

McCabe nodded. He recalled the old sailor's saying: red sky at morning, sailor take warning. He supposed the Indians would have as much folk wisdom about weather as did sailors. "How about the wind?"

"I saw a spider spinning its web on a bush near the camp. It made the web strands long. If there was going to be wind today, it would have made the strands short. And look." He pointed to birds, hardly more than specks in the sky, darting and feeding. "They feed high if the weather will be good, low if the weather will be bad. You must know these things, Mack Cabe. A man who cannot tell the weather is as helpless as a man who cannot find food or water."

"I'm not sure I *could* find water out here." McCabe stared around at the bleak landscape. "I don't see a sign of a river, or a water hole."

"The tracks of animals or the flight of birds will lead you to a water hole. But do not drink if there are bones of animals about, or if no plants grow on its edges, for then the water is poison. There are few water holes anyway. For the hunter or the warrior, water must be found other ways."

"Other ways? How? There doesn't seem to be any water out here at all."

"Where plants grow at the base of rocks or a cliff, or at the bottom of a draw, there you may dig for water. Also dig for water in a dry mud hole, a dry sink, or a riverbed, especially at the bend of a riverbed. If the ground is damp, or muddy, seep water can be found by digging. Also at the base of a sand hill, on the shady side or the steepest side. If willows grow, or elderberries, or cattails, there will be water." Spotted Fox smiled. "You see, my friend, there is much water to be found."

McCabe shook his head. "Well, I doubt if I'd have thought of looking in any one of those places. I have a lot to learn."

"Yes, my friend. You must learn much to survive in this land. You must learn to find water, tell the weather, track game for miles, tell which plants are good to eat, which are good medicine, and which are poison. With nothing but a knife or a sharp piece of stone, you must be able to provide yourself with food, shelter, clothing and weapons. You must. . . ." His recitation trailed off, and he held up a hand for quiet. "In that next patch of brush, there are birds."

McCabe strained his eyes, but could see nothing. "How . . . ?"

"I saw them. Come." Spotted Fox quickly slipped from his horse and moved toward the low bushes as stealthily as his still splintered leg would permit.

"Wait a minute," McCabe called softly. "It's not good for the gun, but I can draw out this rifle ball and load in some shot."

Spotted Fox shook his head. "You white men must be rich indeed, to waste gunpowder on birds."

"Don't tell me you expect to kill them with arrows," McCabe exclaimed.

"Come and see," the other replied. Pulling two heavy, straight sticks from his belt, he resumed his approach to the bushes.

McCabe hefted his rifle doubtfully, then dismounted and followed. As he moved closer to the clump, he gasped. He could see the birds now, though he wondered how Spotted Fox had been able to from horseback.

There were two dozen grey-feathered grouse clustered together beneath the bushes, cocking their heads worriedly at the two men.

Suddenly Spotted Fox hurled one of the sticks, and almost before it had even left his hand he had seized the other and thrown it too. The birds exploded into flight.

"Well, you scared them off, anyway," McCabe grumbled.

Without a word Spotted Fox hobbled into the bushes and plucked three grey shapes from the ground. "Not all of them, Mack Cabe." One of the birds fluttered, and Spotted Fox expertly wrung its neck before tying all their feet together with rawhide.

"I'll be damned."

"Would you like to try, Mack Cabe?"

"I would indeed."

Spotted Fox rejected the next three clumps of brush they came across, though McCabe insisted on dismounting and searching each of them. All he found was a lizard. At the fourth, however, the Indian nodded.

"They are there. Remember," Spotted Fox added as McCabe hurriedly dismounted, "walk as close as you can. Throw at the instant they are ready to fly."

McCabe nodded impatiently and started forward, a throwing stick in each hand. His eyes were on the grey birds, clucking softly to themselves, his right arm cocked. As close as possible, he reminded himself. The birds' heads came up, and he threw at the moment they exploded upward in a burst of feathers. Frantically he hurled the second stick, only to watch it sail through the rising flock of birds and fall beyond the bushes.

"I guess you need practice to be good at anything," McCabe said rue-fully, shaking his head.

"Go look," Spotted Fox replied.

He went on into the clump of brush and found the throwing stick propped against the lower branches of a straggly sagebrush. Three feet away lay a plump grouse. Hefting the bird, he let out a shout and ran back to his friend. "I'll be damned if you weren't right. I did get one. This isn't as hard as it looks."

"Let us find the other throwing stick," Spotted Fox said drily. "Then we may hunt more."

Each man had a dozen birds strung to his saddle by the time Spotted

Fox signaled a halt and pointed to a herd of tiny shapes across the prairie. "Antelope." He slipped to the ground and walked beside his horse, keeping it between him and the distant grazing animals.

After a moment McCabe did the same. "Spotted Fox, do you mean to stalk those animals afoot all that way? They must be a mile and a half off, maybe more."

"Antelope sees very good, Mack Cabe. He recognizes a man, on foot or on a horse, very far away. Then he runs too fast for a horse to catch."

"But they'll see us for sure walking up like this."

"Antelope sees very good, but he cannot count. Four legs or six, it is the same. He sees only horses."

The antelope continued grazing as the two men moved closer. Not until the hunters were less than four hundred yards away did the antelope begin to lift their heads and eye the horses curiously, nostrils flaring to catch a scent. At half that distance they began to drift, trotting slowly to keep their distance, stopping when they were satisfied, moving on as the horses came closer.

"I don't think we'll get any closer," McCabe said finally. He rested his Hawken across his saddle. "But I can make a shot from here."

"I cannot," Spotted Fox admitted. He fumbled under his buckskin shirt and pulled out a length of bright red rag. "They must be drawn inside a hundred paces if I am to make a sure killing shot." Tying the strip of cloth to one end of his bow, he raised it slowly into the air, then began to gently wave it back and forth. "Wait until they are close," he said softly. He gripped two arrows in his teeth and watched the antelope closely.

McCabe shrugged. This time he was certain the other man's superstitions would fail. What kind of animal would be drawn to a red rag waved in the air?

One of the antelope raised its head to look at the horses and froze. Then another did the same. Then another, and another. When the first animal took a cautious step toward them, McCabe swore under his breath. He didn't believe it, even if he *was* seeing it. Slowly, step by halting step, the antelope moved back toward the horses, each of them staring at the waving strip of red. A hundred and fifty yards. A hundred. Their steps became slower, less certain, as they drew nearer. The lead animal swung his head and seemed to tense.

"Now," Spotted Fox grunted, snatching the arrows from his mouth.

As one, the herd of antelope whirled, gathering their powerful haunches under them. McCabe squeezed the trigger, and the heavy rifle slammed back against his shoulder with an earsplitting roar. In the midst of the herd, one animal crashed heavily to the ground. Spotted Fox loosed his first arrow as the animals fled away. Another buck dropped, then began to struggle to its feet, but Spotted Fox had already flung himself into his saddle and raced toward his quarry. The animal went down for good as Spotted Fox's second arrow found its heart.

"Hieaya!" he shouted. "We have meat for many bellies, Mack Cabe!"

McCabe shook his head as he walked his horse to the fallen antelope. "I still don't understand how, though. A red rag?"

Spotted Fox laughed. "The antelope is very curious, Mack Cabe. Very curious. You must learn these things: how, in the mountains, the male deer will send the females across a clearing first to see if there is danger; how the buffalo has poor eyes and will let a man get very close, but will run from the faintest smell. How . . ."

"How the antelope is very curious," McCabe chuckled.

"Yes, Mack Cabe. Come. It is late. We must take the meat back to camp."

The sun was low in the sky by the time they reached the encampment. McCabe was surprised when Spotted Fox stopped and dropped his antelope before the first lodge they came to, then rode on without saying a word! A few lodges later he handed his string of grouse to a woman Mc-Cabe had not seen before.

"Are they relatives of yours, Spotted Fox?" McCabe asked at last.

"Relatives? No, Mack Cabe. The first lodge was that of Bright Sky Woman. Her husband died, and she has no one to hunt for her pot. And Stone Horse, Sweet Water Woman's husband, is a good warrior, but lazy. He does not hunt."

"That's very generous of you, giving your game to them."

Spotted Fox nodded. "That is so. But why should someone go hungry when I have more than I can eat? All men give away their extra meat. If I have no luck at the hunt, I know that someone will see that I still have food. Besides, the more a man gives away, the better he is thought of."

"I'm not sure I understand."

"It is simple. A man who acquires many horses, many silver bracelets, many wives, is admired for his wealth. But a man who acquires these things and gives them away is admired even more. Chiefs give away much. Many times High-backed Wolf has given poor men clothes, lodges, horses, even guns. Just in the way he gave you a lodge and Looking Glass."

"I see," McCabe said thoughtfully. So a generous man was well thought of, was he? It was a good point to remember. "Which is Elk Antler's lodge?"

"That one ahead, with the blue stripe around it. But why do you wish to know?"

McCabe rode ahead without answering. There was no one in front of the lodge. He swung the antelope to the ground. From inside the lodge he heard the sounds of someone moving, but he didn't stop to see if it was Night Bird Woman.

When he rode back, Spotted Fox looked at him strangely.

"What's the matter, Spotted Fox?" he asked. "Did I do something wrong?"

"No," the other said slowly. "But. . . ." He shrugged and let his words trail off. "It is too late to worry now, Mac Cabe. Come. We will go back to your lodge. Tonight I will teach you something else a Cheyenne man must know."

"What's that?"

"How to play the flute for a woman," Spotted Fox laughed. But he cast a worried glance at Elk Antler's lodge as he said it.

The next morning Spotted Fox burst into McCabe's lodge without the customary request to be admitted. "Mack Cabe," he said worriedly, "it is said that you have made a picture of Grey Bear, Three Hatchets and other Bow Strings."

"Yes, I drew them yesterday." He gestured to the place next to him. "Sit, Spotted Fox, I'll do a picture of you."

"Let me see the drawing," Spotted Fox demanded. "Quickly, Mack Cabe."

Mystified, he dug out his sketch box and took out the drawing. The other man took one look at it and shook his head.

"Aieee! This is bad, Mack Cabe. Why did you do it?"

"I don't understand."

"If you make a picture of man when he does not know it, when he cannot guard his spirit, you may catch his spirit in the picture. Come. We must go to Raven quickly."

Clutching the picture in his fist, Spotted Fox hustled McCabe out of the lodge and hurried him across the circle of the encampment.

"But I didn't trap anyone's soul," McCabe protested.

"They will not believe that," Spotted Fox replied. He stopped in front of a lodge decorated with stars and a large black bird. "That is why I have brought you to Raven, the shaman."

From across the camp a shout arose. McCabe looked back to see Grey Bear, Three Hatchets and other Bow Strings running toward him. Spotted Fox quickly called for permission to enter, and pushed McCabe into the lodge.

An old man with an eagle skull fastened in his hair sat before the fire. Shrewd black eyes in a wrinkled face studied the two younger men. Then Raven motioned for his visitors to sit. From outside came an angry shout. Raven answered curtly.

"Grey Bear demands that you be sent out," Spotted Fox said quickly. "Raven refuses." Then, speaking in low, quick Cheyenne, he showed the shaman the drawing. After a minute Raven spoke and Spotted Fox translated. "He wants to know why you did this thing."

"I wanted to show my people what the Cheyenne looked like."

There was another rapid exchange between the two Cheyenne. "Raven says that if your people want to know what the Cheyenne look like, they should come and look for themselves."

"There are too many . . . Where's he going?" McCabe asked as Raven got to his feet, still holding the picture.

"Outside," Spotted Fox replied. "We will follow, but speak softly or not at all."

Outside the tepee a crowd had gathered in a semicircle around the lodge entrance. Grey Bear, his brother and the Bow Strings were in front. When McCabe appeared, they started forward, but Raven uttered a sharp cry and they fell back. Folding his arms, the shaman made a speech, from time to time punctuating his words by nodding toward McCabe or one of the warriors.

"Raven says," Spotted Fox repeated softly, "you had no evil intent. He says you are merely ignorant. You did not want to trap the spirit of anyone. To ensure the safety of the warriors' spirits, however, he will perform a ceremony to free them if they are trapped."

As Raven gathered the implements of his ceremony, Spotted Fox spoke gravely to McCabe. "He will burn the paper. If it burns red, it means you have lied, for red is the color of trapped spirits. If you have lied, you will be forced to leave the Cheyenne."

McCabe watched apprehensively as the old man shuffled around. That Raven could add something to the fire to make it burn red, he had no doubt. But would he? He certainly had no reason to want McCabe to remain.

Raven settled himself in front of a small fire. He held a small bottle of water, which Spotted Fox said would be used to capture the freed spirits so the men could drink them. Molding the paper flat, the shaman sprinkled powder on it in a spiral design, then, on top of that, he made a cross with broken ends. Carefully, so as not to disturb the patterns, he lowered the paper into the fire. The edges curled and blackened, then the whole thing burst into flame. Nauseous smoke rolled up, setting everyone to coughing, and the flames leaped for a moment. They were green.

A satisfied murmur spread through the crowd.

"There was no harm," Spotted Fox sighed in relief.

McCabe heaved a sigh of his own. "Will you thank Raven for helping me?"

Spotted Fox nodded. While he spoke to the shaman, McCabe looked for Grey Bear and the others, but they were already pushing their way through the crowd, grumbling loudly. As relieved as they might be to know their spirits were safe, they seemed not at all happy that McCabe was free to remain.

4

In the days that followed, Night Bird Woman began to appear wherever McCabe was. While writing in his journal, while shaving outside his lodge, and sometimes, to his embarrassment, while bathing in the stream, he would look up to find her standing nearby. The Cheyenne took baths every morning, but men and women bathed in different parts of the stream. Three Hatchets glared at him more and more fiercely every time they met, and Looking Glass began to sulk in the lodge.

Then the camp moved. The lodgepoles were taken down and the large hide covers were folded and packed on horseback. Looking Glass would not let him help her rig travois poles to the pack animals. She took great pride, she said, in showing him that a Dakota woman could do just as well as any Cheyenne woman. The long column trailed away to the northwest, toward the distant mountains. Women, for the most part, rode the animals that were rigged to the travois. Infants were carried on cradleboards in their mothers' arms, while slightly older children rode in bentwood cages to keep them from falling off. Adolescent boys herded the horses, and young girls of that age walked beside their mothers. Men rode wherever they liked, except for a few members of the six societies who fanned out to guard the march and scout the path. For almost a week the long column wound its way slowly northward. Finally, on the seventh day, they built a camp in sight of mountains that stood like blue mist on the horizon.

Making camp was women's work, and McCabe had already discovered that Looking Glass didn't take kindly to his interfering, so he spent his time walking outside the camp circle, where he gathered tiny blue and yellow wildflowers. Lately he had begun to wear the shirt Looking Glass had made for him, and he found the moccasins she had produced were much more comfortable than his boots.

Spring was on the prairie, and soft breezes sweeping in from the mountains seemed to carry the scent of new pine and fir. As he walked back to camp, he found himself drifting toward the lodge of Night Bird Woman's father. Small boys astride sticks, their make-believe horses, circled him on the run and shouted the cries of buffalo hunters. Elk Antler was nowhere in sight, but his daughter and five other women worked outside the lodge over two cooking fires. A pot of thick stew bubbled over one, while a rack of buffalo ribs, suspended on a thong, turned slowly above the other. All five women looked up when he stopped in front of Night Bird Woman.

"I picked these," he said, thrusting the wildflowers at her. "I thought you might like them."

She took them hesitantly, then quickly set them down. "They are very pretty, Mack Cabe. Thank you." She glanced at the pot as if anxious to be back to her cooking. The other women stared at them.

"I didn't mean to interrupt your work," he apologized awkwardly. "I guess I'll be going." He turned away, inwardly cursing himself, calling himself a fool. Just because she was curious about him, a stranger, didn't mean anything. He had probably embarrassed her.

Suddenly Grey Bear swept in front of him on horseback. For an instant the scar-faced warrior pulled up, glaring down at him. Then he was gone.

McCabe stared after him with a shake of his head. If Night Bird Woman was betrothed to the man's brother, perhaps it would be best to stay away from her.

As he started for his lodge, Spotted Fox trotted up on his horse and followed along beside him. "Mack Cabe, I am going hunting. I will be gone for three days. You must be careful while I am gone."

"I'll be careful," he agreed.

"It is not careful to give gifts, even flowers, to Night Bird Woman while Three Hatchets' brother watches."

"You saw that, did you? Well, that's done with. She has no interest in me beyond curiosity, and I've still too much to learn to risk inviting any trouble."

"That is good, but still you must be careful. Until three days, Mack Cabe." He trotted away. But before McCabe reached his lodge, there was another interruption. Otter Belt appeared and signed that he wanted to talk.

"But I can't . . . oh, hell." He spoke the words as he made the signs. It seemed to help. "Let us go to my lodge. My woman can tell me what you say."

The slender young man signed "no" with a show of indignation. McCabe sighed. The man probably thought it was an insult to have his words translated by a woman.

"What do you want?" he said as he formed the hand symbols.

Otter Belt made the signs for "You come hunt with me."

"Hunt?" McCabe said. The other man nodded. "What do you hunt?"

Otter Belt straddled two fingers of his right hand over his left.

"Horses?" McCabe asked, making the sign. "You want me to go with you after horses?"

"Hor-ses," Otter Belt said awkwardly and made the sign again.

"I would enjoy that. When?"

Otter Belt turned the palms of his hands to his body, one above the other.

"Daybreak? At daybreak? I'll be ready." He heaved a sigh of relief when Otter Belt nodded and left. It was damned hard communicating with just the sign. As soon as he reached his lodge, he told Looking Glass that they would have to work harder on his Cheyenne.

"Sit down," she offered, scooping a bowl of venison stew from the steaming kettle over the fire. "It is late."

He took the bowl from her and squatted in front of the lodge. To his surprise he saw that the sky was rapidly deepening to the purple of twilight. "I have to be up early tomorrow. I'm going horse hunting with Otter Belt at daybreak."

She had been settling beside him as he spoke, but at that she gave a small cry. "Horse hunting?"

He nodded and went on eating. "That's right. I guess he and his friends aren't mad at me anymore. In any case, I'm done with mooning over that girl his friend Three Hatchets wants. And I'm not about to let this chance to show my good will go by."

"You are no longer interested in Night Bird Woman?" she asked curiously. "She follows you everywhere around the camp."

"She's just curious. It took me a while to realize it, but it seems logical. I wear a funny hat, and I scrape my face instead of plucking my beard." He laughed. "I suppose to all of you I'm very curious indeed."

"I will see to your horse," she said, rising.

"My horse? Why?"

"Because you have no boy to do it." She stopped to explain patiently. "A warrior always keeps his best horse tethered at his lodge during the night, in case there is an attack. If you are going horse hunting, then you are a warrior."

"If you say so," he laughed. "But I only have the one horse and a pair of mules."

"You will have more," she told him, then disappeared into the night.

Once she was gone, his appetite seemed to go too. Despite what he had said, he didn't *want* Night Bird Woman to be merely curious about him. He tossed his half-finished bowl down beside the fire and crawled into the lodge.

The fire inside was banked low, giving off just enough light for him to fold his clothes and put them away against the wall of the tepee. He rolled into his bedding and pulled a buffalo robe over himself. At first Looking Glass had been going to sleep inside as well, but he explained to her that it wasn't the custom of his people, and he offered to sleep outside. She had refused. She would not be known as a woman whose man slept outside his own lodge. She had bundled her blankets up and gone outside herself.

Now he was just dropping off when she slipped into the lodge. He rolled over to look at her as she knelt by his bed. Her blue blanket was wrapped around her tightly.

"What are you doing here, Looking Glass?" he murmured groggily. "If it's cold outside, put your bedding on the other side of the fire."

"Is Mack Cabe truly too tired?" she demanded, then let the blanket drop. Beneath it she was naked.

Her skin gleamed like copper in the firelight. Her breasts were round and full. Her small waist flared into slender hips and long thighs. He let out a heavy breath and moved the buffalo robe aside. With a smile she slipped in beside him.

The morning was still dark when he left his lodge. He flapped his arms against the cold and stopped in surprise when he saw his horse. The horse already stood saddled and bridled, but in place of his heavy eastern saddle was a simple buffalo-hide saddle pad with rawhide stirrups. The bridle had been replaced by a looped rawhide rope fastened around the horse's lower jaw. He confronted Looking Glass as she left the lodge.

"Where's my saddle? I've never ridden on a contraption like this before."

She handed him his rifle in a fringed buckskin sheath and a fringed deerskin saddlebag. "You must make no noise while horse hunting. Your white man's saddle creaks, and your white man's bridle jingles like the bracelets of a woman."

"I suppose," he admitted grudgingly. He tied the saddlebags on and swung onto his mount. It felt more like riding bareback than any saddle he was used to.

Otter Belt appeared suddenly with a dozen other braves, all mounted. McCabe hesitated when he saw Three Hatchets among them. Their horses frisked, and some made their mounts curvet. Then with a whoop they were off toward the entrance to the camp.

"There is food in the saddlebags," Looking Glass noted.

He dug his heels in and raced after them.

All day they rode northward toward the mountains. That night they camped without seeing another soul or a single horse. The warriors chewed dried meat, making no fire. When McCabe signed to ask how much longer it would be until they found horses, he was answered by three fingers, then four, then five, then a shrug. Three Hatchets laughed as he climbed into his blankets.

On and on toward the mountains they rode. On the third day they passed through towering pines and climbed so high up a ridge that there was a chill in the air, despite the nearness of summer. Then they started down the other side. The horses, McCabe decided, must be on the plains beyond the mountains.

Before they reached the prairie, though, Three Hatchets signaled a halt. Everyone else rode into a sheltered gully and dismounted. Three Hatchets disappeared.

"There are horses here?" McCabe signed to Otter Belt as he spoke. The young Indian signed back "soon," and returned to his friends, who were resting beneath the trees, eating and sharing pemmican. McCabe sat down and leaned against a large fallen pine to wait.

When the sun was falling in the west, Three Hatchets returned. He spoke to the others rapidly, then sank down to take some pemmican from Otter Belt.

McCabe decided not to make a fool of himself. When the others were ready to move, he would find out. But the sun sank until it was a brilliant red globe touching the horizon, and purple shadows crept among the trees, and then it was dark. Even the moon was hidden by scudding clouds. At last Three Hatchets moved.

The muscular Cheyenne pointed to three of the youngest braves, and each of the others handed his reins to one of them. One of the chosen men pointed to McCabe and muttered something, but Three Hatchets retorted angrily. He took McCabe's reins himself and handed them to the one who had complained.

"We're going to hunt for horses on foot," McCabe remarked skeptically. "At night." Three Hatchets gestured at him angrily for silence, and he subsided.

Each man who had not been chosen to hold horses took from his bundle a long, thin stick. One, a young brave named Two Elks, gestured to Mc-

Cabe with his stick and said something quietly. Three Hatchets laughed and broke off a pine branch, which he handed to McCabe. Some of the others laughed too.

The ten men began to creep off to the west. Three Hatchets, who was in the lead, motioned for McCabe to follow behind him. Now wondering what kind of horses they intended to catch with sticks, McCabe fell in behind the Indian.

Quietly they moved down to a valley that opened to the west. The warriors grimaced at every twig that McCabe snapped. Suddenly, Three Hatchets dropped to the ground. The others followed, McCabe a second behind the rest. From there they crawled, pausing frequently while Three Hatchets sniffed the wind.

McCabe used the pauses to strip as many twigs and needles from his branch as he could. He was beginning to think he was the victim of an elaborate practical joke, but if this was a game of some sort, and those thin sticks were part of the play, he intended to have one too.

Three Hatchets froze abruptly. There was a rustle in the bushes ahead. Now, McCabe thought, he would see what sort of prey they hunted. To his surprise a dog appeared, sniffing and growling. Before it could bark, however, Three Hatchets leaped on it, and there was the flash of a knife. Then the Cheyenne crawled on. McCabe sickened as he wriggled past the dog. Its throat had been cut.

He began to imagine he could see a light ahead; then he realized he wasn't imagining. There *was* a light. And a lodge! He lifted up enough to look over the bushes, and bit back a cry. There were tepees all around them, scattered through the trees and rocks. They were in the middle of a camp. He looked around for the Cheyenne who had been following him. They were gone. Ahead, Three Hatchets snaked his way to the lodge and loosed the horse tethered there.

So that was how they hunted horses at night, McCabe thought bitterly. They had tricked him into going along on a rustling raid. He wondered if he could sneak back out the way he had come in.

At that moment a cry sounded in another part of the camp. Three Hatchets vaulted to the horse's back just as an Indian darted from the lodge. Three Hatchets slapped him across the face with his stick, shouting, "Ah haih!" and kicked the horse into a gallop. From all parts of the camp came screams and shouts, and occasionally the vicious cracking of musket fire.

There was no time left to crawl, McCabe thought, and he rose to run. From out of nowhere a dog appeared, launching itself at him with a snarl. He slashed at it with his branch and turned to run the other way. Too late he realized he was heading toward the already roused lodges. A warrior appeared, holding a musket in his hands. He leveled it and fired just as McCabe ducked. McCabe's broad-brimmed hat was jerked into the night.

Desperately he looked for another way to run. All around him was shouting and turmoil and more Indians appearing every second. Loose horses dashed through the camp. Just as another man was pointing his musket, Otter Belt galloped out of the darkness and trampled right over him, then slashed at another man with his stick. *"Ah haih!"* he shouted, and dashed away.

Another group of horses ran by, and McCabe threw himself at them, trying to scramble onto one. He managed to catch at the mane of a flashing grey, but as he tried to hook his heel over the horse's rump, he slipped. Grasping wildly, he clutched at the grey's tail. His feet touched the ground and, holding on for his life, he tried to leap back onto the horse. But the grey moved too fast. McCabe took another bounding leap, then another. He felt hysterical laughter rising as he realized he was taking leaping strides behind the horse, his feet only touching the ground every ten feet as he was pulled through the air between steps. The other horses ran close behind him. Across their backs he could see men from the lodges trying to take aim at him, shaking their fists and shouting as they realized they could not reach him for the horses. And then the lodges were behind. Only darkness surrounded him. His grip on the grey's tail slipped, and he fell, tumbling end over end.

It took long minutes just to get his breath back, and more to get to his feet. Nothing seemed to be broken, but every muscle ached and cramped. When men on horses galloped up, he was too sore to run. He looked up, wondering if he would have a chance to explain before they killed him, and he found himself staring into the furious face of Three Hatchets.

Someone led his horse forward, and he managed to pull himself into the saddle. Otter Belt and several of the others patted him, laughing. He had thought his rifle was gone, but before he could speak, Two Elks pushed it into his hands. He wondered what the man had been doing with it.

But there was no further time to think, for from the camp came the pounding of horses and the shrill cries of pursuers out for blood. The horse thieves leaned low on their mounts and whipped them to a gallop, driving their booty before them.

⬦

During the long ride home, the attitude of many of the braves toward McCabe seemed to change. They no longer avoided him. Sometimes they even offered pemmican, patting his shoulder and laughing. Sourly, he took the offered mix of dried meat, powdered berries and fat. They had succeeded in making a joke of him. They would probably talk and laugh about his escape from the camp long after he had gone.

When they reached the Cheyenne lodges, the stolen horses, forty-two in all, were driven into the camp with much shouting. Three Hatchets stood in his stirrups, arms outstretched, chanting wildly. Otter Belt dropped from his saddle as his mount ran, then sprang back up only to drop again on the other side. He did this again and again all the way to High-backed Wolf's lodge. McCabe, slumped in his saddle, wondered when they would tell the others about him. He saw Spotted Fox and Looking Glass laughing and waving in the gathering crowd. When he saw Night Bird Woman, he winced. She was the last person he wanted to hear of his debacle.

High-backed Wolf raised his hands, and the noise fell to quiet murmuring. One by one the members of the horse-stealing party rode forward, declaiming loudly. As each finished his tale, he rode aside for the next man. Several times one of them pointed to McCabe, and the people all looked. He wondered why they didn't laugh. At last all had spoken except him.

"Mack Cabe," High-backed Wolf said, "it is told of your exploits among the Utes. Many know of your strange reticence of speech, so they have spoken for you. Never has such a thing been done, running with the horses from the camp of the enemy. It is a brave thing. Your name is hard to say, Mack Cabe, and it has no meaning to us. I do not mean to offend you, but among us a man may take his name from a dream, or from a great exploit

50

that he has performed. You will take the name Horse Runner, so that we may say your name clearly."

McCabe looked among the faces of the people watching him, and he had to suppress a desire to laugh. So they didn't think he was such a fool after all. "I am honored," he answered slowly, "to take the name Horse Runner."

High-backed Wolf nodded in approval, then turned back to his lodge. The crowd began to break up, the men into laughing groups that clustered around the returning heroes, and the women back to their work. Night Bird Woman gave McCabe a coy, brief smile before joining the other women. Then Spotted Fox and Looking Glass ran up to him as he dismounted.

"So, Horse Runner," Looking Glass laughed, "I said that you would have many horses, and now you have six, more than anyone else."

"Yes, my friend," Spotted Fox smiled. "They are fine horses. I know the grey horse. It was the horse of Red Bear, a great warrior of the Utes. He used it to make war and to hunt buffalo."

"But they're stolen," McCabe began, then he let the thought trail off. If the Indians wanted to steal each other's horses, he had no right to object. This was, after all, their part of the world, not his. He mused. "Looking Glass, you knew that going on a horse hunt meant raiding another village, didn't you? Why didn't you tell me?"

"I thought that you knew," she said simply.

Spotted Fox looked impatient and surprised with McCabe's remark. "How else would we get horses? It is much easier to steal them than to catch them wild. But it was very foolish for you to go along on the hunt."

"Foolish!" McCabe exclaimed. "But you just said it was the ordinary way. Not that I wanted to steal horses, of course."

"Not to steal horses," the other man broke in. "But to ride with Three Hatchets and Otter Belt. You might not have come back."

He felt a chill as he recalled how Two Elks had appeared with his Hawken. "They didn't expect me to leave the Ute camp," he murmured. "But you said they wouldn't try to kill me."

"They did not have to try to kill you," Spotted Fox replied. "They would have let the Utes do that."

5

A bluebottle fly droned across the journal page in the July morning heat, and McCabe brushed it out of his way. He cursed and blotted a drop of sweat off the paper, then dipped his pen and went on in his best hand, recording all he had learned about Cheyenne government. From each of the ten bands, four civil chiefs were appointed to the Council of Chiefs. Above these were four principal, or tribal, chiefs. The council was supreme in all civil matters, and its members were expected to be wise and generous to a fault, giving aid to anyone in need. When fighting broke out with another tribe, a war chief was chosen. He could not be a civil chief, for his authority lasted only so long as the war.

"Horse Runner," Looking Glass said in Cheyenne, "Spotted Fox is coming with many riders."

"I hear him," he replied in the same language, for he had learned it so well that he had lately found himself thinking in it. He blew on the ink and shut the journal as Spotted Fox reined up outside.

"I see you, Horse Runner," Spotted Fox said in formal greeting.

"I see you, Spotted Fox." He noticed Otter Belt among the score of riders and frowned. All were stripped to breechcloth and moccasins, and each carried a lance or a bow and arrows instead of a musket.

"We go to hunt buffalo, Horse Runner. Stone Elk has seen a herd not far from the camp."

McCabe hadn't seen a buffalo hunt yet, and he had been looking forward to the experience. "I will come," he replied, and set the journal and pen aside. In a moment he had shrugged out of his shirt and stepped out of his leggings. He fastened on his own breechcloth and went out to mount the grey he had taken from the Utes. Looking Glass handed him his lance. It was a gift from High-backed Wolf, and the blade bore the broad arrow stamped SHEFFIELD, as most Indian cutlery was.

Less than ten miles from the camp, McCabe spotted the buffalo in a hollow between two low hills. There were seventy or eighty huge, shaggy brown beasts, many standing taller than the horses, and all at least three times as heavy. They ambled along, raising a cloud of dust, bulls on the outside, cows and calves in the center.

"Ho!" Spotted Fox shouted. "We split now!"

The band divided into two lines and moved apart to approach the buffalo from two flanks. McCabe, riding behind his friend, could smell the heavy, musky scent of the animals long before he reached them.

Gradually the two columns drew closer, the riders shrieking and waving blankets as the buffalo rolled into a lumbering run. The ground drummed beneath the hunters' feet, and they prodded their horses ahead faster to circle in front of the racing herd. When the shaggy animals turned away from the men closest to them, they began to collide with each other, and in moments their flight had been reduced to a confused, milling crowd. The Indians closed in.

Spotted Fox and a few of the others who were bravest forced their horses into the heaving pack, firing their iron-tipped arrows from a distance of inches. Others rode around the perimeter, lancing or shooting any animals that tried to escape.

McCabe saw one shaggy bull lower its heavily horned head and charge out of the mass at a horse. The horse screamed from its wounds as both rider and mount were flipped into the air. In the middle of the pack another horse suddenly went down, its rider scrambling onto the backs of the beasts around him. Like a man running from boulder to boulder across a stream, he tried to run toward safety, but he lost his balance, and with a scream he was gone.

Racing alongside a bull with a hump that towered nearly as high as McCabe's own chest as he sat upon his horse, he leaned forward and thrust with his lance just as Spotted Fox had shown him, behind the last rib and forward into the heart. The impact shook him to his marrow, and the lance quivered in his hands. Immediately he drew rein, letting the buffalo pull free of the weapon. Even as the lance came out, though, the animal wheeled, its great head going down, and it rushed at McCabe, hooking with horns as thick and long as a man's forearm. The grey adroitly stepped aside, and the buffalo rumbled past. Then it turned, and McCabe waited warily for its next charge. The animal's head weaved from side to side, as if trying to anticipate which way the grey horse would dodge. But when it took a step forward, it suddenly fell to the ground in a heap.

McCabe looked around to find that half the buffalo were already down. In the distance he could see the women approaching with the pack animals. The carcasses would be rendered and taken back to camp. Only the hearts of the slain would be left behind, for the Cheyenne believed that would replenish the herd.

Suddenly there was a sharp crack, and a rider slumped across his horse and fell. Screaming and firing, a party of Utes rode over the next hill and down on the buffalo hunters. Some had muskets, but most carried bows, shields and lances. It was immediately apparent that the Cheyenne hunters were outnumbered two to one. The Cheyenne charged.

McCabe didn't hesitate. Looking Glass or Night Bird Woman might be with the approaching women, who were too far from the camp to reach safety.

"*Hieya!*" he screamed, holding his lance level and charging toward the Utes.

A Ute brave galloped toward him, firing arrows as he came, but all of them missed. McCabe's lance did not. It sliced into the warrior's ribs, and with a dull scream the Ute was carried off the back of his horse. McCabe pulled his weapon free and rode on, then, almost in a state of shock, he looked back at the fallen man. He had been caught up in the moment, but now it struck him that he had killed a human being. The thought sickened him.

A howling Ute, swinging a stone-headed club, rode at him as he sat on his horse looking down at the warrior. A buffalo hunter's arrow took the attacker in the throat, and the club whistled harmlessly by McCabe's head. He shook himself. He had to stay alert if he was to stay alive.

The Cheyenne closed in with the Ute and fought hand-to-hand. When McCabe saw half a dozen Utes circling a man on the ground who desperately held them off with his buffalo lance, he again couched his own spear and charged.

Once more the weapon's tip sliced through ribs and sinew, but this time there was a snap, and McCabe found himself left with an eight-foot-long broken shaft. His charge had carried him into the midst of the attackers. Now, holding the lance shaft in both hands, he smashed a Ute in the face. The man dropped, but McCabe had to immediately beat aside the lance of another warrior. A backhand sweep struck the second man's head with a crack, and when that man sagged, clinging to his horse's mane as it dashed away, a third attacker thrust at McCabe with a lance. He had to drop the shaft and grab the Ute's weapon with both hands to keep from being run through. Jerking with all his strength, he pulled the man to him, and then at the last instant, he let go with one hand and smashed the Ute out of his saddle with his fist. An arrow took another attacker in the throat, and the remaining two took flight to search for easier game. McCabe reached down to pull the Cheyenne up behind him and found himself looking into the astonished eyes of Otter Belt. After a moment the young warrior took his succor's hand and pulled himself onto the grey.

McCabe quickly dashed away from the fight to let the other man down. "There is a free horse!" he shouted. "Grab it!"

As he spun to charge back, he saw four or five Cheyenne lying on the field, and several times that many Utes. The rest of the Utes were fleeing as fast as they could, many riding double. A few Cheyenne rode as far as the rise, shaking their lances after the scurrying enemy, but none were foolish enough to follow farther.

The women, who had taken cover in a shallow dale, raced in now. Some dropped to their knees beside the body of a fallen Cheyenne, swaying back and forth, keening, and gashing themselves with the skinning knives they had brought for the buffalo. One woman held her hand up to the sky, her little finger extended.

"Heammawihio!" she cried. "Listen to me, Heammawihio. Buffalo Horn, my man, is dead. I too wish to die." Placing her hand on the ground, she chopped the little finger off. With blood streaming from her hand, she began keening with the others, swaying, her body in mourning.

Other women rushed to the bodies of the dead Utes. Looking Glass and Night Bird Woman were among the first to reach them. Looking Glass pulled the moccasins from the first body she reached, stuffing them into her dress, and she snatched a necklace from under Night Bird Woman's hand. Night Bird Woman snapped at her, but wasted no time in rushing to another body. The women fell on the dead enemy like locusts, taking everything that was usable and scattering the rest. The naked Ute bodies would be left to the ravens that had already appeared. Then the buffalo were attended to.

"Horse Runner!" Otter Belt called as he rode up. "Horse Runner, you have saved my life. You rode among the enemy to take me up on your horse."

"You needed help, Otter Belt."

"And you gave me help, Horse Runner. I have been your enemy, yet you helped me. You did not know Spotted Fox, but you also helped him. You are too generous for an ordinary man. You should be a chief. I will be your enemy no more, Horse Runner. I will ride with you in the hunt, to turn the charge of the buffalo. In battle I will guard your back. This I swear by the Sacred Arrows." The young man sat proudly, waiting.

"But won't your fellow Bow Strings object?"

"I am not a Bow String, but only a friend of the Bow Strings. I have given my oath."

To a Cheyenne, such an oath was too powerful to be taken lightly. He held out his hand. "I will take you as my friend, Otter Belt, to ride by my side."

Otter Belt gripped it with a smile. "We will kill many of the enemy, Horse Runner. We will count many coups."

That night the Cheyenne gathered in the center of the camp around a fire of buffalo chips. Men sat on the inside, the women behind them, and the children behind the women. Near the fire High-backed Wolf sat cross-legged on a blanket, a musket and a gun lying in front of him. The fire blazed high in the dark.

Spotted Fox stood and approached the chief. Touching the pipe, he said, "*Maiyun asts ni ahtu.* Spirit powers, listen to me. *Na nishu.* I touched him." He looked out over the assemblage proudly. "I am Spotted Fox. When the Utes came as we hunted the buffalo, I fought. A Ute with a necklace of silver was shot with an arrow. As he fell I leaned down and touched him with my bow. Another Ute, a man with five feathers in his hair and black stars painted on his face, rode at me with a shield and a stone axe. I took the axe from him and struck him with my hand, then rode away."

He strode back to his place beside McCabe. Already another brave was touching the pipe. *"Maiyun asts ni ahtu."*

McCabe watched in wonder. Man after man made the trek to the center of the circle, but no one mentioned killing a man. No one spoke of being hard-pressed. They told only of their bravest acts: touching an enemy and leaving him alive. Next was to be the first to touch a fallen enemy, for he might be shamming death. To be the second to touch came next, and then to be the third. Killing meant nothing. Anyone could kill. Taking a scalp meant nothing. They were fine trophies, but many left them for whoever wanted to take them. It was the coup, the touching, that was important.

Spotted Fox nudged him. "Go up, my friend." McCabe realized that all the others who had been in the fight had already spoken. Only he remained. Slowly he rose and walked to the fire. He bent to touch the pipe.

"Spiritual powers, listen to me," he said in passable Cheyenne. "I touched him." When he straightened, he hesitated. He could feel the heat of the fire at his back. The watchers sat far enough back so that their faces were indistinct in the dark, but when two men slipped out of the circle and left, he was certain they were Three Hatchets and Grey Bear. "I am Horse Runner. When the Utes came as we hunted buffalo, I fought. I saw that Otter Belt was on the ground and surrounded by Utes. I rode to help him. My lance broke. With the shaft of my lance, I struck a man with red stripes on his face and another with rings in his ears. A third man, whose face was painted red, I struck with my hand. I did not kill any of them. That is what happened." He started back to his place, but High-backed Wolf spoke.

"That is not all that happened, Horse Runner. With enemies all around, you took Otter Belt on your horse." A murmur of approval ran around the circle. From under his robe the chief took a pipe with twin bowls carved of red stone in the shape of two buffalo. "Among us, Horse Runner, such an act is honored. This is a double-horseback pipe. It is given to a man who has done what you have done. Many years ago this one was given to me. I now give it to you."

McCabe was taken by surprise. He should do something, he knew, but he had no idea what. Finally he took the pipe and bowed. The gesture caused a ripple of amusement. Even High-backed Wolf's face cracked in a smile.

As he walked back to his lodge after the ceremony, Spotted Fox joined him. "You have gained much honor, Horse Runner. Never has a white man gained so much among us."

"I do not want it." He fingered the polished stone of the pipe. "I know the honor your people do me, but I am not a Cheyenne. I should not be honored as one."

Spotted Fox shrugged. "Many women are taken captive. No man can say all of his blood is Cheyenne. If his mother was not of another tribe, then her mother was, or his father's mother. Some men have more blood of other tribes than Cheyenne blood, but still they are Cheyenne. Your heart is Cheyenne, Horse Runner. That is enough. Stay with us. You will become a great warrior among us, perhaps even a chief."

McCabe stopped still. Stay with them? "No," he said slowly. "I must return to my own people. I will finish what I came here to do, and then I will go back to them."

6

McCabe stopped outside his lodge to look over the horse Short Bull had tethered there for him. It was one of those he had taken from the Utes; the others now ran free with his mules in the horse herds. The saddle pad and Indian bridle were in place, and his Hawken leaned against the lodge in its fringed buckskin sheath.

When he put on the fur cap that had his three coup feathers fastened to it, he noticed that his hair had grown below his ears again. "Looking Glass, you must cut my hair."

She didn't look up from the deerskin she was sewing into a dress. "You do not let your hair grow properly. Always you want to cut it too short."

"Among my people my hair would be considered long," he replied, but his mind was already off the argument they had been through so many times before. Across the camp, Grey Bear was ducking into the lodge of another Bow String. In the week since the coup ceremony, McCabe knew there had been many conferences among the members of that society.

"I am going to find Spotted Fox," he announced. Spotted Fox would know what was going on.

"He was watching the boys wrestle," she called as he left, then bent back to her sewing.

McCabe followed the shouts of boys and found his friend watching a struggle between two teams of young wrestlers not yet in their teens. There were few rules. Boys on one team could gang up on a boy of the other. Whenever anyone was thrown to the ground, he was out. Half a dozen youngsters, already eliminated, watched the rest. There were almost thirty of them, all struggling for an advantage and kicking up dust and shouting.

"Horse Runner!" Spotted Fox cried as he approached. "Come watch. There are some here who will make good warriors."

"So I see," McCabe shouted back for the boys' benefit. As soon as he was close enough he drew his friend aside. "What is happening among the Bow Strings?"

Spotted Fox shook his head. "I do not know. A society does not speak of its plans to others, unless one of them has boasted to a girl. They plan to do something, though."

A group of women passed, chattering and swinging their root-diggers. Night Bird Woman was among them.

"Night Bird Woman," McCabe suddenly called out.

She stopped, and as the rest of the women hurried on giggling, she looked after them anxiously.

"Night Bird Woman, has Three Hatchets spoken to you about his brother's plans?"

She looked at him in surprise. "That is what you want to say to me?" She shook her head angrily. "No. Three Hatchets has not spoken of his brother." And she darted after the other women.

"There will be trouble," Spotted Fox murmured. "She begins to prefer you to Three Hatchets."

"You are mistaken," McCabe laughed. "She used to follow me, because I seemed strange to her. Now she runs away as soon as I speak."

"Of course. If she behaved too eagerly, you would think she was a loose woman. She runs away so that *you* will be eager."

McCabe stared after the disappearing women in consternation. "Do you mean she has affection for me?"

Spotted Fox snorted. "If she did not, she would stand and talk when you speak to her, and not be angry that you speak of another man."

McCabe was about to reply when a line of horsemen suddenly issued into the center of the camp—forty-eight warriors, each wearing the beaded belt and sash of the Bow Strings. A few carried muskets, but most bore a bow and lance and round leather shield. Grey Bear wheeled out of the line to face McCabe and Spotted Fox with a sneer on his face.

"We will not count coup on worthless Utes, Mack Cabe," he said contemptuously. "We go against a worthy enemy. We go against the Kiowa." Whirling his lance over his head, he barked a sharp cry and galloped back to the line. In single file the Bow Strings rode out of camp to the south.

"There will be trouble from this," Spotted Fox grunted.

"Always you speak of trouble," McCabe laughed. "Soon you will be called Old Woman instead of Spotted Fox." But he frowned after the departing Bow Strings.

For the rest of the day he sat in front of his lodge, carefully checking his Paterson Colts and the heavy-barreled Hawken. He had fired the rifle only at deer, and the Colts had been shot only once—at targets. Powder and ball were too precious on the plains to be wasted. There were few guns, and twenty-five loads of ammunition cost a prime buffalo robe from the white traders; that was as much as three dozen iron arrow points, which could be used again and again.

The departure of the Bow Strings had left him with a dark foreboding. He carefully drew the charges from the Colts and loaded the cylinders anew, sealing each chamber with buffalo tallow and checking the percussion caps to make certain they were firmly set on the nipples before replacing the cylinders in the guns. He had just finished doing the same for the Hawken when a shrill, wavering cry rose outside the camp.

McCabe leaped to his feet as men raced from the lodges and seized horses. Spotted Fox galloped up on a swaybacked pack horse. He carried a bundle of rawhide sacks in his hand.

"Come, Horse Runner!" he shouted. "It is the women. They challenge us. Here, you will need a shield." He threw one of the sacks to McCabe.

With a laugh McCabe swung into the saddle and raced out of the camp with the rest of the men.

A mile from the camp, several parties of root diggers waited near a hill, taunting and waving to the men. A circle had been scribed in the dirt around them; any man who had not counted coup could cross it. Inside the circle with the women were piles of roots, stones and buffalo chips.

Shouting mock battle cries, the men charged and were met by a cloud of rocks and dung. Frantically McCabe deflected every missile that came his way, but Spotted Fox was struck full in the face by a buffalo chip. With a disgusted noise he pulled up.

"I am killed," he shouted as he rode toward the hill. Several other warriors who had been struck were already there. "Avenge me, Horse Runner."

Laughing, McCabe spurred his mount toward the women and leaned out of the saddle to grab a sackful of prairie turnips. Before he could straighten, however, Night Bird Woman darted to grab the sack away from him. He held tightly on to the buckskin with one hand, guffawing as she struggled to pull it free. Suddenly her hand slipped, and she sat down in a pile of buffalo chips. McCabe roared with laughter.

"You laugh at me!" she shouted, feeling ridiculous and trying to sound angry. "I will teach you to laugh at me." Scrambling up out of the crushed dung, she grabbed his leg with both hands. "Ah haih! I am first! I count coup on you!"

For an instant, their eyes met and locked dreamily. Then a dozen more women were crowding around, struggling to touch him and count coup. Flogging at his horse with the sack of turnips he dashed out of the circle, pursued by a hail of dung.

"Ho, Horse Runner," Otter Belt called as McCabe galloped up the hill. He waved a sack of turnips also. "We are the only ones brave enough to break in among the enemy. Shall we share with these old women who were driven off?" He gestured to the dung-spattered braves gathered on the hilltop.

"Let us share with them," McCabe answered. He took a turnip for himself and threw the sack to the others. "Perhaps they will be inspired by our example, and do better next time."

Otter Belt chortled as he too tossed his sack to the others. Below them the last of the braves were fleeing from the pelting. Hefting their sacks of turnips, the women marched toward the camp, chanting like victorious warriors. As they went, McCabe was sure he saw Night Bird Woman turn and look back at him.

"Spotted Fox," he asked, "how does a man go about getting married in your tribe?" Otter Belt and some of the others rolled on the ground laughing.

Spotted Fox cast a shrewd eye after the woman and answered. "First you must go to Elk Antler."

"I did not mention a name."

"You did not?" Spotted Fox pretended to ponder the question. "I wonder where I heard it." The laughter redoubled among the others. "It is of no matter. Go to the father of the girl who has no name. Ask him for his daughter, and he will tell you her bride price. You will give him the horses he asks for. If she does not want you, she will have the horses sent back. If she does want you, she will have the horses mixed with those of her father, and it is done."

"You mean a wife is bought like a slave?"

"Not at all." Spotted Fox seemed shocked. "A wife is not a slave. She can refuse by returning the horses, and if you mistreat her, she may return to her parents, taking all that she has brought to the marriage, all of her horses and any of their increase. You give a bride price to show that you think she is worth much to you. After you are married, her father will give you the same number of horses, to make certain that you will have a prosperous life."

"Among my people a marriage requires words from a holy man. A blackrobe."

"I saw a blackrobe once," Otter Belt said doubtfully. "It was many years ago. He lived among the Crow."

McCabe shook his head. Well, he thought, he had been given a Cheyenne name, and the warriors called him brother. Maybe a Cheyenne marriage would count as much for him as a Christian one.

That night, as he lay in his blankets with Looking Glass, he whispered, "I am thinking of marrying."

She stiffened slightly, but replied. "That will be well. It will be good to have someone to talk to as I work."

"I cannot have two women," He said. "Once I am married, my wife will . . . you will be given your freedom, Looking Glass."

"You will set me aside?" Furiously she rolled over, presenting him with her back. He touched her shoulder, but she shrugged his hand off.

"But Looking Glass, after what we have been to one another, surely you would not want to go back to being just a servant." He thought he heard her growl, but he wasn't sure.

After a while he rolled onto his side and pressed his back against hers. She was still stiff and angry. He sighed, wondering if he would ever understand women.

7

When he awoke in the morning, Looking Glass was already up and doing her chores. He lay for a time staring up through the open smoke flap of the tepee. If he wanted to marry Night Bird Woman, the problems to be solved were not simple ones. What would he do with Looking Glass? He could free her, give her a few horses. Some women did have their own lodges. But to pay the bride price for Night Bird Woman might mean losing almost everything he had. He had the feeling that Night Bird Woman would not come cheaply. He was willing to accept whatever ceremony the Cheyenne performed until a minister could be found. The Indian belief of a Creator who existed in everything was not that different from his own. But a minister must be found before he took her back to Boston. Indian marriage ceremonies would certainly be frowned upon there. That left only the matter of asking for her hand and paying the bride price. The last worried him most of all. Suppose he didn't have enough horses? It didn't matter that he would get them back after the marriage. They must be given to her father beforehand. And there were only two ways to get horses: trap wild ones or steal somebody else's. If only he could find some other way to pay the bride price. Some other way.

"The corn," he whispered, and a smile spread across his face. Hurriedly he began searching, pulling sacks and bundles away from the walls of the lodge. He felt a little ashamed that for all his plans he had hardly thought of the corn until then. "Looking Glass! Come here!" He found one gunny sack under the winter bedding and ripped it open. The seed still seemed all right, but he couldn't find the other three sacks. "Looking Glass!" he shouted again. She ducked through the entrance, and he went on before she could speak. "Where are the other bags like this one? Bags of corn." He dug among the stored bundles again.

"I have seen them," she replied. "I have used them."

He turned to face her slowly. "Used them? You used the seed corn?"

"What is seed corn? It looked like any other corn, only with a bigger kernel. I have ground it to make your pemmican, and to put in the stew."

"I have been eating the seed corn," he whispered. He looked doubtfully at the single sack. One sack would have to be enough. He carefully took a handful and set the bag aside. "I am going to see High-backed Wolf," he told her, then hurried out.

"Horse Runner," she called after him, "are you all right?"

He trotted out across the camp without bothering to answer. The corn could be more than just his means of paying the bride price. If he could talk High-backed Wolf into keeping the camp in one place long enough to grow one crop, he would kill two birds with one stone, for he could use the occasion to show the Indians the advantages of growing food for themselves.

High-backed Wolf, his eyelids closed, squatted in front of his lodge, smoking a pipe. He motioned for McCabe to sit, then passed the pipe to him. Carefully holding the stem upright, McCabe offered the smoke to the sky and the earth before taking a draw. The thick fumes were redolent of the juniper berries that had been added for sweetness, and of the powdered buffalo dung scattered atop the tobacco to ensure quick lighting. He exhaled the pungent vapors, then passed the pipe back to the chief. For a time they sat in silence.

"You seek me," the chief said at last. He tapped out the ash and dottle into a small box and slid both box and pipe into a beaded pouch.

"I have come to ask you to keep the camp in one place long enough for me to grow a crop of corn. I know the season is old, but I think it is not yet too late."

"We do not grow corn, Horse Runner. If we want corn, we trade with our friends—the Blue Cloud people, the Arapaho—who trade with the Pawnee for corn and beans and squash. We do not need to grow these things."

"But you could," McCabe insisted, holding out the handful of corn. "This is not the stunted corn the Pawnee grow. This comes from the East. Each ear is four or five times as big as an ear of Pawnee corn."

High-backed Wolf did not even look at the kernels. "We are not Pawnee. We are not Mandan. We are Cheyenne. We do not grub in the earth."

"But . . ."

"No!" There was a stern finality in the chief's voice. "If you wish to grub in the earth, Horse Runner, do so. When it is time for the camp to move, the camp will move. I have spoken." With slow dignity he stood and went into his lodge.

McCabe sat there dolefully until Spotted Fox appeared from behind the lodge and patted him on the shoulder. "I have heard you speak to the chief, Horse Runner. Your words are strange."

"What is so strange about wanting to grow some corn?" McCabe poured the grain from hand to hand. "Do you never wish to stay in one place, to stop your constant wandering and fighting?"

"No," declared Spotted Fox. "Come with me. I cannot tell stories, but Raven will tell you how we lost the corn."

"Lost the corn? What does that mean?"

"Come with me to Raven, Horse Runner."

McCabe shrugged, but he followed the other man to the shaman's lodge. The tepee had been freshly whited, and the stars and raven repainted.

"Raven," Spotted Fox called from in front of the lodge, "I am Spotted Fox. Horse Runner is with me. We wish to speak with you."

"Enter my lodge, Spotted Fox," the old voice answered. "Enter my lodge, Horse Runner."

McCabe ducked through the flap and waited until the wrinkled shaman motioned them to take seats at his left. The back edge of the tepee was raised on props to allow a breeze through.

"Raven," Spotted Fox said, "Horse Runner wishes us to grow corn."

Raven stared at them. McCabe wasn't sure if he saw astonishment or amusement in the old man's eyes. I brought him to you so that you could tell him how we lost the corn.

"Ah." The old man nodded. He settled into a half-chant, as if the story was often told. "I will tell you, Horse Runner. In the time before our grandfathers' grandfathers, the Cheyenne lived far to the east, beyond the great rivers, where there are trees everywhere, like the hairs on a buffalo, and many lakes. We lived in villages and did not move from place to place. We planted corn and beans and squash and pumpkins. But our enemies traded with the white man, who lived still farther to the east, for guns. When they attacked us, they always won, for we had no guns. Finally the chiefs decided that we could either travel to the west, or we could die. Our people packed their belongings on their backs, and on their dogs, for we had few horses, and we began the great journey. At many places did we try to make our villages, but nowhere did we find men who would accept us in peace. Always we were attacked and driven away, for now we had few arrows. We fought only with clubs and spears. Many men were killed. Many women were taken captive. The chiefs sat together again and said, 'Everywhere, the people want to fight. There is no peace. We must make war or die.' Again we were attacked, but this time we did not flee. We followed our enemies back to their camp and attacked them in the night. Many of the enemy were slain. We took their women. We took their horses. Ever since, all tribes saving only the Arapaho, are our enemies, and we may take their women and their horses when we find them. All know the Cheyenne. All fear the Cheyenne. No one comes to drive us from our land again."

For a moment after the old man had finished, McCabe was silent. At last he said, "Do you not see that you may regain the peace you spoke of? You could again live as you once did."

Raven shook his head. "The river flows one way only. It cannot be turned back on itself."

"It cannot be," Spotted Fox agreed. "To plant, we would have to stay in one place. Our enemies could then find us easily. And would they fear us if we grubbed in the earth? If we stayed in one place, we could not hunt the buffalo. Everything we have comes from the buffalo, Horse Runner. The lodge cover and the cords which bind it to the lodgepoles. The robes we sit on. Your shirt and your leggings. Your breechcloth and your moccasins. The shoulder blade makes the woman's digging stick. The horn gives a cup or ladle. The sinew is thread, and the hoof makes glue. Even the dung makes our fires. Without the buffalo we have nothing."

"I can see I have much still to learn," McCabe said sadly.

"Wisdom comes with years," Raven replied.

Outside the lodge, McCabe started to pour the corn into his belt pouch, then stopped. It didn't seem to have much importance now. He dropped it into Raven's cooking pot instead.

8

Shouting and gesturing, a group of women in a circle caught McCabe's eye as he left his lodge. He had intended to hunt, but instead he strolled over to see what they were doing. Some of the women giggled as he walked up, and he thought he heard someone murmur, "Corn." In the week since he had spoken to High-backed Wolf and Raven, the story of the corn had spread, but the Cheyenne seemed to regard it as just another of his eccentricities, like scraping his face or refusing to let his hair grow. The women were watching two teams of girls play the awl game. Shouts of betting ran around the circle, and they loudly encouraged the teams they backed. He stayed because Night Bird Woman was among the players.

On the ground to the north, south, east, and west, lines had been drawn. Those to the north and south were called rivers, those to the east and west dry rivers. On both sides of each river, three awls had been driven into the ground. A woman stood at each awl, and one at a time each would throw four sticks at a large stone in the middle of the playing surface. If the stick landed flat side up, it was a point for her team. If the stick had an awl carved on it, that woman got to throw again. If the stick landed in a river, however, or hit an awl where a woman of the other team was standing, the thrower had to start over. The first team that advanced all of its women around the circle was the winner. Women often bet jewelry or even horses on the game. Men never even bothered to watch it. The fact that McCabe did was another of his eccentricities.

Night Bird Woman eyed him as she moved around the circle. His watching seemed to unnerve her. The first time she threw, she landed in a river and had to go back. A few groans went up, and some of her teammates frowned at her, but her play didn't improve. She looked over at McCabe before every throw, and her efforts began to go wild, some missing the awl stone altogether, some hitting the awls of the other team. When all the other women of both teams had completed the circle, she was left less than halfway around. Quickly she gathered up her sticks and her awl, and hurried away.

He ran to catch up with her. "You had bad luck. Did you lose much?"

She stopped and glowered at him angrily. Finally she said, "A bracelet of silver and my third-best dress." She walked on. He followed.

"I am sorry that you lost."

She became furious. "Why are you sorry? Do you think that you are to blame? Do you think that I could not play because you were watching me?"

"No. No, of course not." Once more she hurried on, and he had to follow. "Night Bird Woman, I must talk to you. It is important. Do you have any feeling for me?"

"I like you," she replied nonchalantly. "I like Spotted Fox too. And Otter Belt is very nice."

"Do not play with me," he pleaded. "If I come to your father for you, will you marry me?"

Her face was very serious, but a smile played around her lips. "My bride price will be very high, Horse Runner."

"Whatever it is, I will pay it. . . . If you want to marry me."

"Go to my father and see. Perhaps I will send your horses back," she laughed. Suddenly she danced away, laughing over her shoulder at him. "I am not an easy catch, Horse Runner."

He shook his head ruefully She was most definitely not an easy catch. She'd make him commit himself fully before she gave even a hint. But he didn't want an easy catch, like Isobel would have been. He wanted only Night Bird Woman.

He turned back toward his lodge, but Spotted Fox bounded up, out of breath. "Come," he gasped. "You are wanted by High-backed Wolf."

McCabe reluctantly let himself be led along. "What is it? What's happened?"

"There are white men outside the camp."

For all of Spotted Fox's worry, the old chief was calm. He motioned for them both to sit with him before his lodge.

"Some of your people are here, Horse Runner," he told McCabe.

"What do they want?" For some reason, he found himself resenting the presence of other white men.

"It was Spotted Fox who spoke with them. He will tell you what he saw."

"I rode out to hunt this morning," Spotted Fox said soberly. "As I returned, I saw them. There are not many. Perhaps thirty. They have the boxes on wheels the white men use. I spoke to them. Some seemed afraid. Some seemed angry. One of them wanted to trade for the deer I had killed."

"But who are they?" McCabe insisted.

Spotted Fox frowned at the interruption. "Some wore blue coats. They said they were soldiers. Three men wore long coats like the traders at Bent's Fort, but they did not act like the traders. They stared at me as if they had never seen a man before. One, a red-hair-face, wanted to trade for my shirt. Who would trade for the shirt a man wears?"

"I do not know," McCabe replied, but he was thinking furiously. Soldiers escorting civilians, it sounded like, and on the plains, civilians only belonged to three classes: traders, trappers and missionaries "Will they be allowed to stay?" he asked the chief.

High-backed Wolf looked at him, then nodded reluctantly. "If they do not cause trouble, they may camp there. But they may not come into the

Cheyenne camp. At Bent's Fort, the traders often give the young men fire-water, then cheat them in trading when their wits are fuddled. I do not want my young men robbed."

"I will tell them," McCabe agreed. "They will remain in their own camp."

When he returned to his lodge, Looking Glass stood outside, her brow furrowed. He tied his Hawken in its sheath to his saddle and untethered the grey.

"There is a camp of your people nearby," she said suddenly. "I have heard it."

"There is," he admitted. He gripped the horse's mane and vaulted up onto its back.

"If you go to your people, you will not come back."

"Of course I will." He leaned from the saddle to touch her cheek. "It is only a small camp. I will come back. I promise."

She gave him a doubtful nod, and he galloped out of the camp.

The soldiers' camp wasn't hard to find. The sentry, standing atop a low hill, could be seen from miles away. Horses and mules were picketed in a long line across the side of the hill, and below them were scattered a dozen large-wheeled wagons and twice that many pup tents. Two larger tents of dirty grey canvas stood a little way from the rest. As McCabe rode up to the sentry, the beefy, red-faced man stared, then cocked his musket.

"Captain!" he shouted. "It's another one of them savages. You there, Injun! Halt!"

"I'm not an Indian," McCabe called back, but he pulled up his horse. The English words felt rusty in his mouth.

At the sentry's shout, soldiers, with their shirts off and their suspenders pulled up over long underwear, dropped their shovels and their currycombs to grab muskets. From one of the large tents bustled three men in civilian clothes, and from the other hurried an officer, buckling his sword belt over an undone tunic.

"What is it?" the officer called. His gaunt cheeks were blue with stubble.

"Another savage, Captain Early," the sentry stormed, pointing.

"I'm not an Indian," McCabe calmly repeated.

The captain took a step closer. "My God!" he exclaimed. "You're a white man. Are you a captive?"

"A captive would hardly be allowed to keep his gun," McCabe replied, brandishing the Hawken. "My name is Thomas McCabe. I'm here to make a report on the Cheyenne for the Office of Indian Affairs."

"From the inside," the red-bearded civilian murmured, running an eye over McCabe's garb.

"I'm Captain Peter Early," the officer said, "United States Cavalry. This is Professor Henry Chalmers of the College of New Jersey"—he indicated the man with the red beard—"and Mr. Franklin Smith and Mr. John Le-land, government mapmakers."

"Then none of you is a missionary?"

Early looked at him quizzically. "Why, no. Are you in need of one?"

McCabe shook his head. "It's of no matter. I have a message for you from High-backed Wolf, principal chief of the Cheyenne. He's given you permission to camp here as long as you want to, but none of you is to come into the Cheyenne camp."

"Why not?" Chalmers demanded. "I wanted to see the savages up close. I intend to give a series of lectures when I return on the culture and habits of the savages of the American West."

"I'd think it was enough that they didn't want you," McCabe said quietly. "Some of their warriors don't particularly like whites. They might kill a man who poked his nose into the wrong hole."

Chalmers seemed more indignant than afraid, but Smith's pudgy mouth fell open with alarm. "Why, this is the United States of America. Those savages should be taught they can't kill Americans." He blinked his watery blue eyes at Early. "They should be taught."

"I'm not doing any teaching with thirty horsesoldiers," Early said. "Mr. McCabe, perhaps you'd like to come into my tent and have a bite of civilized food?"

McCabe hesitated. Leland, who had said nothing, took a deep breath and stared at McCabe owlishly. None of the strangers was very prepossessing. On the other hand, he hadn't spoken to another white man in. . . . With a shock he realized he didn't know exactly how long it had been. He stepped down, cradling his Hawken in the crook of his arm.

"I thank you, Captain Early." He frowned. "If you don't mind, could you tell me what month it is?"

Early blinked in surprise; Chalmers smirked. "It's September," the captain said. "September 9, 1837."

"I knew the year," he said, following them to one of the big tents. "It was the month I wasn't sure of." It had been five months since he'd left Russell on the Arkansas. It felt like five years.

"You must know these savages pretty well," Chalmers commented. They squeezed in around a table, and McCabe dropped into a camp chair. It felt vaguely uncomfortable.

"They're not savages, Mr. Chalmers," he said calmly. The remark never failed to irk him, but he was determined to keep his temper. He was grateful for the chance to hear fluent English spoken.

"*Professor* Chalmers," the red-beard corrected fastidiously. "Professor of Natural History at the College of New Jersey. Now, you sound like a man with at least some education. . . ."

"Yale, class of 1832." He was pleased with Chalmers' stare at that, but the man recovered quickly.

"Well, then. As a man of education, how can you observe these people surviving by murder, rape and theft, and living lives of filth in those hovels they call tepees, and then call them anything but savage?"

Ever since he had entered the tent, McCabe had been aware of an odor, but it wasn't until he saw Smith scratching surreptitiously that he realized it was the stale body odors of the other four. They must not have washed since they left St. Louis, he thought.

"They're not filthy," he said pointedly. "They bathe every morning, if there's water nearby."

None of the whites seemed to understand. Smith scratched harder.

"That wasn't my meaning, as you're well aware," Chalmers insisted. "And what about the rest of what I said?"

"They do kill," McCabe replied carefully, "but only their enemies. Our soldiers do as much, and in the Cheyenne way of life every man is a soldier by necessity." Chalmers snorted; McCabe ignored him. "They also steal, but again only from their enemies. It seems to me I've heard of American and European soldiers doing a little looting of their own. And I've never heard of one of their braves committing rape. A Cheyenne who raped a woman, even an enemy, would be beaten and would have to pay reparations to that woman. He'd be lucky not to be killed."

"What about the women, then?" Leland asked suddenly. He leered. "I've heard you can buy one of these women for a few nails, or a bag of beans."

"Not a Cheyenne woman," McCabe said flatly.

Leland snickered. "I saw some of them going out by themselves. No men. They didn't look like much, but I'll wager once you got all those blankets peeled off . . ."

"Leland," McCabe broke in, "if you touch one of those women, the Cheyenne will kill you for sure. They might kill everyone in this camp."

There was a long minute of silence, then Early spoke. "Mr. McCabe, I'd appreciate it if you stopped trying to scare these men with all this talk of killing. Mr. Leland won't be touching any of those women, but if he did, I'd handle it, not the Indians. This is the United States of America, after all."

"To the Cheyenne," McCabe said quietly, "this is their land. They only let us cross over it as a favor, and they're more than a little concerned about just how many whites have been taking advantage of their generosity."

They might as well get used to it," Early said.

"People are beginning to immigrate to Oregon. That means wagon roads. That's why I'm here with Mr. Smith and Mr. Leland, to map this territory for a road."

"The Cheyenne won't like that. Neither will the Kiowa, the Comanche, or any of the other tribes you may come across."

"Like I said, McCabe, they'll have to get used to it. If they try to interfere, they'll be stopped. I may not be able to do much with thirty troopers, but if it takes three hundred or three thousand to ensure safe passage for the settlers, they'll be sent. You can bank on that."

McCabe felt a chill. The soldiers would be sent, three thousand or ten times that number, and if the soldiers came, the Cheyenne would fight. Against such numbers, all armed with guns, they could not win. But they would fight.

"That's enough talk of fighting," Chalmers grumbled. He produced a square bottle from under the table. "I have a more pleasant way to pass the time. Try this." He poured a tin cup full and pushed it across the table to his quirt so hard that it broke with a loud crack. "How could the Kiowa kill all of the Bow Strings?"

"South of the Antelope Hills," the chief explained, "they were set upon by Sitting Bear, the Kiowa war chief, and many warriors. All were killed and scalped." The women's wailing rose in volume.

"We must avenge them," Three Hatchets growled.

"We must make war on the Kiowa!" Otter Belt shouted.

"War," echoed Spotted Fox.

McCabe stared at his two friends in astonishment as the same shout went up throughout the crowd and across the camp.

High-backed Wolf waited patiently for the noise to fall. "My people, war is a matter that must be discussed at the Council of Chiefs. I will send riders to all of the other bands, to the Omissis and the Hevataniu and the rest. I will ask the chiefs to consider. I have spoken."

As the crowd broke up, McCabe spoke to his friends. "Why did you call for war? I have seen others killed on raids, but never has there been a call for war."

Spotted Fox looked frustrated. "This was different, Horse Runner. These men were members of a society."

"And all were killed," Otter Belt added. "All. They must be avenged."

"I suppose they must," McCabe sighed.

"Horse Runner," Spotted Fox said, "if so many of your own people were killed by your enemies, would you not go to war?"

"I accept that you must do this," McCabe answered. "But I wish it were not so. How soon will you go?"

"It will not be soon," Spotted Fox told him. "Many messages must be sent. The chiefs must meet. Many guns must be traded for, with the traders at Bent's Fort. All will not be ready until the winter, and no one can fight in the winter."

"We will not carry the Sacred Arrows south until the snow melts," Otter Belt said.

"Then there will be time for you to help me. I am going to ask Elk Antler for Night Bird Woman."

Otter Belt gave a joyous whoop, but Spotted Fox looked at him quizzically. "You will marry now? When war comes?"

"Yes. Is there some law or custom against it?"

McCabe. The others held out their own cups eagerly, tossing out coffee grounds for the whiskey.

McCabe took a swallow and almost gagged. It was pure fire going down. "I'd better go easy," he said when he had his breath back. "I'm not used to this anymore." The others only grunted, but Chalmers smiled maliciously.

"I've been admiring your hat, Mr. McCabe, especially those feathers. I'll need a few artifacts for my lectures. Perhaps you'd like to sell it?"

McCabe smiled bitterly. "Been talking to some traders, have you? Well, I'm not an Indian. I don't want to sell. And a little whiskey won't change my mind."

"Oh, I didn't mean to confuse you with whiskey," Chalmers said innocently. "I'll pay a good price. Five dollars? Ten? I'll double what it cost you."

"I don't think you could meet that price, Mr. Chalmers."

One of the soldiers pushed into the tent to set a kettle and a stack of tin plates on the table.

Early brought spoons and bread, and slopped a lumpy brown stew onto the plates. The others fell to eating with a will, but McCabe took a spoonful and pushed the rest around on his plate while the others wolfed theirs down. There were large bites of what he thought was dried beef, but mainly there was the taste of flour.

Early paused long enough to say, "Good to get some civilized food after eating that offal those savages make, isn't it?"

McCabe smiled back and kept on pushing his stew around with the bread. Even if there had been some taste to it, the smell in the tent was enough to ruin his appetite.

When the stew was gone, Chalmers pulled out his bottle once more. "A little something to wash it down? But you haven't even finished your first."

"No, thank you," McCabe said. He pushed back from the table. "I have to be going."

Chalmers followed him outside. "I really do need artifacts, McCabe. If you won't sell, maybe you know one of the savages who will."

McCabe mounted without answering and rode away without looking back.

"You'd better look out, McCabe," Chalmers shouted after him. "If you aren't careful, you might find your own skin turning red."

❖

At the camp McCabe rode straight to his lodge. He dropped to a squat in front of the cooking fire. Looking Glass took one look at his frowning face and stayed away from him.

Savages, are they? he thought angrily. He watched the girls kicking their ball, some others playing the awl game. Some of the smaller boys were being chosen by girls who wanted to play mother. A knot of bigger boys, racing stick horses, dashed by. Those men, sitting in their stink, had called the Cheyenne filthy. Could he have been away so long that he no longer saw the same things as other whites? It couldn't be. The men in the camp had to be just an unsavory bunch. But even Early, the best of them, had talked as if the Indians were no more than rowdies and roughnecks who had to be kept in line. For long hours he squatted, worrying, while the sun fell.

"Horse Runner," Looking Glass blared suddenly. "Look!" There is a man on foot."

McCabe started and peered around at the lengthening shadow, then got to his feet. A Cheyenne man never walked if he could ride. It must be one of the whites, and he had no wish to get involved with them again.

When he looked, though, he could see that the man stumbling toward the camp was naked except for a breechcloth, and was weaving from side to side, as if hurt. Then the figure abruptly fell. With a sudden suspicion, McCabe ran toward him.

It was Otter Belt, lying on his back, giggling. Except for the breechcloth, not even his coup feathers or his bear-claw necklace remained. Beside him on the ground lay one of Chalmers' square bottles.

"Where is your horse?" McCabe asked. "Where is your bow, and your clothes?"

Otter Belt waved a hand at the sunset. "Off there. Somewhere." He seemed to see McCabe for the first time. "Horse Runner! You must drink with me." He fumbled for the bottle, but McCabe grabbed it and shattered it against a rock. Otter Belt lifted his head to look around. "The bottle, Horse Runner. Your people gave me a fine bottle. Where is it?"

McCabe hoisted the young man onto his own shoulders. "Not my people," he muttered. "Not mine." And he started back to the camp.

9

❖

Two days after the whites departed, seven Arapaho rode into the camp. McCabe looked at them with interest. They were generally of shorter stature than the Cheyenne, and they looked less warlike. They were called the Blue Cloud people because they were friends with everyone, though the Cheyenne were their particular friends. They filed into High-backed Wolf's lodge where McCabe joined Spotted Fox and Otter Belt in the crowd of watchers.

In a short time the chief came out. He waited until all of the Arapaho had followed before he spoke. "Our brothers, the Blue Clouds, bring us word of the Bow Strings. They have seen the scalps of the Bow Strings in the camp of the Kiowa." A moan ran through the onlookers. Some of the women began keening and tearing at their clothes.

"How did this thing happen?" Three Hatchets demanded. He gripped

"No," Spotted Fox answered slowly.

"It is time to talk of important things," Otter Belt broke in. "We must see that you are dressed in your finest. Come."

McCabe found himself pulled to his lodge by the two men, who laughed as they ran him along. The two men fell on his belongings immediately, pulling out this garment and that, commenting loudly on whether or not it was fine enough. Looking Glass stood staring at them in confusion.

"I am going to ask for Night Bird Woman," McCabe explained. "They are helping me to find the best clothes."

"You must impress Elk Antler," Otter Belt cried as he discarded a pair of leggings. "You must show him that you are an important man."

"Yes," Looking Glass agreed. "You must impress him. Sit, and I will comb your hair." She produced a beaded comb made from the tail of a porcupine. He sat, and she began to run it through his hair, which he had finally allowed to grow long. It now hung below his jaw.

With much shouting and bickering Spotted Fox and Otter Belt decided on McCabe's garb and saw that he was dressed. The long shirt had quillwork spirals down the arms, and beaded horses ran across the front. The leggings had been beaten and bleached until the supple buckskin was almost white, with tufts of elk fur down the outer sides. The moccasins reached high above the ankle and were quilled in yellow and black. Finally, his fur cap was set on his head, and a wolfskin robe was laid around his shoulders.

Spotted Fox nodded. "You are ready, Horse Runner."

McCabe felt flutters in his stomach as the two men escorted him to Elk Antler's lodge. Along the way they coached him in what he should say. People who saw him immediately realized the reason for his fancy clothing, and they laughed and waved. Three Hatchets came out of his lodge as they approached, and his face went pale with anger. He stalked after them.

In front of Elk Antler's lodge, McCabe had to quell a sudden desire to run. He cleared his throat. "Elk Antler! I am Horse Runner. I want to talk with you about your daughter."

"Enter my lodge, Horse Runner," came his reply, "and we will talk."

McCabe took a deep breath and ducked through the entrance.

Elk Antler, leathery-faced, his hair streaked with grey, sat cross-legged on the other side of the fire, facing the entrance. Night Bird Woman knelt to her father's right, in the family part of the lodge. She pretended to sew, but her eyes continually strayed to McCabe.

Elk Antler, motioning for McCabe to take a place to his left, waited for the supplicant to sit. "You want to speak of my daughter, Horse Runner? What do you want to say of her?"

"I want to marry her," he said simply.

The older man nodded impassively. "She is a fine girl. Very pretty. This will be her eighteenth winter."

"I know," McCabe acknowledged. Then her father continued to extol her virtues.

"She is a member of the Quillers' Society. Her work is praised at their feasts. Her garments are fine. By herself she can skin and dress a buffalo in less than two hours. She can carry many loads of firewood and water without complaining. I do not have to beat her too much. She digs my turnips and gathers many berries. Her pot is always filled with good stew. Her hips are wide and will bear many children."

"Yes," McCabe interrupted. "I know of all of her virtues."

The old man seemed disappointed at not being left to enumerate the rest, but McCabe decided it was time to list his own good points. "I have a fine lodge, seven horses and two mules. There is always meat for my pot, and my pot is always there for those who are hungry. I fetch many furs. I am a good hunter."

"And a brave warrior," Night Bird Woman added. She colored and returned to her sewing when her father stared at her sternly.

"My daughter," the old man went on, "will marry only if she chooses to. I will not give her to a man she does not want, as some fathers do. Speak, daughter. Will you have this man?"

Slowly she raised her dark eyes to McCabe's, studying him. "I will have him, Father," she said at last. "But my bride price must be fifty horses."

The jaws of both men dropped. Even a chief's daughter would cost only half that.

"My daughter," Elk Antler scolded, "it is not your place to set your own bride price."

"I must be certain that he wants me," she said calmly. Her eyes never left McCabe's. "When he first came to our camp, his eyes followed me always. Then they did not. Now again he seems to want me."

"But I did not understand," McCabe protested. "I thought that you were not interested. I thought you did not like me."

"I must be certain," she maintained. "I do not want to be sent away if you decide you want another instead."

Her father nodded. "That is her right, Horse Runner. Her price is fifty horses."

"Night Bird Woman," McCabe said insistently, "I *do* want you. Only you. I have already arranged to give Looking Glass her freedom."

"That is how you prove your faithfulness?" she responded scornfully. "By sending her away? Perhaps you will do the same to me."

McCabe felt like tearing at his hair. "Don't you want me to send Looking Glass away?"

"Do you want me to do all the work alone, when I could have someone to help me? Am I to have no one to talk to? Who will warm your blankets when I am with child, or in my time?"

"I . . . I will keep her, then, if that is your wish."

She nodded decisively. "If we become friends, she and I, perhaps in a year or two you will marry her. I would not mind so long as I am first wife."

"Of course," he agreed hollowly.

"If I do not like her," she went on, "I will ask you not to marry her, so that I may beat her when she displeases me.

"Night Bird Woman," he began hesitantly, "I am not certain. That is, among my people it is the custom to have only one wife at a time."

"Only one?" she queried. "But how can that be?"

"It is our way. Our custom."

"It is a foolish custom. You are a Cheyenne now, Horse Runner. You must follow Cheyenne custom. The importance of a man is known not only by his coups, but by the number of his wives. My father has five," she told him proudly.

McCabe blinked. The five women he had often seen about the old man's lodge ranged from a fat, jolly woman almost as old as Elk Antler to a slender girl not much older than Night Bird Woman.

"Good wives," Elk Antler remarked, nodding.

"I see," McCabe said. "It will take me time to get the fifty horses, Elk Antler, but I will do it. I will get them, Night Bird Woman."

She leaned forward to touch his hand briefly. "If you come this evening we may sit together."

He had often seen the courting couples sitting together, shyly holding hands. McCabe had often wondered how a man could stand the watchful gaze of the girl's parents and the giggles of children and girls who made it a point to pass by. "I will come," he said.

Spotted Fox and Otter Belt were waiting expectantly when he emerged from the lodge. "She said yes," he announced, and they began to whoop and dance. "Her bride price is fifty horses."

The two men stopped their dance and stared.

"I could marry any girl in the camp for five horses," Spotted Fox exclaimed.

Otter Belt shook his head gravely. "Elk Antler's brains must be faded with age. If High-backed Wolf had a daughter, he would ask no more than twenty or twenty-five horses."

"You will never get them, Mack Cabe," called Three Hatchets, who was marching arrogantly up to McCabe. The heavyset warrior's muscular shoulders had been rubbed with buffalo grease to make them glisten. "You will never have Night Bird Woman. Elk Antler sets such a price so his daughter will not go to a *white*." He spat out the last word.

"It was Night Bird Woman who set the price," McCabe answered quietly.

His friends gasped at the impropriety. Three Hatchets smiled confidently and turned to the lodge. "Elk Antler! I am Three Hatchets. I would like to speak with you of your daughter."

"Enter my lodge, Three Hatchets, and we will talk."

The muscular warrior sneered at McCabe and pushed through the door flap. Spotted Fox and Otter Belt looked at each other doubtfully. McCabe kept his eyes on the lodge. In a few minutes the voices grew louder inside. Suddenly Three Hatchets stormed out, glaring at McCabe.

"You will not have her, Mack Cabe!" he shouted, and stalked off.

McCabe sighed with relief. For a minute he had had the suspicion that Three Hatchets might have been right. "Now I must get the horses," he told Spotted Fox and Otter Belt.

"We could steal them from the Utes," Spotted Fox suggested. "Or the Crow. They are not far."

"The Crow!" Otter Belt exclaimed. "You would steal from men who let a woman lead them in battle? They call her Woman Chief, Horse Runner. These old women of the Crow count her as a war chief."

"We will not steal the horses," McCabe declared. "I will trade for them."

Both men fell silent. Finally Spotted Fox said, "Horse Runner, if there were fifty horses to be traded at Bent's Fort, they would cost four hundred good buffalo robes."

"That is almost three years' work for five women," Otter Belt remarked with downcast eyes.

"I did not say I would trade buffalo robes," McCabe barked.

"What then?" Spotted Fox asked.

"Something. You both have beaver traps, but you do not use them. Lend me your traps, and I will give you some of the furs I take."

Spotted Fox looked doubtful. "Have you ever trapped beaver?"

"The beaver dwindle, Horse Runner," Otter Belt cautioned. "A winter of trapping takes only as many as could once be had in a single month. And there are many Utes in the mountains, many Crow. It is better if we steal the horses."

"Will you lend me the traps?" McCabe repeated.

The two men looked at each other, and Spotted Fox smiled. "We will lend you the traps, Horse Runner," he said. "And we will come with you. Together we will take many beaver."

10

◈

The wind died down, and McCabe cocked his ear to listen for any sounds. A crow flapped up across the stream, cawing. Spotted Fox pulled his horse back into the willows. Nothing else moved. The stream rippled its way through the pine-covered banks toward the Colorado. McCabe rode out of the trees and down into a rocky hollow nearby. Otter Belt and Looking Glass followed, tugging the leads of the pack animals, and Spotted Fox galloped through the water.

"You will scare the beaver away," McCabe called out.

"We will not trap near the camp," Spotted Fox said. He leaped down and began untying the bags on Otter Belt's pack horse that held their traps. "Tell your woman to make a lodge of saplings against the bank of hollow, and we will show you how to set the traps."

At a word from McCabe, Looking Glass climbed down from her mare and set off to cut the saplings. Otter Belt took a bag of six traps from Spotted Fox and handed one to McCabe.

McCabe was also given a bundle of dried hardwood stakes to carry. He was beginning to feel like one of the pack animals, but the other two had to be able to set the traps. McCabe and Otter Belt put the sixty-pound sacks on their shoulders as they waded into the icy stream. McCabe's rifle and the others' muskets were slung on rawhide cords across their backs. Spotted Fox carried only a buffalo-horn flask on a cord and an axe thrust through his belt.

"The water is cold," McCabe grumbled. "Can we not walk along the bank?"

Otter Belt shook his head. "We must leave no scent to scare the beaver."

McCabe adjusted the bag of traps on his shoulder and nodded sourly. Spotted Fox took the lead, studying the bank as they waded through water that was now above waist-level. McCabe's buckskins, chilled with the water, grew cold and stiff against his skin. When they were a mile farther upstream, Spotted Fox suddenly stopped and pointed to a patch of scraped dirt on the bank.

"That is where the beaver enters the stream. See his sign beyond the turned earth? We will make a set here."

Setting his bag down in the water, Spotted Fox took out one of the traps and unwound it from its chain. The V-shaped springs on either side had to be unfolded, and then the trap could be set on the bottom of the river. Spotted Fox stepped on the springs to depress them, opened the rectangular jaws, and slipped in the catch. When a beaver stepped on the pan, the trap would spring.

"See," Spotted Fox directed, placing the trap. "It must lie with the width of a man's hand below the surface. No more and no less. If necessary, cut away some of the bank, or dig a hole in the river bottom. Hand me a stake, Horse Runner."

Taking the stake, he unwound the six-foot chain into deeper water. A rawhide lashing secured the last ring of the chain to the stake, which he drove into the streambed.

"Here," Otter Belt said, wading carefully from the other side of the stream where he had cut a willow switch.

"The bait," Spotted Fox responded. Peeling the top of the switch, he uncorked the buffalo-horn flask and poured a little liquid on it, holding it away so none fell on him. "The scent of beaver glands. Man cannot smell it, but the beaver can." He thrust the stick into the bank so that the end was six inches above the trap, at the surface of the water.

"It is set," Otter Belt said with satisfaction. "Let us go on, for the water is cold."

As they waded on, McCabe looked back. There was nothing to be seen except two innocuous sticks and the wind riffling the water's surface.

Setting the rest of the traps took them until early afternoon. The three men, cold and stiff, returned to camp only to find Looking Glass laboring over a half-completed framework of bent willow saplings. A bubbling pot sat over a small fire. They rushed to the stew, wolfing it down and huddling around the flames for warmth. That night all four slept huddled together for warmth.

At first light the three men waded upstream from the camp. The first set seemed undisturbed to McCabe as they approached, though the willow stick was twisted a little to one side, and the stake leaned a bit.

As soon as Spotted Fox saw the stake, he broke into a huge grin. "Ho, Horse Runner. We have something." He went over to the stake and felt along the chain, which now led toward deeper water. With a sudden shout he straightened, the trap in his hand, a beaver dangling from it by a foreleg. Quickly he depressed the springs enough to free the animal, and handed it to McCabe. "Skin it on the far bank, so the scent of blood will not frighten others away. I will reset the trap."

"Take the tail, too," Otter Belt instructed. "It is very good to eat."

A mile or so away from the stream, a flurry of crows suddenly sprang up, cawing furiously. The three men froze. The sounds receded as the birds flapped away.

"It was a deer," Spotted Fox said finally.

"Or a bear," Otter Belt offered.

"Yes," McCabe said. "A deer. Or a bear." But he noticed that both of the others now had their muskets in their hands instead of on their backs.

They waded to shore, and McCabe bent to do the skinning, but he kept a wary eye running along the banks and into the depths of the pine forest. His knife made a quick slit down the belly of the beaver, and two more to each leg. The feet and tail were cut off, and the hide peeled away from the carcass. Then he stuffed the pelt into his rawhide sack.

Before the morning was out, they had run the twelve traps and found twelve beaver. "It is like the days of our fathers!" Otter Belt shouted when the last skin was taken.

Something splashed upstream, and McCabe whirled, thumbing back the hammer on his Hawken. A deer skittered back into the woods before he could fire. Out of the corner of his eye he could see the others lowering their muskets.

Spotted Fox eased the hammer down on his musket and hefted the gun absently. "We will check the sets again when the sun is falling. We must make certain they are not too easily seen."

McCabe led off back down the stream, the water swirling and splashing around his knees. All the way back to the camp his eyes searched the willows.

◇

McCabe examined the beaver skins, which had been propped up near the fire in the lodge. They were thawed. He began cutting them loose from the willow hoops they had been stretched on. Outside, the wind rose to a howl and faded again.

"We do well," Otter Belt declared. As quickly as McCabe cut a skin loose, he laid it in the press that crowded one side of the lodge. Six upright poles were lashed together by a framework at the top. Another, the lever, lay beside them. "In less than three moons we have taken close to four hundred beaver."

Spotted Fox sat checking the sinew string of his bow. "Perhaps we will have what we need by the end of winter."

"Perhaps," McCabe returned. "If we are lucky."

As the last pelt was placed between the poles, McCabe laid rawhide cords across the top of the bundle. Other cords had been laid before the first hide was placed in the press. "Come help us," he told Spotted Fox.

The lever was put over the top of the furs, tilted up as steeply as it could be inside the lodge, and the low end was fastened with braided rawhide rope.

"Now," McCabe commanded. All three men grabbed the lever simultaneously and jumped. As the bundle of furs slowly compressed, the three men wriggled onto the lever, leaning across it and bouncing to force it a little lower. Finally the furs could be compressed no more by their crude machine. "Quickly, Looking Glass," McCabe shouted. "The cords."

Leaving her cooking pot, she darted over to tie the cords. McCabe and the others got down from the lever. The rawhide creaked, and the pack expanded a trifle and was still. Quickly McCabe unlashed the top framework, and the other two men helped him lift out the pack of furs. Sixty pelts, he thought. Close to one hundred pounds of beaver. It would fetch three hundred dollars at Bent's Fort, or six horses. And there were six more packs outside in the lean-to that sheltered the horses from the snow.

"You spend much time with the beaver," Looking Glass observed. "You should spend more time with the elk."

"What do you mean?" McCabe asked. He checked the small pot, in which the castoreum glands of many beaver were boiling to make bait scent.

"The last of the venison is cooking. If you do not hunt today, tomorrow we must eat what is in your pot."

McCabe nodded slowly. They had done little hunting, though deer, elk and even a bear had been taken while they ran the traps. More than once they had eaten beaver, but even Otter Belt had begun to say he no longer cared for beaver tail. McCabe began to fasten snowshoes to his moccasins. "I will hunt."

"I will go with you," Spotted Fox proposed. "It is better not to waste powder and lead."

The snow had now stopped, but the wind still blew fiercely. McCabe pulled the hood of his wolfskin coat closer around his cheeks as they shuffled past the lean-to where the horses huddled, tails pulled tight against the wind. Fresh snow covered the landscape, and some of the small rivulets running into the stream were covered with ice.

"The big streams will not freeze," Spotted Fox said, his words coming in a cloud of vapor.

As they walked abreast, clumsy in their snowshoes, McCabe scanned the ground for sign, while Spotted Fox kept watch around them, Deer or elk could often he sighted stretching for low leaves, especially now that the ground forage was covered.

"Ho, Horse Runner," Spotted Fox called softly, pointing at the snow to his left. "Tracks. A deer."

They curved off after the tracks. Several times they came to places where the animal had stopped to crop at leaves growing on a low-hanging branch.

McCabe caught a flash of movement ahead and pointed silently. Two hundred yards through the trees a big buck moved warily, his huge antlers swinging as he lifted his nose to test the wind. The wind blew toward the men, though, and did not carry their scent. Carefully they began to stalk, crouching low and moving from bare bushes to fallen trees, always keeping a tree or a bush between them and the buck in case it looked back. The deer continued its slow drift. After an hour they had come no closer than fifty yards.

"I am going to try a shot," McCabe whispered. He fumbled his right hand out of its mitten and checked the cap on his Hawken. At that range the rifle shot almost flatly, and the heavy lead ball would make a sure kill.

"The noise," Spotted Fox said quietly. "There are others in these mountains."

"We have seen no one," McCabe answered. "We have seen no sign." He thumbed back the hammer and drew a bead on the animal.

But before he could squeeze the trigger there was a sharp crack, and both men froze. The deer took one staggering step and fell. McCabe crouched against the trunk of an ash, looking for the shooter.

A man swathed in furs ran heavily through the snow to the fallen animal. McCabe realized with a start that he had a beard. He was a white trapper.

"I got him," the trapper shouted. Five more men floundered up on horses, leading a saddled horse and pack mules. Two of them jumped down and fell on the deer, wielding their knives.

"They are your people," Spotted Fox whispered. "Perhaps they will give us some of the deer."

McCabe put a hand on his arm as he started to rise. "No." The mounted men held their rifles ready, peering carefully about them.

"I have twice been to their gatherings in the summer," Spotted Fox insisted, "on the Sis-ke-dee, what they call the Green River. They will trade with us."

"And what if they decide they would like four hundred more pelts?" McCabe asked quietly. "They are six to our three, and their packs are small. I do not think their trapping has been so good as ours."

"But they are your people."

"I am no longer so certain. We will find another deer and kill it with the bow." He drew Spotted Fox away.

As they slipped through the trees, he took one last look back. Who were his people?

❖

It had to be past the first of the year, McCabe thought as he slipped under the bearskin beside Looking Glass. Three weeks had passed since they had seen the trappers, and two more bales of pelts rested in the lean-to with the horses.

"Soon you will have all the furs you need," Looking Glass said softly.

"I did not know you were still awake." She snuggled closer, pressing her breasts against him. He put his arm around her.

The fire had dwindled to glowing coals, and the other two men were sleeping beneath their furs. One of them snored.

"I have not spoken to you about my getting married to Night Bird Woman, Looking Glass, and you have said nothing."

"It is good for a man to marry," she said simply.

"I wanted to give you your freedom, but Night Bird Woman says I should not."

She gazed at him dreamily. "Why should you send me away, Horse Runner? Have I not pleased you?"

"You have, very much. But I am taking a wife."

"And you would make her do all the work when I could help? Who will come to your blankets when she is ill, or tired?"

"She said the same thing," he laughed.

"Of course."

"But it is not the way of my people."

"Many Cheyenne have more than one wife."

"But I am not . . ." He sighed and touched her cheek.

She giggled suddenly. "Will you talk all night? The others are asleep and cannot hear what we do."

"I will not talk," he laughed, and pulled her closer.

He woke in the darkness, wondering what had startled him from sleep. Looking Glass remained still, sleeping contentedly by his side, and the only sound was the light snoring of one of the men. He was about to close his eyes again when something creaked at the lodge door.

His hand snaked from under the bearskin and pulled back the hammer on his rifle. Suddenly there was a shriek and a long-haired warrior pushed into the lodge, a tomahawk in his hand. McCabe lifted the gun and fired one-handed. The .50-caliber lead ball smashed the Indian back through the door flap.

From outside came abrupt shouts, then musket shots crashed through the walls of the lodge. Spotted Fox leaped to his feet, then drooped again as a ball burned across his cheek. Looking Glass screamed, and Otter Belt scrambled for his musket.

McCabe snatched the two Paterson Colts from where they lay beside his bed and rolled to the door. In the dim morning light he could see a dozen shapes, some mounted nearby, and there were more in the distance. Thrusting the guns through the door, he fired as fast as he could draw a bead and thumb back the hammer. Men dropped in the snow, and the shouts turned to screams. Abruptly they were gone, melting into the morning mist. Four still shapes lay outside the lodge. Another man struggled to crawl away. The hair of these warriors was partially shaved from their heads, but it fell almost to their waists.

McCabe squatted just outside the lodge, his eyes searching the trees around the camp, and he hurriedly reloaded. Otter Belt, wearing only his breechcloth, ran to the struggling man and crushed his head with the butt of his musket.

"They are Crow," Spotted Fox observed.

Looking Glass peered out of the lodge, clutching her robes around her. "What will we do?" Her voice shook.

"Pack everything," McCabe concluded, "and move. We will camp far from here until the Crow are gone."

"But the traps," Otter Belt protested.

"We will come back for the traps later," McCabe promised. "Better to lose the traps than our lives."

"These are yours, Horse Runner," Spotted Fox said. "Do you want the scalps?"

"No," McCabe replied. As he hurried into his clothes, the other two whipped out their knives and bent down over the dead Crow.

From the camp they went directly into the stream. The four pack horses were strung together so that Looking Glass could lead them while the men had their hands free to use their weapons. The Crow would soon figure out why there were no tracks leaving the camp but they would still have to decide whether they had gone upstream or downstream. He hoped they would puzzle over it long enough to give him and the others a lead.

McCabe took the lead, Hawken held ready and Colts in his belt. Otter Belt rode close behind, musket in hand. His bow, which he would always use after the first shot, hung by a thong from his saddle. Looking Glass followed with the pack horses, and Spotted Fox covered their rear. Everyone watched the banks cautiously.

"In another half mile," McCabe said, "we will start marking false trails from the stream."

"That is good," Otter Belt attested. At that moment the Crow charged.

McCabe brought up the Hawken and fired. The lead Crow, taking the ball full in the chest, seemed to suddenly stop while his horse ran out from under him. With his left hand McCabe slung the rifle on his back, while with his right he pulled a pistol from his belt. Spotted Fox and Otter Belt were already loosing arrows as fast as they could nock them. One took a Crow in the throat, and another man went down with a shaft sticking out from his eye.

A knot of the warriors rushed at McCabe. He fired and missed, and the group, expecting a single pistol shot, began to whoop victoriously. His second shot caught a warrior in the chest, and the third bullet clipped the feathers from another warrior's head. He clawed his tomahawk from his belt as they closed in, desperately blocking a lance that was thrust at him. Sticking the muzzle close to—almost in—a passing warrior's mouth, he fired. The warrior fell off his horse, his face a bloody mess. The man with the lance came at him again, but this time McCabe had his tomahawk ready and swung it into the side of the warrior's head. McCabe's last two shots left powder burns on the hunting coat of the final attacker.

"Horse Runner!" Looking Glass screamed behind him.

He whirled his horse to find her frantically using her knife to fend off another Crow who was equipped with a lance. She released the rope on the pack animals as her horse reared. The horse backed all the way into a water hole and went down, dumping Looking Glass in the process. She struggled to her feet in the muddy water. Her knife was gone.

With a cry, McCabe kicked his horse forward. Hastily he replaced the empty Colt in his belt and drew the other one, firing as the Crow raised his lance above Looking Glass.

A black hole appeared in the man's red-quilled coat. He jerked suddenly, but somehow retained his seat. His lance swept away from the girl toward McCabe, and he charged.

McCabe quickly drew rein to give himself a steady seat. Taking deliberate aim, he fired. Another hole sprang up in the Crow's shirt, but still he came on. Again McCabe fired, and again. The Crow jerked at each impact and blood poured down the front of his shirt, but still he came. McCabe watched the point of the lance rush closer—thirty feet, twenty, ten. He fired again. A bloody hole bloomed between the Crow's eyes, and he tumbled off his horse.

"Looking Glass!" McCabe shouted, leaning out of the saddle. He swung the horse closer to her as she ran to him with uplifted arms, and he pulled her up behind him.

As he settled her, an arrow struck his left arm, passing all the way through so that the stone head projected behind him. Quickly he broke off the shaft at the front and, gritting his teeth, he seized the arrow behind the head and pulled it on through with a deep groan.

The pack horses had wandered loose in the stream, and the fight was becoming desperate. There would be no chance to reload his weapons. He could see that the others were hard-pressed too. Both men still fought, but Spotted Fox had blood running down his face, and an arrow shaft stuck out of Otter Belts thigh.

"Spotted Fox!" he shouted. "Otter Belt! Run! Come on!" As the two men broke away from the Crow, he dug his heels into his horse's flanks and splashed down the stream, Looking Glass clinging to his waist.

A triumphant shout went up from the Crow. Arrows whistled around the fleeing horses. McCabe risked a look over his shoulder, and then drew rein. They were no longer being chased.

Half a mile back up the creek out of range of arrows and muskets, twenty Crow milled around the pack horses, shouting victoriously. One rode a little way toward them, waving something over his head tauntingly.

"The traps!" Otter Belt cried. "They have the traps."

Spotted Fox only shook his head.

McCabe drew a shuddering breath and lowered his voice. "We can recover nothing. If we try, we will only die. I am going back to my lodge."

Without another word he turned his horse out of the stream and rode into the woods. After a few minutes the others followed.

11

For two days after they had returned to the Cheyenne camp, McCabe remained in his lodge. Then, on the third day, he emerged to find Otter Belt and Spotted Fox sitting outside, robes drawn against the cold.

"We have respected your wish to be left alone, Horse Runner," Spotted Fox said.

Otter Belt nodded. "We did not know if you were ill."

"I am well," McCabe replied. "have you seen Night Bird Woman?"

"She came the day we returned," Spotted Fox replied, "after you had gone into your lodge. We told her of the Crow, and she ran back to her father's lodge crying."

"I am going to get the horses," McCabe stated grimly. "Ask among the young men of the camp who will come with me."

Otter Belt gave a whoop and began to laugh in delight, but Spotted Fox looked serious. "Is it a good time to do this thing?" he asked.

The younger man's laughter stopped. "Spotted Fox speaks wisely," Otter Belt admitted. "The tribe is preparing for war."

"To avenge the Bow Strings?" asked McCabe.

Spotted Fox nodded. "Already men trade at Bent's Fort for guns. In two moons all the bands will assemble. We will advance the Sacred Arrows against the Kiowa."

"Two moons. Then there is still time. Ask the young men."

After they had gone, Looking Glass came out of the lodge. "I heard your words to Spotted Fox and Otter Belt," she told him as she looked into the cooking pot.

"And?" He squatted and began oiling the lock on the Hawken.

"There is anger in you. It is not good to go horse hunting when there is anger in you."

"The Crow stole my furs, the furs I would have traded for horses. I will take the horses I need from the Crow in payment."

"Evil will come from this," she warned.

He laughed. "You begin to sound like Spotted Fox when I first knew him. He too always said bad things would come. But they never did."

She slammed the ladle into the cooking pot. "Do not laugh at me, Horse Runner. I have dreamed of a black buffalo bull driving you before it. In the dreams, you do not know the bull is there. You think that you run where you want to, but it is the bull who drives you." And she rushed into the lodge.

He got up to follow, but as he stood, two young braves, Buffalo Horn and No Tail, walked up and sat in front of the lodge. On their heels were Spotted Fox and Otter Belt and Walks Wide of His Horses. Soon thirty men sat cross-legged in a wide semicircle. Three Hatchets stood to the rear, watching.

"I intend to go horse hunting among the Crow," McCabe announced.

A low murmur rippled through the assembled men.

"War comes with the Kiowa," Buffalo Horn said, standing. He was a slender man, and he wore his hair in four long braids. "The Crow are far away. Why should we go against them now?" He sat down again.

"What need is there of reason to go against the Crow?" McCabe answered. "The Cheyenne have always taken horses from anyone they wished. We will return before the people go south to war, with many horses."

Walks Wide of His Horses stood next. His shirt and leggings were fringed with the scalps of men he had killed in battle. "War comes with the Kiowa. If we go horse hunting among the Crow, some men will not return. Every man will be needed against the Kiowa, for their number is as great as the blades of grass in a field."

"I do not intend to lose any warriors," McCabe responded as the other man sat down. "We go to steal horses, not count coup. I have to plan so that the Crow will run in circles while we steal their horses and ride away."

"Horse Runner is a brave warrior," No Tail said, getting to his feet. "It is known that you fight well. But it is not known if you plan well. How will you do this thing?"

"I will tell the plan only to those who come with me. I trust only men who trust me. I lead this raid."

"You lead this raid," Three Hatchets sneered. A few turned to look at him. "Mack Cabe thinks like a white man. He goes against the Crow because he let them steal his furs in the mountains. Remember, those of you who are thinking of going with him, that Mack Cabe brings trouble with him on his back. We go to war because of Mack Cabe."

There was a shocked silence. McCabe tried to keep his voice cool. "The Cheyenne go to war because Grey Bear talked forty-seven other Bow Strings into riding to their deaths."

"It was because of you!" Three Hatchets shouted angrily. "Mack Cabe was given honors no white man should have been given. Some had begun to talk as if Mack Cabe were a Cheyenne. Grey Bear had to show what a true Cheyenne is. Mack Cabe is not a Cheyenne. Mack Cabe is a white man. Go away, Mack Cabe. Leave us to fight the war you have brought."

"Here I am called Horse Runner," McCabe replied.

"Mack Cabe," Three Hatchets sneered. "You are Mack Cabe."

"High-backed Wolf himself gave me that name. Do you challenge his right?"

Three Hatchets hesitated. Challenging the chief was more than he dared. A sly grin spread across his face. "No, Mack Cabe. I challenge you." Quickly he shed his shirt and leggings so he was wearing only his breechcloth. His shoulders and arms stood out with firm muscles. He snatched his knife from his belt and waved it in the air. "I challenge you, Mack Cabe." With a final sneer he strode toward the center of the camp.

"I do not wish to fight Three Hatchets," McCabe said.

Some of the braves stirred uneasily, and Spotted Fox hurried to whisper in his ear. "You must fight him. I know that it is some foolish custom of your people to refuse a fight but the others will not understand. They will think you are afraid. No one will ride with a coward, Horse Runner. Elk Antler will not give his daughter to you if he thinks you are afraid of Three Hatchets."

McCabe looked at the other man with dismay. If he fought, he might well have to kill or be killed, and whatever the Cheyenne custom, it would be murder in his own mind. But if he did not fight, he would lose Night Bird Woman.

Slowly, reluctantly, he took off his shirt and leggings. Spotted Fox handed him his knife, and the warriors followed him to the middle of the camp. No matter what they thought, he decided, he had to make one more effort to stop this.

"Three Hatchets," he began as he came up to the other man, but suddenly Three Hatchets' knife dug a gash across his chest, and McCabe leaped back.

The muscular Indian sank into a crouch and began to circle. McCabe imitated him, holding his blade with the point turned slightly up. A line of fire burned across his chest, and he could feel the warm blood slowly spreading down from it. Three Hatchets growled and grimaced as he moved, taunting McCabe to come on, feinting a thrust, kicking up puffs of dust with his feet.

McCabe moved cautiously, keeping his eyes on Three Hatchets. He knew nothing of knife-fighting, and the other man obviously did. His only hope was to get Three Hatchets' knife away from him and fight hand-to-hand. But a look at the man's heavy muscles gave him a sinking feeling about that too.

Three Hatchets' knife flickered in the sunlight and came straight at McCabe. He danced back and let Three Hatchets go past, but there was another burning sensation, this one along his side. Before McCabe could recover, the Indian was back on guard.

Again the other man waved his blade in a snakelike motion while weaving and darting about McCabe. With a hair-raising shriek, Three Hatchets rushed at him. This time, instead of jumping aside, McCabe managed to knock the attacking knife-hand aside, and he grappled with his opponent. Instantly they were locked, each gripping the other's wrist, straining against each other.

Three Hatchets fell backwards abruptly, pulling McCabe with him. As the Indian landed on his back, his feet caught McCabe in the stomach, lifted him up and threw him.

McCabe hit the ground hard. As he struggled for breath, he realized he no longer had his knife. Desperately he rolled over, but Three Hatchets was already at his feet, and even as McCabe made it to one knee, the Indian grabbed the knife and threw it over the heads of the onlookers. Laughing, he darted at McCabe, who was trying to roll away. The Indian was looming over him when McCabe grabbed a handful of dust from the ground and threw it at the man's face. Three Hatchets coughed and stepped back, rubbing his eyes while McCabe scrambled to his feet.

Both men were breathing hard now. Three Hatchets no longer laughed. He circled grimly. McCabe searched for an opening. The blade began to flicker, flicker again, feint, then thrust. Suddenly, McCabe launched a kick. His foot connected with the Indian's wrist. The knife flew out of Three Hatchets' hand, and before he could move, McCabe stepped in and smashed first a left to his face, then a right. Three Hatchets staggered back, his upper lip cut badly. McCabe followed him. Pain shot up his back, but he had to ignore it. The heavyset Indian tried to ready himself to fight again, but McCabe stabbed two stiff lefts to his face, then followed with a sharp right. He felt the man's nose crunch beneath his fist. Three Hatchets managed one step toward McCabe, then his eyes rolled back in a daze and he dropped to the ground. His attempts to rise were fruitless as he remained in the dust.

The stunned watchers stood staring at McCabe, their mouths hanging open.

"I have never seen such fighting," Spotted Fox said at last. "Beating a man so with his fists."

"High-backed Wolf," Otter Belt whispered suddenly. McCabe turned to discover the chief watching them.

"What happens here?" the chief asked. He bent with an interested look to pick up one of the knives from the ground.

"Three Hatchets challenged Horse Runner," Buffalo Horn revealed, "and they fought. Horse Runner hit him with his hands."

High-backed Wolf Looked at Three Hatchets, who had by now struggled to one knee. Blood ran from his mouth and his swelling nose. Two braves helped him to his feet.

"You would fight with knives?" High-backed Wolf asked Three Hatchets. "If you had killed him, it would have been murder. But if he had killed you, because you challenged him, it would have been self defence."

"It would not be murder," Three Hatchets managed thickly. "Mack Cabe is a white man."

"Horse Runner is a Cheyenne," the chief countered.

Three Hatchets glared at the chief, and then at McCabe. Then he angrily shrugged free from his helpers and staggered away toward his lodge.

High-backed Wolf shook his head and turned to McCabe. "You have done this to his face with your hands? How did you do this?"

"It is a way of fighting," McCabe explained. "Among my people, it is taught as a sport."

"I do not think he will forgive this," the chief counseled. "You must be careful of him. Both of you will be needed when we go against the Kiowa. I will have no more trouble between you."

"There will be no trouble from me," McCabe pledged.

High-backed Wolf ran a careful eye over the watchers, and then he nodded. "I will say the same to Three Hatchets. No trouble between you or your friends."

When the chief left, McCabe faced the others. "Now we can talk of the horse hunting."

"We have decided," Walks Wide of His Horses said. "Those of us who will not go want you to know that we do not believe Three Hatchets. If Grey Bear did what he did because he was jealous of you, it is not your fault. We do not go because there are to be no coups counted. There may be many horses, but I have enough horses." He walked away, and sixteen braves followed him. Except for his friends, the men who stayed were the youngest warriors of the tribe.

"Come to my lodge," McCabe told them.

Looking Glass choked back a scream when she saw him, blood and dust drying on his chest and ribs, but he waved her away. There were more important matters at hand.

He sat and motioned the others to sit in a circle with him. Then he took his tobacco pouch and filled the red buffalo bowls of his double-horseback pipe with a mixture of wild tobacco, sumac leaves and bearberries, then sprinkled ground buffalo waste on top. The tobacco lit at the first try. He offered the smoke to the sky, to the earth, and then to the north, east, south and west. Then he took a long draw and passed it to Spotted Fox, the stem held precisely skyward. Spotted Fox took a puff and passed it to Otter Belt, who did the same. And so the pipe went around the circle until it finally returned to McCabe.

"I will tell you now," he said, "of how we will hunt the Crow horses. There will never be another horse hunt such as this. Hear now my plan. . . ."

As night fell across the Crow village, McCabe watched closely from among the trees on a hill nearby. Perhaps a hundred lodges were scattered in haphazard fashion across an open space. Cooking fires outside the lodges were banked with ashes, and dogs slunk through the camp looking for scraps. Finally, the last man disappeared into his lodge.

Suddenly, from another hill, three musket shots rang out in quick succession. McCabe did not move. The two young braves behind him shifted uneasily on their saddles and hefted their muskets. The camp broke into pandemonium. From every lodge, long-haired men ran clutching weapons. Some leaped onto their horses. Dogs barked, then yelped as shouting women kicked them away. There was no more sound from the hills. The mounted men looked at one another hesitantly, then climbed slowly down. One by one they disappeared into their lodges, and the camp was once more abandoned to the scrawny dogs.

Half an hour later, four shots sounded from another hill. Again the camp exploded. This time some of the mounted men rode out of the camp and circled it a short distance from the lodges, peering into the dark.

The women shouted louder, and in their pique, smacked the dogs for their constant barking. At last, though, the camp settled down once more, the men grumbling and shouting to one another as they again retired.

An hour later three more shots were fired. And so it continued throughout the night. Whenever the camp had been quiet for an hour or so, three or four rapid musket shots would split the silence. By the hour before dawn only a few men stuck their heads from their lodges, shaking their fists at the hills and shouting dire threats against whoever was playing these tricks.

"It is time," McCabe announced, and he led the two men toward the next hill.

As they rode, McCabe gave a low whistle, and Spotted Fox appeared with three more young men. "Now?" he asked excitedly. McCabe nodded.

One by one they gathered the other groups and rode around the camp to find the village horse herd. In the dimness of the early morning, over five hundred mares and stallions began to stir in the large pasture of tall grass, as three adolescent boys on sway-backed nags dozed.

"Remember," McCabe said quietly. "Over their heads." Some of the nods were reluctant, so he repeated himself. "Over their heads," he insisted. "We are warriors. We do not kill children. Now be ready for my word." Everyone checked his musket. McCabe slung his Hawken and drew a Paterson Colt. "Now," he commanded.

The raiding party fired a ragged volley. McCabe triggered the two Colts as fast as he could thumb back the hammers. To the boys guarding the horses, it sounded like a full-fledged battle breaking out. They gave one startled look around and flogged their sorry mounts back toward the village. The horse herd milled and tensed.

McCabe waited until the boys were out of sight, so they could not report how many were in the party, then shouted, "Ride!"

Whooping, yipping, and waving their arms, they galloped down on the herd. The horses darted this way and that, then abruptly thundered ahead of the charge. A few broke off to one side, and some of the Cheyenne started after them, but McCabe glared, "Let them go! There is no time!"

All day they kept the horses moving, abandoning those that broke free or fell behind. Every stream, every plate of hardpan, every stretch of sand that could be scribbled over with branches, McCabe used to confuse pursuers. In the afternoon Spotted Fox and Otter Belt dropped back to check their trail, and they returned in two hours to report that there was no pursuit.

"None?" McCabe exclaimed in disbelief. "No pursuit at all?"

Spotted Fox shrugged. "By the time the boys convinced them it was not another joke, perhaps they were just too far behind. Or perhaps they have no horses to ride."

"Perhaps they were afraid," Otter Belt laughed. It must take many brave warriors to steal five hundred horses."

"We have not so many as that now," McCabe said. He considered briefly, then told them, "We must keep moving until dark. If we see no sign of pursuit by then, we will stop."

"You grow to be an old woman in your age," Otter Belt joked, but then he joined the rest in pushing the herd on.

Shortly before dark they drove the horses into a blind canyon and fenced it off with rawhide ropes. Spotted Fox watched the horses go in and shook his head in wonderment.

"There must be four hundred of them," He speculated. "Truly, there has never been a horse hunting like this one." Otter Belt wailed suddenly, and he looked at him with astonishment. "What is the matter with you?"

"If only we could have kept all of them. One horse for each pelt they took. That would be a revenge to sing of."

"I am satisfied," McCabe laughed.

As the last rope was knotted, a lanky young man named Dull Knife approached them. "Horse Runner," he said, "you have given me a horse hunting I will tell my children of, and my grandchildren. Accept my gift of half my share of the horses."

Before McCabe could speak, another man appeared. "Horse Runner, I am Pulls His Horse. I have never before heard of such a horse hunting. For my gratitude I gave you half my share of the horses."

One by one the others appeared, each giving McCabe half of his horses. And then Spotted Fox spoke. "I too give you half of my share."

"And I," Otter Belt joined in. "You are a man of wealth now, Horse Runner."

"But why?" McCabe asked. "You, all these others . . . I do not understand."

"Each of us wants to give you a gift," Spotted Fox explained. "Each of us knows the price you must pay for Night Bird Woman."

"We show respect and generosity toward a great leader," Otter Belt added. "It is the way of the Cheyenne."

McCabe grabbed each of them by a shoulder. "My friends," he began, but he couldn't go on. Each of them then grasped his shoulder in turn, and he knew they understood.

12

When the raiders returned to camp, all bands of the Cheyenne had assembled there. Over a thousand lodges stretched around the camp circle, which was now over two miles in diameter. Nearly four thousand people filled the camp, a quarter of them warriors. The entire Cheyenne nation had joined together.

Shouts rang out as the returning men were spotted, turning to cries of wonder as the horses were driven into the camp circle. McCabe saw Night Bird Woman smiling and waving at him furiously. Three Hatchets, his broken nose bent to one side, spat and turned away when McCabe looked at him triumphantly. In the tumult, the story spread quickly, the young men leaning from their saddles to tell of the raid. McCabe heard his name mentioned more than once as he rode to his lodge. Horse Runner. There he is. Horse Runner.

Looking Glass ran out to meet him as he climbed down. He swung her into the air. "No trouble," he laughed, spinning her so that her feet couldn't touch the ground. "No black buffalo bull, and no trouble."

"I will say it," she grinned. "You are a great warrior. Now put me down."

He dropped her to her feet. "I have the horses. Now I can pay Night Bird Woman's bride price."

"After the war," she said.

"Now. Why should I wait until after the war? In fact, why should I wait at all? I will go to Elk Antler now."

"Horse Runner," she called after him, but he set off across the camp to find Elk Antler's lodge.

On his way, many people stopped him to offer their congratulations, but at last he arrived at the lodge near the north end of the circle.

"Elk Antler," he called. "I am Horse Runner. I come to talk to you about your daughter."

"Enter my lodge, Horse Runner."

Night Bird Woman ran up just as he started in. He held the entrance flap for her, and she laughed as she darted past him into the lodge. Elk Antler motioned McCabe to sit, and said, "We will talk of your horse hunting, and of the arrow renewal that begins tomorrow."

"Arrow renewal?" McCabe queried. "I have not seen that ceremony."

"Only when our way of life, our existence as a people, is threatened, is the arrow renewal held. For four days we will observe the rituals to renew the power of the Sacred Arrows given to our people by Sweet Medicine. Two have power over men, and two over buffalo. They are the spirit of our people. Horse Runner. But we will talk of that later. Let us talk of your horse hunting."

"I have the horses," McCabe told him. "I will send them to you tomorrow."

"During the arrow renewal!" The old man appeared to be deeply shocked.

"Then after," McCabe offered. "In four days, when the ceremony is finished, I will send the fifty horses to you. I am eager to marry your daughter, Elk Antler."

"That is good. It is good for a young man to be eager. But that must wait till after the war."

"That was what Looking Glass said," he responded. "Is there a custom I do not know of, that a man may not marry when war is coming?"

"It is not a custom," Elk Antler replied, "but I do not want to give my daughter to a man who may soon die. When you come back, I will take your horses, and give you mine and my daughter."

For a long moment McCabe sat quietly. Then he turned to Night Bird Woman. "And do you also want me to wait until . . . until I come back from war?"

She nodded immediately. "Of course, Horse Runner. I too am eager to be yours, but if I marry you now and you die fighting the Kiowa, it will be said that I married you only to inherit your possessions."

"I see," McCabe said softly. "You will marry me, but only after I come back from the war."

"I cannot marry you if you do not come back."

"Would you marry me if I did not go?"

"Yes," she answered. Then her forehead creased in a frown. "But why would you not go?"

McCabe shook his head and stood up. "I must go to talk with my friends."

"But we have not talked of the horse hunting," Elk Antler complained.

"We will talk of it another time. I must go."

McCabe found Spotted Fox and Otter Belt in the center of an admiring circle of warriors. The men listened gravely to the two of them as they related their exploits with McCabe. Curious girls sat wide-eyed behind the group, hoping to catch parts of the tale. McCabe pushed his way into the circle.

"I must have a talk with you, Spotted Fox and Otter Belt. I must speak with you." He looked around at the disappointed listeners. "I am sorry," he added as he pulled the two men away.

"What is the matter?" Spotted Fox inquired.

"Has Elk Antler refused you?" Otter Belt asked. "I saw you going into his lodge."

"I must ask a question of both of you. Even though I am a white man and not of your tribe, do you expect me to ride with you against the Kiowa?"

"Of course," Otter Belt answered immediately. "We will all ride together."

Spotted Fox looked more thoughtful. "No one is forced to go."

"But what if I do not go? What then, between us?"

"Why would you not go?" Otter Belt asked. "I do not understand."

"Otter Belt and I will go," Spotted Fox said. "When we return, it will be between us as it has always been."

"But we are friends," Otter Belt protested. "Brothers. How can you refuse to fight beside us? We will count many coups among the Kiowa."

"I do not know what to do," McCabe confessed. "This is not my war. But you two are my friends." He shook his head slowly. "I wish there were some wise man I could talk to, a sage who could tell me what is right."

Spotted Fox clasped his arm. "Raven is the oldest of our band. There is wisdom in a man's years. Besides, he is a shaman. Many secrets are known to him."

"Perhaps you are right," McCabe returned. "I need to talk to someone. Perhaps I will go to Raven."

He wandered away from them, though, with no idea where he was going. The triumph of his return only an hour before had already soured. He could ride into a war he had no part in, or he could desert his friends. He drifted through the camp, wrapped in the darkness of his thoughts, and ignored the shouts of well-wishers that came wherever he went. At last he looked up and found himself in front of the lodge with the black raven painted on it.

"Why not?" he whispered. Then he exclaimed, "Raven! I am Horse Runner. I want to speak with you."

"Enter my lodge, Horse Runner," came the old man's reply.

When he stepped into the lodge, he found that Raven was not alone. High-backed Wolf sat in the honored position to the shaman's left. Raven motioned McCabe to sit next to the chief. If it was wisdom he sought, perhaps it was just as well that High-backed Wolf was there, he thought. Fools did not become chiefs of the Cheyenne.

"You wish to speak to me," Raven said. "I see in your face that your heart is troubled. Tell me your troubles."

He glanced at the chief and began slowly. High-backed Wolf listened impassively, while Raven leaned forward to catch each word.

"I have lived among the Cheyenne for almost a year, though sometimes it feels as if I were born among you. I have made fast friends—Otter Belt and Spotted Fox. I love Night Bird Woman, and I want to marry her. And perhaps I love Looking Glass too. The people call me warrior. They say I have become a Cheyenne."

"I hear no problem in this," Raven told him. "This is reason for rejoicing. Why do you waste my time?"

"Because I am not Cheyenne!" McCabe shouted. Raven's mouth dropped open, but High-backed Wolf still watched and listened patiently. McCabe lowered his voice. "I am not a Cheyenne. Now the Cheyenne ride to war. Night Bird Woman expects me to go to fight, as do Otter Belt and Spotted Fox. I could see it in their faces. They expect me to go, but I am not Cheyenne, and it is not my war."

"No man must go to war," High-backed Wolf replied abruptly. "Men of the Cheyenne are not forced to go. It is true, you were not born a Cheyenne. Therefore there is little reason for you to ride against the Kiowa. Hunt in the mountains until we return."

"He fears he will lose the woman," Raven told the chief. "If he does not go, perhaps she will not have him."

McCabe shook his head. "She has told me she will marry me, whether I go or not."

"Then do as High-backed Wolf suggests," Raven said. "There are many warriors among the Cheyenne. One more or less will make no difference."

"But even High-backed Wolf said he expected me to go." The chief looked at him quizzically, and McCabe explained. "When Three Hatchets and I fought, you told me that you needed both of us for the war."

"That is true," the chief agreed. "You are a good fighter, Horse Runner. But that does not mean you will be forced to ride against the Kiowa. As you have said, it is not your war."

"Then why do I feel as if I will be deserting my friends if I do not go? We are like brothers. If they go without me, I fear they will leave part of themselves behind. And part of me will go with them to be lost forever if they die and I am not there."

"Your answer lies inside, Horse Runner," Raven imparted. "High-backed Wolf cannot tell you what you must do. I cannot tell you what you must do. You have to search inside."

Search inside, McCabe thought as he left the shaman's lodge. That's where all the conflicts are. Were the Cheyenne his people? He still wasn't sure, but the people he cared for, the people he loved most in this world were all Cheyenne. And those people were going to war, to fight, perhaps even to die.

Spotted Fox and Otter Belt found him squatting on the prairie outside the camp. They sat on either side of him.

"It is lonely out here," Spotted Fox observed as he looked out over the open land.

"There is laughing in the camp," Otter Belt told McCabe. "Already some begin to feast and celebrate our horse hunt."

McCabe searched their faces, but he wasn't sure what he was looking for. They seemed concerned that he was alone when there was a feast in his honor.

"My friends," he said finally, "I cannot let you ride against the Kiowa alone."

"We will not be alone," Spotted Fox said. "Many warriors will ride with us."

"If I did not go, I would feel that I had sent you against them alone."

Otter Belt tilted his head in confusion. "Does that mean that you are coming?"

McCabe nodded, and his two friends broke out in smiles.

"Then why do we just stay here like sticks in the ground?" Otter Belt cried. In the camp, a drum began to beat in a slow rhythm. He sprang to his feet. "Come. The celebration has begun."

"Come," said Spotted Fox, offering a hand.

With a laugh McCabe let himself be pulled to his feet, and together they ran into the camp.

The next morning, the arrow renewal rite began. Before dawn, the sacred lodge, a yellow tepee twice as tall and three times as broad as any other, was erected. The Council of Chiefs entered, followed by the shamans, who carried the Sacred Arrows in a buffalo-skin bundle. From the sacred lodge came the deep, booming sound of drumming, of prayers and songs chanted with wavering voices. Throughout the rest of the camp, a solemn quiet prevailed.

Women and children stayed inside their tepees. Men did no hunting or trading. The Dog Soldiers stalked through the camp with clubs to see that everyone followed the rules, that no unnecessary noise was made.

On each day of the ceremony, the bundle was opened for the arrows to be checked. Bear Paw, a brave selected for his bravery and good temper, was called to the sacred lodge to repair the feathers on the ancient shafts. On the third day, tally sticks were cut from the branches of a willow, one for each family in which no member had ever murdered another Cheyenne. The sticks were passed through the smoke of incense fires to purify and bless each lodge. On the fourth day, the sun was greeted by a long cry from the sacred lodge. Then the drums stopped.

McCabe kissed Looking Glass and left the lodge. He wore his best clothing, but carried no weapon, not even a knife. From other lodges, other men came—old men who had to lean on the shoulders of the young; older men who had to be carried on blankets; infant boys, crying for their mothers' breasts, who had to be carried in their fathers' arms. Each man wore his best. Even the babes had been decked with strings of beads. McCabe stood in the crowd outside the sacred lodge, watching their entrance.

High-backed Wolf stepped out, resplendent in his war bonnet, which hung behind him and trailed along the ground. He carried a staff covered with eagle feathers, each feather testifying to his bravery. Behind him came Grey Hair, and then Grey Thunder, and so on until all forty-four chiefs of the Cheyenne stood facing their people. The shaman of each band followed the chiefs. Raven carried in his arms the buffalo-skin bundle.

Suddenly High-backed Wolf thrust the bundle into the air, letting the skin fall open so that he clutched the sacred arrows over his head through a handful of skin. A gasp of wonder went through the men as they watched the old shaman. Fathers held their children up to see better; old men stood straighter. Even McCabe could sense the age of the arrows. The striped shafts were dry and withered, the stone points chipped and broken with antiquity. To McCabe they seemed a reaffirmation of the life of the Cheyenne. As long as those arrows existed, so would the Cheyenne nation.

"A man has been chosen," High backed Wolf announced. "A man has been chosen to carry the Sacred Arrows against the Kiowa."

Grey Thunder reached inside the sacred lodge and brought out a lance. Grey Hair reverently took the arrows from Raven, then both men went to High-backed Wolf with their burdens. The arrows were placed just behind the head of the lance and tied with four buffalo-hide thongs, each wrapped four times. High-backed Wolf took the lance and held it aloft.

"Three Hatchets!" he called.

There was a stir in the crowd as Three Hatchets pushed forward. His nose was still red, and slightly bent. He wore a shirt that was quilled and embroidered over its entire surface.

"To carry the Sacred Arrows," High-backed Wolf proclaimed, "above all a man must be brave. If he should lose the arrows in the fighting, he would bring about the end of the Cheyenne. He must hold the arrows above his own life." He held the lance out to Three Hatchets.

Three Hatchets took the lance slowly, then whirled and thrust it at the sky. As the Sacred Arrows rose, a roar went up among the Cheyenne, and McCabe suddenly realized he was shouting as hard as the rest.

13

The sun had been up for an hour when McCabe scrambled up the sand hill and peered through the scrub growing on its crest. Below lay Wolf Creek, at the far side of which the Kiowa were camped. Hundreds of their lodges were set over a large field overgrown with low brush.

"There are many," Spotted Fox said as he climbed up to the hilltop. His face was painted completely red except for one black line that ran from his chin to his forehead. "I have never seen a camp so large."

McCabe studied the camp carefully. People seemed to go about their daily lives much as did the Cheyenne in their own camp: women cooked, children played, men met in council. Horses were tethered outside every lodge, but no one seemed to be keeping special watch.

"They do not know we are coming," McCabe said finally. "If we can strike them before they realize. . . ." He cut off as shots sounded to the north. He waited. Another ragged volley carried through the morning still-ness. We must go back to the others. Something has happened."

He scrambled down the hill and leaped into the saddle. Spotted Fox came close behind.

The main body of the Cheyenne was still riding toward Wolf Creek in a huge mass that snaked back for miles. First came the chiefs, and then the warriors, all except the soldiers of the six societies, who ranged out in a fan on either side of the march, guarding and policing the long line of women and children following behind with the lodges and pack horses. Young boys, diving the vast horse herds, brought up the rear. The Cheyenne na-tion had been traveling south for days, joined by three bands of their allies, the Arapaho.

When he rode up, Three Hatchets and some of the rest were brandish-ing bloody scalps. The muscular warrior had one tied to his lance below the Sacred Arrows.

"High-backed Wolf," McCabe called. He pulled in to ride beside the chief. "What has happened? Have we been attacked?"

"No," the chief replied. Six red lines were painted across his face. "Three Hatchets found some Kiowa hunting buffalo. Thirty of them were killed."

"The shooting may have warned the main village. We must hurry to at-tack them."

"And leave the women and the herds unprotected?" High-back Wolf shook his head. "What will happen will happen. If we have done the ritu-als properly, we will win."

With a slowness McCabe found infuriating, the Cheyenne continued to move south. When they came short of the creek, the women and chil-dren broke away toward a nearby hill. The six societies joined with the main body of warriors, and they splashed across the creek below the Kiowa camp. Still there was no sign of reaction from the Kiowa.

McCabe felt the percussion cap on his rifle to make certain it was in place and checked the Colts in his belt.

"Ho!" Otter Belt called, riding up beside him. The young warrior had painted the black horns of a buffalo sweeping up from his chin across his cheeks. "There are root diggers ahead!"

Down the bank McCabe spotted a few dozen women digging. As they saw the Cheyenne, they scattered, screaming. The Cheyenne went into a gallop.

McCabe leaned low in his saddle. It was too much to hope that the Kiowa would be taken by surprise now. The killing of the buffalo hunters might have gone unnoticed, but the women screaming and the drumming of a thousand horses' hooves would not.

The Cheyenne rode between two hills and rounded toward the Kiowa camp just as Kiowa warriors came rushing out to meet them. On the plain before the camp, the two masses met.

Within seconds, a warrior with a necklace of silver circles around his neck charged at McCabe with a lowered lance. McCabe fired from the waist, and the heavy ball from the Hawken smashed the other man from his saddle. All around him the battle swirled. Quickly he slung the Hawken across his back and drew one of the Colts. Arrows brushed his sleeve, and a musket ball tugged at his shirt, but he seemed to be blessed with luck. One tall Kiowa, grinning viciously, sprang at him with an axe, but was cut down by a stray arrow from a Kiowa bow. Another, who had his hair plaited on his forehead, had drawn a bead on McCabe with his bow when a Cheyenne warrior, charging with his lance, rode between to take the arrow. Then Spotted Fox appeared and did away with the Kiowa. McCabe rode through the melee, paying almost no attention to defending himself. He pistol-whipped a Kiowa from Otter Belt's back and shot another who was attacking Spotted Fox with a lance. Wherever his friends went, he followed, guarding their backs, aiding when they were hard pressed.

Abruptly the Kiowa broke ranks and retreated. Their warriors streamed from the field so suddenly that the Cheyenne were left standing in confusion for a moment before they could gather to follow. The women had been working in the camp. Breastworks had been thrown up in the sandy soil. Small trees and bushes had been cut down to make barricades against charging horses.

Shouting their battle cries, the Cheyenne charged the camp. A murderous hail of musket balls and arrows met them, but they fought through to the breastworks.

McCabe rode in among the barricades after his friends. Suddenly a shot burned his cheek, and with a shrill yell a Kiowa ran at McCabe with a knife. There was no time to shoot. McCabe whipped a pistol around as the man darted in, and he clubbed him with the barrel.

Suddenly High-backed Wolf called to his braves to retreat.

Reluctantly, the Cheyenne pulled back from the barricades. As they did, the Kiowa swept out after them. The Cheyenne regrouped at the hills, turned on their pursuers, then charged. Back and forth across the plain the battle raged, from the barricades at the camp to the hills upriver and back again. McCabe saw Grey Hair fall, his skull split by a tomahawk, and he saw Grey Thunder take a musket ball in the face. The dead of both sides littered the ground.

As the sun touched the horizon in the west, High-backed Wolf called the Cheyenne to retreat for the last time. The Kiowa did not follow.

In a daze McCabe rode back across the creek to the hill where the women had pitched the lodges. His ears still seemed to ring with the shouts of the dying as he rode into the camp. Darkness had almost fallen, but the women were taking down the tepees. He looked for Looking Glass and found her pulling the last of the pins from his lodge to let the cover fall away from the lifting pole.

"What are you doing?" he asked. "Why are the lodges being taken down?"

"High-backed Wolf has said we will move before dark," she replied without stopping. She pulled the lifting pole down and began folding the lodge cover hurriedly.

McCabe pulled his horse around and went looking for High-backed Wolf. He found him holding a council on horseback with the surviving chiefs.

"High-backed Wolf!" he called. "I am Horse Runner. I would like to talk with you."

The chief motioned for the others to wait, then rode aside with McCabe. "What do you want, Horse Runner?"

"The camp is moving, and it is nearly dark. If the Kiowa attack us tonight while we are moving, they will destroy us."

"They will not attack us. They would have followed us if they intended to attack. They are in their camp, licking their wounds." The chief sighed heavily. "More Kiowa have died than Cheyenne, but it has not been a good war."

"It will get better," McCabe said. "If they are not going to attack tonight, let some of us. . . ."

"The war is over, Horse Runner. We will move throughout this night and tomorrow. We are going home."

"Over!" McCabe said incredulously. "We have fought only one battle, and we have not yet captured their village. If we attack them again tomorrow, we may finish them."

"We have fought the battle, Horse Runner, and that is the war. Would you have us go on until all of the young men are killed?"

"Then all this has been for nothing! Men have died, and we have gained nothing."

"We have gained honor. We have gained revenge for the Bow Strings."

"And the next time? Don't the Cheyenne and the Kiowa live too close together for there not to be a next time? Will there not be another war where the only things that are gained are honor and dead men?"

High-backed Wolf looked troubled. "Already we speak of this in the council, Horse Runner. But no one knows what to do."

"Make peace," McCabe said simply.

"With the Kiowa? And if we make peace with them, we must make peace with their allies, the Comanche. They too are our enemies."

"Among my people, there are many nations, but each knows the other is just as strong. The nations make treaties so they won't fight. It does not mean they have stopped hating each other. But they have agreed not to kill each other."

"And they keep these agreements? Even though they hate each other?"

"If the leaders of the people are good, the agreements are kept. If they are not, sometimes, they are broken."

"To make peace with the Kiowa and the Comanche would be a strange thing," High-backed Wolf mused. "Still, I will talk of it to the council."

When the chief returned to the council, Spotted Fox and Otter Belt found McCabe.

"Ho, Horse Runner," Otter Belt shouted, riding up. "We have won the war. I saw you in the fighting. You counted many coups and killed many Kiowa."

"It is a pity we do not have something more than coups to show for the war," McCabe replied drily.

Spotted Fox took him at his word and nodded. "It is said by some that the reason we did not destroy more of our enemy was Three Hatchets."

"Three Hatchets!" McCabe exclaimed. "But I saw him always where the fighting was thickest."

"He did not advance the Sacred Arrows properly," Otter Belt said.

"Do you mean," McCabe grumbled, "you actually believe that if it weren't for Three Hatchets we would have won the battle?"

"We did win," Spotted Fox answered, "but if he had advanced the arrows better, we would have won better."

That night the Cheyenne nation, which had come south so proudly, started back home in the dark, grieving the loss of so many of its men.

14

Once they were north of the Arrowpoint River, which the white men called the Arkansas, the bands of Cheyenne divided once more. High-backed Wolf's band turned to the west.

At the first camp the bride price was sent to Elk Antler. McCabe worriedly stalked up and down the line of horses. One end of the lead rope was held by Otter Belt, the other by Spotted Fox. He had chosen the horses carefully, curried them till their coats glistened, combed every tangle from their manes and tails. But he still was afraid there was something he had missed.

"Let us go," Spotted Fox pleaded. "If the woman really wants you, they could all be lame and swaybacked, and she would not send them back."

"I know," McCabe sighed, "but. . . ." He ran a hand down a mare's foreleg, then patted a stallion on the neck.

"It is the fear," Otter Belt laughed. "I have seen it before. A man who has no fear when riding in the camp of the Comanche will sweat on this day."

"All right," McCabe growled as Spotted Fox joined Otter Belt in mirth. "Take them. Go on."

The two snickering men led the horses away, and McCabe went to sit sullenly in front of his lodge. Looking Glass brought him a bowl of stew, but he set it down untouched.

"I am going to stay this night with Elk Antler's wives," she told him.

"What? Oh, yes. It is good stew," he said, peering off toward Elk Antler's lodge.

With an amused snort, Looking Glass turned and walked away.

McCabe sat staring at the lodge until Spotted Fox and Otter Belt appeared. He leaped to his feet. "It is done?"

The two men stared at him with long faces.

"What is the matter?"

"We are sorry, Horse Runner," Spotted Fox said, shaking his head.

"It could not be helped," Otter Belt murmured.

"What are you talking about?" McCabe shouted. "Did she refuse the horses? Has she changed her mind? What happened?"

Spotted Fox shrugged as if denying fault. "She sent the horses to her father's herd."

"She sent the horses—" McCabe began to shout in agitation, then realized what the other man had told him. "She sent the horses . . . to her father's herd?" he repeated quietly.

They both nodded.

"And you let me think something had gone wrong?"

Again they nodded, smiles beginning to appear on their faces.

"Why you," McCabe howled, but he couldn't finish as he was filled with laughter. "She accepted!" he shouted. He grabbed them both by the shoulder and shook them. "She accepted!"

"Come," Spotted Fox said. "You must get ready. Your bride will soon come."

Quickly they hustled him into the lodge and unwrapped the wedding garb they had brought for him: shirt, leggings and moccasins of elkskin, with brightly colored quillwork. Then they bound his hair back from his face with an elkskin band.

"Hurry," Otter Belt pleaded. "I hear them coming."

"I am hurrying," McCabe returned. "You hurry." He ducked outside, and in a few moments the others followed. He could hear a bridal drum beating across the camp.

"We wish you well," Spotted Fox smiled, and Otter Belt repeated the sentiment before both left him standing there to meet his bride.

The sound of the drumbeat grew closer. Now he could see the drum. A woman walked across the camp, carrying it in her arm. She was beating it with a stick. Behind her followed more women, as many as could crowd together to carry the blanket that Night Bird Woman sat on. They held the blanket taut, and with every step they took, the woman bounced. As they came closer, McCabe could hear their wordless chant rising and falling.

When the procession reached his lodge, the woman with the drum motioned him to go in. As he did, the women with the blanket crowded close to the entrance to let Night Bird Woman slide from the blanket into the tent. It was the first time her feet had touched the ground since she had left her father's lodge.

As she stood, six of the women crowded in behind her, all carrying bundles wrapped in hide. Quickly they surrounded her, almost blocking her entirely from his sight. Some of the bundles were unwrapped, and the clothes she was wearing were tossed out of the circle. Finally the women backed away, scurrying out, leaving Night Bird Woman standing in a brand-new dress that was covered with colorful beadwork, quilled moccasins and a red shawl. Her hair was braided, and silver rings and bracelets decorated her wrists and fingers. A large red dot was painted on each cheek.

When he realized she was looking up to the top of the lodge, he followed her gaze. An elk skull, complete with antlers, had been suspended there.

"Is that part of the ceremony?" he asked. "I do not remember being told of it."

Night Bird Woman blushed. "It is a joke by your friends, my husband, signifying the same thing as the groom's elkskin wedding clothes. The elk is much admired for his prowess in attracting a large number of mates and keeping them . . . satisfied." She demurely covered her face with her hands, but dropped them almost immediately. "My husband. I like to say that to you."

"I like to hear you say it. My wife." He untied the door flap and let it drop. It was as simple as that. They were now husband and wife. "Would you like. . . ." he began, then stopped as he turned back to her.

Without looking at him she had begun to remove her clothes. His face reddened as he watched. The deerskin dress dropped to the ground, baring her slim body, round hips and delicate breasts. The firelight highlighted her skin, making it gleam like satin. She wore a braided deerskin cord that passed down between her legs and rose across her rounded buttocks, fastened in front and back to a waistband. Quickly she unfastened this and tossed it aside.

"Are you not hot in those garments, my husband?" she murmured.

"Yes," he said slowly, "I am." He grinned. "Yes, I am." He tugged off his shirt, and suddenly she was next to him, pulling at the fastenings of his leggings.

As they fell to the sleeping mats together, McCabe felt his desire for her begin to grow fierce, but he had never held her close before this moment, and he felt timid, reluctant, like a shy young boy with her. He embraced her awkwardly, as if afraid that he might hurt her. She looked curiously into his deep blue eyes and giggled. He brushed her lips briefly with his own, then stroked her long black hair gently with his fingertips, barely touching. . . . The warmth of her breathing fluttered on his cheek as lightly as a hummingbird's wing, and as her arms went around him, he became aware of the frantic, rhythmic demand of his own heaving breath. He wanted to possess her, to be within her, to become part of her, and as if their passion had suddenly been kindled from spark to flame, they touched and embraced each other in the dark. Their bodies arched, strained and yearned for each other, and with the power and abandon of hungry young lovers, they made love through the night.

15

The first months of their marriage passed smoothly, even after Looking Glass returned to the lodge. The two women seemed to size each other up, and afterward they spoke only in low tones when working together. To be on the safe side, McCabe made sure he didn't look at Looking Glass in any way that might make Night Bird Woman jealous. On the one night Looking Glass tried to enter his bed, he quickly told her that he had to check his horse outside and asked her to leave. By the time he returned to the lodge, Night Bird Woman was there and the danger was averted. Despite what she had said before their marriage, he was leery of her true feelings about the captive girl.

In the late summer, as he was writing in his journal, Spotted Fox came up and sat beside him, his face drawn. McCabe put the book aside. "You have a problem, my friend. Tell me of it, and I will help you if I can."

"I am troubled by that which worries all of us," Spotted Fox sighed.

McCabe nodded. Few men of the Cheyenne had not been worried since returning from Wolf Creek. Some way to make peace had to be found, or the Cheyenne and the Kiowa would destroy one another.

"I have had a dream," Spotted Fox went on. "I have dreamed this dream every night for nine months. I have told Raven of it, and he says it is a true dream."

"What is your dream?"

"I dream of the Sun Dance. I dream that I dance in the Sun Dance, Horse Runner, and that you do also. And I dream that a vision will come in the dance to tell us the way we must go."

"I have never seen the Sun Dance," McCabe said slowly. "But I have heard of it. The flesh of the dancer's chest is pierced with skewers, and he must dance until the skewers are pulled free."

"Most men who dance may stop when they choose. They are not fastened to the sacred pole. Only pledged dancers like me must go on."

"And like me," McCabe added quietly.

"You, Horse Runner? The Sun Dance is not a thing to be taken lightly. To horse hunt, to ride to war, these are decisions any boy can make. But to dance the Sun Dance must be considered carefully, for not only is a man's life in danger when he dances, but his spirit as well."

"I must, if your dream is to be fulfilled."

"Yes," Spotted Fox admitted. "that is true. But Raven did not speak of this. And I have never heard of a man being called to dance by another man's dream."

"Nevertheless, I will dance."

After Spotted Fox had gone, McCabe sat for a time staring at the dry ground before him. He absently put a hand under his shirt and felt his chest, pinching a fold of skin. He wondered how painful the ordeal would be. He did not want to find out, but neither did he want his friends to die. There was no telling what sort of things men would say or imagine after dancing for three days without food or drink. There had to be a vision that called for peace. And he intended to provide it.

From the front of his lodge McCabe watched the parties that were sent to prepare for the dance. Two Elks, the young brave, rode out with his wife. They were to return with the hide of a buffalo killed by a single arrow. A dozen men went in search of brush and wood to build a sweat lodge, while twice as many went to look for the same materials to construct the Sun Dance lodge. Another group went to bring back the ceremonial lodgepole for the Sun Dance itself. They would fashion it from a cottonwood tree about twenty-five feet high. Shouting war cries, they would count coup on it and fell it as an enemy. Near the center of the camp, young men chosen by Raven for their good health and pure spirit worked under the shaman's direction to raise a ceremonial tepee of yellow buckskin.

The sweat lodge, to be used by only the pledged dancers, was finished first. A low, round structure, it was covered with buffalo hides to make it airtight. Nearby, the remains of a large fire smoldered. Rocks that had been heated the previous night in the fire were placed inside the lodge, along with water in which herbs had been steeped. The dancers would purify their bodies and their sprits in the steam.

McCabe joined the other dancers outside the lodge early that morning. Spotted Fox was there, and Kills by the Camp, a man of middle years who had pledged to dance in thanks for his life after a Kiowa musket had misfired when pressed against his head at Wolf Creek. The fourth dancer was Three Hatchets.

Three Hatchets, scowling at everyone, shifted impatiently from one foot to the other. The others avoided his gaze. It was known in the camp that Three Hatchets resented the rumors that the battle had been lost because of him. Many said he had decided to pledge to regain lost prestige. This was not a proper reason to dance, and so Spotted Fox and Kills by the Camp avoided him. McCabe didn't look at him for a different reason. If Three Hatchets had a poor reason to dance, McCabe's reason was a complete lie.

Raven looked each of them in the eye and nodded. "Let us go into the sweat lodge." The shaman shed his clothes and entered the low hut naked.

McCabe dropped his own clothes beside Raven's and followed him in, sitting cross-legged in front of the pile of hot stones. As soon as Kills by the Camp, the last man, was in, the entrance was closed with a heavy buffalo robe.

Raven waited until Kills by the Camp was seated, then scooped up a ladle of water and threw it on the rocks. As it hissed into steam he threw another ladleful, then another, continuing until the lodge was filled with thick, aromatic mist. No one spoke. Silence was required until they were ready to leave.

McCabe found he had to draw in deeply just to inhale enough of the thick steam to breathe. But it did seem to cleanse his lungs. Gradually his breathing began to feel lighter, despite the heavy, hot mist. Sweat rolled down his body; rivulets streamed down his face and stung his eyes, but the burning didn't seem to bother him. He wondered absently if there was something in the herbs that was affecting him.

Finally Raven signaled the end of the cleansing by rising to his feet. McCabe had no idea of how long they had been inside. When Raven pushed back the robe over the entrance, they filed out one by one. McCabe was surprised to discover that the sun was already past its zenith. He had been in the lodge for hours.

From the sweat lodge Raven led them to the tepee he had erected. Inside they sat in a line before him, still naked, and he began to speak.

"To the Cheyenne, to all the peoples of the plains, the ceremony of the Sun Dance is a ceremony of renewal, of rebirth. The sun represents Heammawihio, the Wise One Above, but Heammawihio is more powerful than the sun, for he knows all things. Through the Sun Dance we make our pleas to Heammawihio for wisdom and guidance. The lodgepole is the connection between the world of the living and the world of the spirits. It is the axis of the world, the center of the universe. Through it our supplications pass, not only to Heammawihio, but to Aktunawhihio, the Wise One Below. Thus are the harmonies restored, the balances made right. The world dies and is reborn. In the Sun Dance each man dies and is reborn. Wisdom, health and fertility are restored. The supernatural powers that aid us are renewed. In all the world a man owns only one thing: his body. When a man gives his pain in the Sun Dance, he gives the only gift that is truly his to give."

He fell silent, and the others sat in meditation. Death and rebirth, McCabe thought. A balance in the universe. Spirits that dwelt in all things. It was not so far from his own belief that God existed in everything, and that a balance existed between good and evil. Even death and rebirth were basic to Christianity.

"Dress," Raven ordered, and began to don a suit of yellow buckskin.

McCabe put on a fresh breechcloth that had been left at his place. Then he waited where he stood.

The shaman fastened around each man's waist a kilt of yellow buckskin, but in such a way that the breechcloth hung outside and over it. A sage bracelet was put on each wrist, and a sage wreath, standing stiffly upright like a war bonnet, was placed on every head. Finally he handed each man a branch of cedar and a whistle made from the wing bone of an eagle. From each whistle an eagle feather hung.

McCabe put the whistle in his mouth and gripped the branch in his right hand as he followed Raven from the medicine lodge. Many men were waiting expectantly around the Sun Dance lodge in white buckskin kilts. This lodge, at the center of the camp, was a large dome built of brush and timber, with rafters reaching up to the great central pole. Boughs covered the walls and the lower third of the roof. The rest was left open to the sun.

Each dancer, facing east as he entered, carefully put his feet on the flat rock set at the entrance. McCabe touched the rock and moved to his place on the west side. The floor was covered with fine sand, and more was heaped around the base of the lodgepole. Behind him were two shallow holes walled with mud, out of which rose the smoke of incense fires. The buffalo hide that Two Elks and his wife had brought was suspended from the tip of the lodgepole. Tied below that were a bundle of brush, a roll of red cloth, and offerings of food. Also from the top of the pole hung eight long leather thongs, reaching all the way down to coil on the ground. At the end of each thong was a four-inch-long skewer as thick as a man's finger.

McCabe couldn't stop staring. These were the instruments that would be driven through the flesh of his chest, and there was no longer any way to escape the ordeal. A part of him accepted that. He had made the pledge as the other dancers had, as his friend Spotted Fox had. He had told Raven he would dance.

He watched the shaman grasp a fold of skin on Spotted Fox's chest and drive the first skewer through. Spotted Fox let out a long breath and tensed for the next. That one brought another long, hissing breath. Kills by the Camp grunted as each of his skewers was driven in. Three Hatchets made no sound at all.

Raven's dry hand forced the skin and flesh on McCabe's chest into a ridge. McCabe stared over the shaman's head and across the lodge at Spotted Fox. The sudden fire lanced through him. He managed to choke back his scream, and he emitted a low moan. Raven peered at him before thrusting the second skewer in place. McCabe trembled and clenched his teeth.

From outside came a slow drumbeat, and the dance began.

McCabe fell into the rhythm, concentrating mightily on it in an effort to forget the searing pain in his chest. At first all the dancers stood in one place, then bent their knees, rose up on their toes, bent their knees, rose up on their toes—all in time to the drumbeat. Slowly, they began to shuffle forward. McCabe heard the long, shrill screech of the whistles, and he began to blow on his own. In time with the drum, he shuffled across the sand to the lodgepole, and as soon as he reached it, he started back again. The thongs stretched out, lifted, grew taught, pulled at the wooden slivers in his chest. With his full weight he leaned back, and a long blast sounded on the eagle-bone whistle.

As they stretched forward again, other dancers entered—men dressed in white kilts, there to fulfill their obligations. These men danced among the pledged dancers, swaying back and forth in the same steady rhythm and pattern. They had no whistles, they wore no sage, and there were no skewers driven through their chests. They danced for one hour, for three, for five, and left when they felt they had danced enough. But for the four men attached to the thongs, there was no leaving. There was no food, no water, and no rest.

In an endless pattern they danced as the sun fell, and they continued on through the night. The fires of fatigue began to worm through McCabe's legs, but he ignored them. If he could stand the pain in his chest, he could stand anything. Throughout the night he kept his eyes fixed on the buffalo robe, and as the edge of the sun rose over the open center of the roof, he transferred his gaze to that. Needles seemed to pierce his eyes, but this was the way of the dance. When the sun could not be seen, the buffalo robe was the object of the dancer's concentration, but when the sun was visible, the dancer directed his eyes to it.

The pains grew worse, from eyes and legs and chest, all merging with and overwhelming one another. His shuffling steps faltered into a shamble, and then a stagger, but he kept moving, always following the drum. The pain drove away any thought of food, but thirst clawed at his tongue, and his dry breath, as he blew on the whistle, seared his throat.

He lost count of the times he had seen the sun. Twice? Three times? Four? Was the ceremony being allowed to go on longer than the four pre-scribed days? Images flickered in his mind, confused, jumbled, without meaning. Desperately he pushed them out of his thoughts. There was no time for anything but the dance. And the sun.

Somewhere in this he heard a scream, and vaguely became aware that Kills by the Camp was lying on the ground, one hand feebly touching his chest. The skewers were gone. He had pulled free. Men rushed to carry him away, but McCabe barely noticed. For him there was only the dance.

After a time he realized that Spotted Fox was gone. Now only he and Three Hatchets still danced. Not even the men in the white kilts were there. And then Three Hatchets danced back to the ends of his thongs and fell backwards, the skewers ripping from him. McCabe danced alone.

The pain was gone now. He did not feel his arms or legs. His hand was frozen to the cedar branch, and he seemed to float back and forth, as if his legs were gone. There was no fire in his lungs, no agony in his chest. He danced in limbo, where time and space and pain did not exist.

Suddenly he fell backwards. One hand fumbled to his chest and touched the bloody patches where the skewers had been.

As men rushed to gather him up, he sank into a haze of unconscious-ness.

"Horse Runner! I am Otter Belt. I must speak with you."

McCabe, impatiently motioning Looking Glass and Night Bird Woman away when they moved toward him to help him, struggled upright on his bed. "Enter my lodge, Otter Belt."

When Otter Belt was seated, he said, "I have come from High-backed Wolf. As your friend, I have the right to ask you. Did you have a vision while you danced?"

McCabe took a long time to answer. He had entered the dance intend-ing to lie, to claim a vision of peace. Many strange hallucinations had come, though, and he was no longer certain that a lie was necessary—or even that he would lie if it became necessary. "I saw visions, Spotted Fox, but I do not know what they meant."

"High-backed Wolf and Raven will interpret them. Can you come to the medicine lodge?"

"I will come," McCabe nodded. He managed to get to his feet, then followed the other man outside.

In the center of the camp the yellow medicine lodge still stood, but the sweat lodge and the Sun Dance lodge were gone. Spotted Fox remained outside while he entered. The three other dancers were already there, sitting cross-legged. Three Hatchets, a little apart from the others, faced High-backed Wolf and Raven across a small fire that smelled of herbs. All three dancers looked drawn; they too had been pushed to the limits of endurance.

High-backed Wolf motioned McCabe to sit in the space between Spotted Fox and Three Hatchets.

"You have danced," Raven said abruptly. "You have danced, and you have seen visions. Tell us of the visions you have seen." He indicated Kills by the Camp.

"I have danced," Kills by the Camp stated. "I have danced, and I have seen a vision. A spirit came to me as I danced. I knew he was a spirit because although he looked like a man, his body was covered with hair and his eyebrows hung down either side of his face to the ground.

"He said to me, 'Come with me and I will show you the doom of your people.'

"'I will come with you,' I said, and he snatched me up in his arms and ran. He ran like the wind, and it was a mile between each step of his moccasins. At last we came to his home in the Black Hills, atop a rock spire. There he pointed to two small white birds. 'Clutch one to your breast,' he said, 'and fly with me. We must hurry, and I can carry you no longer.' I told him that I could not, for the bird was too small to carry me. But again he said, 'We must hurry, and I can carry you no longer.'

"I clutched the bird to my breast and leaped from the spire. Instantly the small white bird became a giant white eagle and bore me on his back. The eagle flew upward, higher, and higher, and the spirit followed, standing on the back of the other white bird, which was still small.

"At last the spirit pointed down, and we began to descend. 'Look down,' the spirit cried, 'and see the doom of your people.' I looked down and saw a great camp. It was on the banks of the Greasy Grass. In the camp were many warriors of the Dakota. Nearby was another camp, that of the Cheyenne. Suddenly white soldiers came, riding on horses, and the Dakota and the Cheyenne rode out and fell on them. All of the white soldiers were killed. Not one of them was left alive. Even their horses were killed. 'See the doom of your people,' the spirit cried. I saw no more."

The others listened solemnly. McCabe had to refrain from shaking his head in wonder. How much of the dream did Kills by the Camp actually remember, and how much had he made up? In any case, it was a fantastic tale.

Raven conferred with the chief before speaking. Finally he said, "Your dream is for another, Kills by the Camp. There are few white soldiers west of the Great River, and they do not attack us. We do not camp on the Greasy Grass, nor do the Dakota. It is the land of the Shoshone and the Crow, who call it the Little Big Horn. Spotted Fox, what was your vision?"

"I have danced," Spotted Fox began. "I have danced, and I have seen two visions. In the first vision, I saw a spirit who looked like a man, but he had two heads, and one of them was a buffalo's head. The spirit drank from a large clay pot, but only with the human head. The buffalo head looked at me. 'What are you drinking?' I asked, and the buffalo head replied, 'It is blood.' 'What kind of blood?' I asked. 'Human blood,' the buffalo head told me. 'He likes it very much, but I will not drink.' That is the first vision."

Raven considered the dream for a long time. "there is a message for us," he said at last. "The meaning is clear. There are two paths we may follow: the way of the buffalo is the good path, for the buffalo represents life. He warns us of the other path. If that path is taken, many people will die. What is your second vision?"

"I saw myself," Spotted Fox admitted reluctantly. "I looked as I do now, but I wore a strange hat. It was high and round and black and shiny, and it had a rim at the bottom like a white man's hat, but narrow. I rode wearing it into the camp of the Pawnee, and I carried only a coup stick. It was daylight, but I rode through the camp, touching many men. I saw no more."

Again the shaman consulted with the chief. They murmured with their heads together for only a moment before Raven straightened with a satisfied grunt. "This vision may be a true vision, Spotted Fox, or it may not be. You will know if you ever see the hat of your dream. I have never seen such a hat, but you must watch for it. Horse Runner, what is your vision?"

McCabe hesitated, then tried to recall for the others what he had seen. "I have danced. I have danced and I have seen two visions. In the first vision I saw myself. I was old. My hair was grey, and I knew that there were many scars on my body. I wore a long black coat and a black hat with a wide brim, and I held a gun in my hand. The gun was like my pistols—they could shoot many times. But in some way it was different. There was a piece of metal on the coat, like a round badge, and there was blood down the side of the coat. I put the gun into a holster at my waist. And I walked away."

"You have seen yourself as an old man," Raven concluded. "Many even see the way of their death as old men. You will live to be an old man, but there will be much fighting in your life. Before you die, you will return to your own people."

"I am not certain I want to return to them," McCabe mused.

High-backed Wolf and Raven both blinked at the impropriety. "You had a second vision," Raven prompted.

McCabe nodded. The second vision was the important one. If only they interpreted it the way he wanted them to. "In the second vision I saw four men. They were men, not spirits. One was Cheyenne, one Arapaho, one Kiowa, and the last Comanche. They stood in a river that was knee-deep, and they clasped each other by the arm. A huge herd of horses splashed across the stream behind them, and they looked at the horses and smiled. Then they clasped arms again. I saw no more."

The chief and the shaman put their heads together for a long time, talking with much excited nodding and gesturing. Finally Raven sighed and straightened. "I do not know if your vision is for this time or for another. It says that one day the four peoples you have named will fight no more."

"It is a false vision!" Three Hatchets cried. Raven shook his head at the interruption. High-backed Wolf frowned and gestured for Three Hatchets to be silent.

"He is white!" Three Hatchets went on. "He should never have been allowed to dance!"

"Be silent!" the chief growled. "You break the proper forms."

"I must," Three Hatchets insisted. "This white man will lead us to destruction with his white man's vision. Even his first vision shows that he is white, not Cheyenne."

"You will be silent!" Raven shouted. Even Three Hatchets' arrogance seemed to quail before the old man's fury. "This is the medicine lodge. It is you who will bring evil to the Cheyenne with your breaking of the proper ways. Here only the visions may be spoken of, and only in the proper forms. You will observe them, or I will summon spirits to come in the night to torment you, now and after you have died. You will never know rest again."

Three Hatchets licked his lips as he stared at the shaman, who suddenly seemed to loom like a great shadow over them all. With a visible effort, he forced his eyes away and was silent. Raven nodded and turned back to McCabe. Once more he seemed like only a frail old man. "Your vision is a true vision. But whether it is for this time or another, I cannot say." He turned to Three Hatchets. "What was your vision?"

Three Hatchets looked at the others before he spoke. He gave a glare at McCabe, and as he spoke, his old arrogance seemed to return. "I have danced. I have danced, and I have seen three visions. In the first a spirit came to me. He looked like a man, but the horns of an elk grew from his forehead. 'Look at the past,' he told me. I looked, and I saw a dog fighting a giant wolf. The wolf drove the dog away from its den, then lay down to rest. The spirit said to me, 'See the future,' and I looked again. I saw the dog return to the wolf's den and attack it. This time the dog killed the wolf. That is what I saw."

Raven nodded thoughtfully. "What is the second vision?"

Three Hatchets seemed annoyed that the first vision wasn't interpreted, but he went on. "In the second vision I saw another spirit. He had no hair above his waist, but below his waist he was covered with it. 'Look at what is gone,' he said, and I looked. I saw an eagle fighting a hawk, but the hawk was as big as a buffalo. The hawk drove the eagle away. 'Look at what is to come,' the spirit said. I saw the eagle return. Again they fought, and the eagle drove the hawk away."

"It is interesting," Raven noted, "that your first two visions were so much alike. Perhaps their message is powerful. What is the third vision?"

"Why will you not interpret them?" Three Hatchets demanded. "It is clear what they mean."

Raven's face tightened. "The third vision."

"in the third vision again a spirit came to me. He looked like a man, but he had two heads, and his feet did not touch the ground. 'See what has been,' one head said. And I saw two buffalo bulls fighting. One was huge and black, the other white. The black buffalo drove the white buffalo away. The spirit's other head said, "See what will be.' I saw the white buffalo return. Again they fought, and this time the black buffalo was vanquished, running away bloody."

"These are visions of power," Raven judged. "They say that the Cheyenne should attack the Kiowa again, that this time the Kiowa will be destroyed. But Horse Runner's vision was also a vision of power, and it says that peace is the way. This must be pondered." He stood to signal that the ceremony had ended.

Outside the lodge McCabe found Spotted Fox. "Three Hatchets wants war very much," McCabe reported.

The young warrior had a preoccupied frown on his face. "What? Yes, he wants war."

"Doe he want war badly enough to lie about his visions during the Sun Dance?"

Spotted Fox stared. "No one would lie about a vision of the Sun Dance. No. No mater how much he wanted war, he would not lie. He saw what he said he saw." He sighed. "And I saw what I saw. I saw the way I will die, in the camp of the Pawnee."

"Of course not," McCabe countered. "Not if you take care not to wear a black hat or to ride into the Pawnee camp in the daylight."

Spotted Fox looked at him, his face expressionless. He slowly shook his head. "You do not understand."

McCabe watched his downcast friend walk slowly away. Nothing had come out as he had hoped. Spotted Fox was convinced he was going to die. McCabe had told the truth about what he had seen, only to have Three Hatchets contradict the message of his visions—with a lie, he was certain, despite what Spotted Fox said. He was tired of it all. The mountains were not too far away. Perhaps his friends would come with him for a winter trapping. Even if they would not, he decided, he would go with Night Bird Woman and Looking Glass. He would go away from the troubles that seemed certain to end in another war.

16

As McCabe walked into the camp, the women glanced up at him, then bent back to their work when he dropped wearily to the ground.

"Is my husband tired?" Night Bird Woman asked. She was quilling a new shirt for him, and she didn't take her attention from her work.

"Your husband is very tired," McCabe grunted. He took the bag that had been slung at his waist and tossed it to Looking Glass.

She drew out three beaver pelts and began to make a willow hoop on which to stretch the first one. "Ten traps are too many for one man to run," she told him. "You should have talked Otter Belt and Spotted Fox into coming with you."

"They didn't want to come," he grumbled irritably. "Spotted Fox sits all day worrying that he is going to be killed by the Pawnee, and Otter Belt intends to spend the winter trying to get more powerful medicine for the war. He is sitting on a hilltop talking to the spirits. I have told you this ten times already."

"I am sorry," Looking Glass murmured.

"She is right," Night Bird Woman remarked, "and you will not change it by getting angry. Ten traps are too many for one man."

"Nine," he said.

"What?"

"Nine. I said nine. Nine traps, not ten. A cougar got into one."

Both women looked at him worriedly.

"You were not hurt?" Looking Glass asked anxiously.

"It was not there when I arrived. I found the tracks. I guess the cougar stepped into the trap, then managed to pull the stake loose from the river bottom, and got away with my trap still on its foot. I tracked it for two hours, but I lost it when it doubled back over the river. Fool cat probably drowned trying to cross. Why would a cougar step in a beaver trap, any-way?" He heard a suspicious noise and looked up. Both women were star-ing at him with straight faces.

"Perhaps, my husband," Night Bird Woman offered, "if you told the cougars they were not supposed to step in your beaver traps. . . ."

"Or sent messages to the beaver to come before the cougars," Looking Glass added. She began to giggle, and then Night Bird Woman began to giggle too. In minutes both doubled over, rolling on the ground in laughter.

McCabe stared at them angrily. But then a chuckle escaped his throat, and he fell back laughing just as hard.

◇

In autumn the leaves on the trees were turning to shades of red and gold and orange and brown. A red fox trotting across a clearing ahead caught McCabe's eye. His hand went to the hammer of the Hawken, then he pulled it back in disgust. Trapping hadn't been good so far, but to think of wasting powder and lead on a fox was ridiculous. A prime red fox pelt was only equal to half a beaver pelt, and that was without .50-caliber holes in it.

He stalked back into the trees, but as he did his horse suddenly flared its nostrils and shied violently. Standing ten feet from him was a bear, a nine-and-a-half-foot grizzly, its dark brown coat tipped with silver. With a

139

shrill scream the horse reared and twisted in its effort to escape, and then toppled clumsily.

McCabe lost his breath with a gasp when he hit the ground, but he quickly got it back as his horse thrashed about before gaining its feet and dashed away, wide-eyed with terror.

The bear coughed and started toward McCabe.

Desperately he looked around for the Hawken. It lay a dozen feet away. He pushed himself to his feet, took a step, and fell again. The bear growled behind him. He could hear its feet rustling in the fallen leaves. With his hands and his good leg he scrambled and clawed across the grass to the rifle. As his hands fell on it he thumbed back the hammer and rolled over.

No more than six feet away, the bear loomed over him. He drew the gun to his shoulder and fired. The heavy ball smashed into the bear's massive chest, and the animal screamed with pain and anger. McCabe fumbled for his pistols. They were gone. Frantically he pulled out his knife. He had no wish to get closer to the fangs and jaws below those fiery eyes or to the sharp claws in those hairy paws. He had seen a man whose face had been left a one-eyed twisted mass of scars by a grapple with a dying bear. But now there was no choice.

As the bear shambled forward with a roar, McCabe brought his good leg under him and threw himself at the beast. He felt the wind from a swiping paw whip through his hair, but then he was against the animal's torso, gripping the shaggy fur with his free hand, wrapping his legs around it, sinking his teeth into its hide to keep his face tight into the bear's chest. Claws scraped across his back. The creature twisted itself, trying to get McCabe's head in its jaw. The fur cap was torn away savagely. If the bear managed to pull McCabe loose from his grip for even an instant, he would be torn to shreds. With all his strength he thrust his knife into the bear, seeking the heart. The animal roared, its paws beating at him like clubs, its claws tattering his hunting shirt and cutting into his back. He pulled the blade free and stabbed again. And again. And again. And he continued to stab the bear's flesh until the animal slowly toppled.

Even when it lay on the ground he would not release his hold. He kept himself pressed against its chest, listening to the last beats of the great heart. Finally, when he could hear no more, he let himself fall free.

He had no idea how long he had lain there, the gentle breeze blowing dry leaves over him, but at last he struggled to a sitting position. Carefully he probed at his leg, then tried to bend it. It was not broken, he decided, but the bruise was severe. The cuts on his back throbbed, but the bleeding was slowly beginning to subside as the remains of his shirt helped to check the flow of blood. He looked at the clouds creeping low over the mountain peaks. It would be a cold night; perhaps the first frost would come. But on foot, with his leg so painfully injured, there was no way to make it back to the camp. He heard wolves howl in the distance and shivered. The Indians said the wolves were smart, that they hardly ever attacked men since men had started carrying guns. But he also knew that they seemed to sense helplessness or injury. He had seen them pick out and close in on an injured buffalo, even when it seemed outwardly as strong as any other. They always took the easiest prey, and tonight, gun or no gun, he might well be that prey.

Gingerly he reached around to touch his back, and stopped after the first try. The effort set his whole body on fire. What he had touched beneath his fingers felt like raw meat slashed with razors. The scent of blood would help to attract the wolves.

Forcing himself to move quickly despite his pain, he found his pistols and put them back in his belt. Next he reloaded the Hawken. Then, straining every muscle, he pushed the bear's carcass over onto its back and began to skin it. It was enough work for two or three people, but he forced himself to wrestle the skin loose and finally freed it from under the animal.

The wind freshened, carrying with it the breath of the snow from the high mountains. Shivering, he pulled the skin around himself. The wolves howled again. They were closer. They smelled the bear carcass, he thought, and he set himself into a shambling run.

His breath came in short pants, but he pushed himself forward. The mountain valley was wide and treacherous. He trotted across the meadows, startling deer and foxes, and used the Hawken for a crutch in working his way up the hills and down the far sides.

As dark began to fall, he started looking for a place to hole up. Wherever he stopped, the place had to be defensible. The wolves might linger over the bear, but they would soon pick up his scent as well. Even as he thought of it he saw a thick tree with one heavy branch six feet above the ground and a fork twice that high. It took a straining effort to make it with the rifle and bear hide to the fork, but he finally settled himself in to wait with the hide wrapped around him.

An hour after dark the wolves came, and they snuffled around the base of the tree, whining eagerly like dogs. They quickly realized he was in the tree, and most of them settled down around the base to wait him out. A few, more impatient, reared up with their front feet on the tree trunk to see if they could reach him. One began to leap.

McCabe watched the leaper warily. The animal fell short every time, but it wouldn't give up. Again and again it gathered itself and jumped. Just as he was settling back, sure that it couldn't reach him, it jumped high enough on one of its leaps to hook its front paws and the front half of its body across the lower limb. With a scramble of its hind paws it stood on the thick lower branch. Tentatively it began to gather itself for another jump.

McCabe quickly shot it off the limb. The others scattered at the sound of the shot, but he could hear them in the darkness, toenails clicking on outcroppings of rock. When the clouds shifted to let the moon through, he caught glimpses of their grey shifting shadows and gleaming eyes. As the wind grew colder, he pulled the skin tighter, thankful for the insulation of the fat still on it.

By dawn the wolves had gone. He looked around carefully, but there was no sign of them except for the single dead wolf beneath the tree. Stirring stiffly, he climbed down. To his astonishment, he saw Night Bird Woman and Looking Glass riding toward him, leading a saddled horse.

"My husband!" Night Bird Woman cried as she saw him.

"What were you doing in that tree?" Looking Glass called. "Why did you not return to the camp?"

They stopped in amazement as they drew close enough to get a good look at him.

"Skin the wolf," he said, and only half-listened to their exclamations at discovering the animal as he painfully pulled himself into the saddle.

"When did you shoot this wolf?" Night Bird Woman asked. The two women pulled out their skinning knives and set to work.

"Last night," he replied. "He climbed into the tree with me."

The two women stared at each other, then looked at him worriedly.

"Are you truly all right?" Night Bird Woman demanded.

"I am all right," he answered. "Hurry. I must see to something." When they were back on their horses, he led them to the bear's carcass.

The wolf pack had ravaged it, stripped away its flesh, scattering and cracking its bones till what remained had little resemblance to the great brute McCabe had faced. He pulled the bearskin from around his shoulders and dropped it on what was left of the carcass. The women screamed when they saw his back.

"I bring you back your skin," he said, looking down at the remains of the bear. "I had to borrow it, but I bring it back."

"The bear did that to your back?" Looking Glass inquired. "And you still live?"

"We fought," he replied without looking at the women. "My knife against his claws. But I shot him first, so I killed him."

"With a knife," Night Bird Woman remarked wonderingly.

"The skin," Looking Glass prompted. "It is too valuable to leave here. Let me take it back to the camp with the wolfskin. I will scrape them both today."

He shook his head. "I came into the bear's land. I did not want his flesh to eat, or his skin to warm me, but I came into his land, and he tried to defend it. I had to kill him, or he would have killed me, but I came looking for nothing from him, and I will take nothing. What are you doing?" he asked as Night Bird Woman got down and took out her knife again.

She began rummaging through the scattered parts, putting this part and that in a buffalo-hide sack. "I am gathering the bear's teeth and his claws. You must make a necklace of them and wear it."

"I said I would take nothing."

"You must." She straightened, holding the skull, tatters of bloody flesh still clinging to the bone. The teeth, as long as his forefinger, still seemed ready to bite. "This was a great bear. The great bear is not like the little bears. There is a song about him." Her voice rose in a plaintive chant. "Your heart is black, you great bear. Your heart is as black as your deeds, you murderer of men."

"I still want nothing from him."

"The great bear has a powerful spirit, Horse Runner. If you do not make the necklace of his teeth and claws, his spirit will pursue yours and swallow it up."

143

As he stared at the bloody skull, he could almost imagine that the beast would indeed pursue its enemies even after death. "Bring them," he said at last. "I will make the necklace."

McCabe tossed the empty trap into the water with a sigh, then set it back where it was supposed to be and freshened the bait scent on the willow stick that was secured in the bank. He had been in the wilderness for weeks now and had hardly any pelts to show for it. The half-healed claw wounds on his back itched, but at least they no longer kept him awake at night. Slinging the empty pelt sack on his back, he waded back downstream to the campsite.

As he came out of the river near their willow-framed lodge, he stopped in astonishment. Looking Glass and Night Bird Woman were playing the awl game, laughing at each other as they made a point or were forced to start over.

Night Bird Woman saw him first and ran to him. "Come and play, Horse Runner. You spend too much time with your traps."

"I have to spend time with the traps," he protested. "Would you have me play a woman's game?"

"Of course not," she said scornfully. "We will play the button game."

"All right," he grinned. He scooped up a pebble from the bank. "I have my button. Get yours."

Night Bird Woman grabbed a stone as well. "Come, Looking Glass. We will play the button game with him."

"But I have only two hands," he complained. "If both of you play, you will have four hands on your team."

"You are a man," Looking Glass smiled, "and so much smarter than us poor women. What will our advantage really do for us?"

He laughed as they sat side by side, waiting, and he dropped down to face them. Immediately they began passing Night Bird Woman's stone back and forth behind their backs. After a minute of this they brought their fists in front of them.

"Which hand?" Looking Glass quizzed.

He touched her right hand. She turned it over and opened it. There was no stone. "The point is ours," she laughed. Giggling, they put their hands behind their backs again.

"Which hand?" Night Bird Woman asked, and he touched her left hand. Again there was no stone. Nine times more the women passed the stone back and forth before he chose the correct hand.

"Very well," Night Bird Woman said. "We have ten points. It is your turn."

Putting his hands behind his back, he passed the pebble from one to the other. With a quick move he tucked the stone into a fold of his shirt and brought his fists in front of him. "Which hand?"

They conferred too softly for him to hear, then Looking Glass touched his left hand. He turned it up empty. Quickly he put his hands behind his back again and made as if shifting the rock. This time Night Bird Woman chose his right hand. She shook her head and muttered to herself when she saw his empty palm. He piled up ten points, twenty, thirty.

"Let me see your button," Night Bird Woman requested suddenly as he was putting his hands behind his back yet again.

He deftly plucked the pebble from its hiding place and showed it to her. When he pretended to shuttle the rock from hand to hand once more, he again slipped it into the fold of his shirt, then presented his closed fists to the women. Looking Glass touched his left hand. He opened it to reveal nothing, and she muttered to herself. But before he could put his hands behind his back again, Night Bird Woman suddenly threw herself on him, seizing his right wrist.

"Help me, Looking Glass!" she shouted. "Force his hand open." Looking Glass stared at him with sudden suspicion and leaped to help the other woman.

Laughing, McCabe halfheartedly tried to fend them off as they pried at his clenched fingers, slowly forcing his fist open. Then they stared in consternation when they realized the hand was empty.

"You cheated," Looking Glass cried.

Shrieking like eagles, they turned and began to pummel him in the ribs with their fists. He threw up his arms to protect himself, and backed away so they wouldn't be able to reach the pebble.

"Wait," Night Bird Woman appealed. "Is your back all right?"

"My back is fine," he replied, and they immediately fell upon him again. Flinging an arm around each of them, he managed to catch one hand of each woman in his own and trap the two other hands beneath his back. Their heads were caught between his arms.

"It is said that women sometimes become violent in their lovemaking," he laughed. One of them tried to bite him through his buckskin hunting shirt. "Some even bite like beavers." There was a flurry of punches from both women, and yelps as they tried to kick him, missed, and banged their toes on the hard ground. Night Bird Woman squalled into his armpit.

"Will you admit that I won the game?" he asked.

Looking Glass managed to twist her face free of his hunting shirt enough to pant, "You cheated."

"But I won."

Night Bird Woman struggled to her feet, but McCabe still held her by the arm. "Let us go. There is work to be done."

"Say that I won the game."

"You cheated," Looking Glass insisted.

He sighed as if settling down for a long rest. "But did I win the game?"

"You won the game," Night Bird woman moaned resignedly.

"He cheated!" Looking Glass cried.

"He won the game," Night Bird Woman repeated. "If he did not win the game, we will be here all day."

Looking Glass finally relented. "You won the game."

Immediately he released both of them. "You are wrong," he stated immediately. "I did not win the game. How could I? I cheated."

Leaping to his feet, he ran between the trees for cover from a pelting of dirt clods and rocks. When he timidly peered back out a few minutes later, the women were laughing so hard that they had to hang on to one another to keep from falling over. He grinned and pulled back into the trees. If he showed himself too soon, he'd likely get another pelting.

There was a sharp pain in his back. He dug the hidden pebble out of the fold of his shirt and was about to throw it away when something caught his eye. There were glitters in the pebble. Golden glitters. Small flecks and streaks of gold studded the stone.

146

Taking a deep breath, he pulled out his knife and dug at one of the streaks. It cut. It was soft. It had to be gold.

Frantically he tried to remember where he had picked it up. Right at the edge of the river, directly in front of the camp.

He raced down to the spot and searched along the bank. There they were, other pebbles gleaming with the same golden flecks. He dug in the rocky soil, and more turned up. Gold.

"Why are you digging in the dirt?" Night Bird Woman called. She and Looking Glass, standing in front of the lodge, peered at him curiously.

"Gold!" he shouted back.

They walked slowly down to squat by his side. "What is this gold?" Looking Glass asked.

"Yellow metal," he answered. He began to pick up pebbles, keeping those that showed signs of color in a small pile and throwing the rest over his shoulder into the river. "It is very valuable. Very valuable."

"Like silver?" Night Bird Woman asked. "There are people far to the south who dig in the ground for silver."

"Yes," he agreed, "like silver. But more valuable." He sat back on his heels suddenly. "This is not the right way, picking up pebbles. I have seen pictures. I must built a long box to put the dirt in, then cover it with water from the river. The dirt will wash away and leave the pebbles behind . . . with the gold."

"I do not understand," Night Bird Woman said. "You will not trap beaver anymore? You will dig in the ground for this gold instead?"

"I will dig in the ground for this gold, but I will still trap beaver," he said with a frown. What he knew of mining came from scant reading. There could be a great deal more gold here, or only a small amount. An experienced miner might know, but he had no clue. "I will do both."

"It will snow this night," Looking Glass judged with a glance at the granite-grey sky. "The ground will freeze."

He sprang to his feet, sizing up the trees around the camp. "Get me the axe, Looking Glass. Night Bird Woman, get the spade. While I cut timbers for the box, the two of you begin digging here. Pile the dirt to one side. Quickly."

He paused to look once more at the ground where the gold lay buried.

With luck, he might find enough to make up for the poor trapping. He took the axe from Looking Glass and hurried into the woods.

—◇—

McCabe clambered wearily out of the icy river and stumbled past the sluice box and pit into the camp. The crust on the snow cracked under his feet. From inside the low, wooden lean-to the women looked at him with concern as he pushed aside the door flap and tossed his sack in. A warm fire burned brightly inside.

"Come in, my husband," Night Bird Woman said. "Warm yourself."

"I have no time," he told her. Looking Glass dug into the sack and looked up at him in surprise when she found three unskinned beaver. "One of you skin them. Keep the tails and the meat. I will try to get a deer in a day or two."

"You work yourself too hard," Looking Glass returned.

"She speaks the truth, my husband. You must rest."

"There is no time," he replied heavily. "In the morning I must run the traps. In the afternoon I must dig for gold. Only the night is left for sleep."

"Then do not dig for the gold," Night Bird Woman said simply. "It does not seem proper to see you grub in the dirt so much."

"Or if you must dig," Looking Glass appealed, "do not trap. There are few beaver this year. Many days the traps are empty."

"I must do both," he insisted. "There is only a little gold too, but the gold and the beaver together will make this a profitable winter. One alone will not."

"Why must there be a profit?" Night Bird Woman inquired. "If there are few beaver this year, there will be more next. You have acted very strangely since you found this gold."

"I have no time to argue," he concluded.

"But my husband. . . ."

He let the flap fall, ignoring her words, and turned back toward the river. It had taken three tries to design a sluice box that worked. It was a plain rectangular crate of roughhewn wood, standing on four legs with one end over the water. That end of the box was made of a half dozen thin slats that fitted tightly into a groove. When the box was filled with dirt and water, he would stir it up into a muddy soup, then remove the top slat.

The water and loose dirt flowed away. Then the process was repeated until finally he would have only pebbles left, often bearing gold.

The ground was frozen all the time now. He calculated the month to be December, or perhaps January. Every morning he labored with axe and spade to break up the clods of dirt that had frozen during the night, and he shoveled them into the box and pounded at them again and again until he had smashed them into pebble-sized pieces. Then he had to carry bucket after bucket of water to fill the sluice.

Pebbles with the milky look of quartz went into the sack even if they showed no glittering color. They would be broken open with the rest at night. Occasionally he would find a sparkling flake, a single tiny grain of gold sand. These he put into a pouch hanging about his neck.

On this night, he stumbled to the lodge and dropped heavily beside the fire, his arms so stiff from the cold that he could barely manage to shrug out of his heavy buffalo-hide coat.

"You must rest now," Night Bird Woman instructed.

Looking Glass held a bowl of stew out to him, but he pushed it away. "I am not hungry." He worked his numb fingers before the fire, but before any feeling was restored, he rummaged in the sack for a pebble.

The small chunk of quartz was placed on a flat rock, then pounded to fragments with a heavy, round river rock. Usually the debris was brushed aside onto a hide. But now and again the pile of powder and splinters gave up a twisted thread of gold. These he placed, along with the grains and flakes from the pouch around his neck, in a pouch he kept hidden in a corner of the lodge, behind a pile of furs in a hollow space in the wall of the lodge itself.

Looking Glass and Night Bird Woman, watching him as he worked, slowed in their own tasks. Shivers racked him as he twisted and pried the thin filaments of gold from the stone. He couldn't seem to get any warmth from the fire. His frozen clothes had begun to thaw, and icy water mixed with his sweat.

"Now you will rest," Night Bird Woman commanded as at last he tucked the pouch away.

"I still have to. . . ."

"No," she said sharply. "I cannot watch you harm yourself, my husband. You are chilled, but you sit in your cold clothes. Will you let yourself get sick? Who then will dig for your gold?"

"All right," he mumbled. "I will rest." He felt too drained to argue. It was an effort to drag off his buckskin leggings and hunting shirt. He crawled beneath a pile of furs, but the chill stayed with him. It seemed to creep into his bones.

Suddenly he was aware of two warm bodies burrowing under the furs beside him. He looked in astonishment as Night Bird Woman's head popped up on one side of him and Looking Glass' on the other. The two women pressed themselves against him. They were both naked.

"Let us warm you," Night Bird Woman said.

With a sigh he sank deeper in the furs, absently putting an arm around each woman to cup a breast. In the space of two breaths, exhaustion claimed him. He slept.

When he awoke the next morning, he lay alone in the lodge. The fire had been built high to give a cheery warmth. The previous night had been the first in a long time when his sleep hadn't been broken by worries over how many beaver he would take for the season, or how much gold he could get out of the ground.

He stretched and slowly dressed. Outside, the sun was bright and warm on his face, but a cold veil of snow still covered the land.

Looking Glass carried forage to the horses in the lean-to attached to the side of the lodge. She stopped to look at him as she moved around each horse. Night Bird Woman came up from the river with a bark bucket full of water.

"Good morning, my husband," she greeted. "You slept well?"

"I slept very well," he smiled. He regarded her for a moment. "Perhaps," he said slowly, "I have pushed myself too hard. I will no longer. The trap line must still be run, but I will not dig so much. There will be time again for games and laughing."

"That is good, my husband, for Looking Glass wept all last night."

"She did?" He looked back to where the other woman was feeding the horses. She paused, one hand absently stroking the grey, but when she saw that he was looking at her, she colored and scurried into the lean-to. "I will tell her what I have just told you."

"My husband, you are as strong as a buffalo bull, but sometimes not as smart. She did not cry for you last night. She cried for herself."

"I do not understand."

"I did not understand, either, until she told me she had not been to your blankets since I became your wife."

He sighed heavily. "I should have done as I wanted to in the first place. I promise that when we return to the camp, she will have her own lodge. And I will give her enough horses so that she will soon get a husband."

"Why do you make matters so difficult?" she asked, shaking her head. "Take her to your blankets."

"Take her?" he began uncomfortably, and trailed off into a cough. "Among my people. . . ."

"You have told me of your people, my husband. You are among the Cheyenne now."

"Night Bird Woman, I do not want to bring trouble. We cannot live in the same lodge if there is jealousy."

"Jealousy!" she fumed. "Looking Glass is my sister, as you are my husband. How can I be jealous of my sister? Go to her now."

"I have to run the trap line," he said awkwardly.

"I will run the trap line," she replied. "Go to her." Quickly, McCabe's wife gathered up the sack for pelts, a hatchet for driving stakes, and then the horn bottle of castoreum gland solution. "Go to her," she repeated, and waded into the chilly river.

He watched her disappear upstream before he turned to the lean-to. Looking Glass had come out to look curiously after Night Bird Woman.

"We talked," he told her. She jumped at the sound of his voice. "Night Bird Woman and I talked."

"Is she going to check the traps?" she asked with a small frown.

"Yes. She said. . . ." He stopped to clear his throat. "That is, she told me . . . Looking Glass, would you come into the lodge with me?"

A slow smile spread across her face. "I will."

Scooping her into his arms, he carried her in to the furs.

With spring came the echoing cracks of ice breaking up in the high mountains. Finding gold had become a rare event, and beaver remained scarce.

McCabe finished skinning out the pelt and added it to the one already in his sack. Absently he wondered how Solomon had managed with his many wives. Keeping up with two women was almost more than he could manage. For a time he squatted, staring at the river. The water sparkled and rippled now with the run-off from the melt in the mountain peaks that loomed all about him. It had been a fight, wading in those waters today, and he decided it had been for the last time.

A long winter of trapping had taken only a hundred beaver. Otter Belt and Spotted Fox had warned him the year before. The beaver just weren't there in the numbers they once had been. The demand for hats in the East and in Europe had driven hundreds of white trappers to the mountains, and hundreds of Indians had joined in the slaughter once they found that pelts could be traded. Hundreds of thousands of the animals had been taken every year, until there were hardly any of the creatures left. Now the white trappers were deserting the trade in droves, and the Indians were hunting for other ways to buy the white man's trade goods.

Even the gold wouldn't balance things out, he thought ruefully. He would hardly make enough in trade to buy powder, ammunition and supplies, let alone extra food for the winter. All his work had netted him, as near as he could figure, sixteen ounces, worth three hundred and twenty dollars; that was a little more than sixty prime beaver pelts . . . if the price of beaver had not gone down again.

There was a thrashing in the trees on the far bank. He tossed the carcass into the willows, and scrambled quietly behind one broad trunk. He had not seen any Crow or Utes this winter, but that didn't mean they weren't nearby. He checked the cap on his rifle and thumbed the hammer back.

The thrashing sounded again, and then Looking Glass appeared, running and then falling. With an oath he ran to the bank. "Looking Glass! What is the matter?"

Wild-eyed, she glanced about to find him. When she did, she threw herself into the river, struggling to wade across. The current caught her, pulling her off her feet. She fought to regain her footing, and went down again.

"Hang on!" he shouted, running down the bank. When he reached a point opposite her, he jumped in. Re-entering the freezing water sent a shock through him that forced a gasp to his lips. The swift water almost jerked him down, but he leaned against it as he fought his way to her. She was falling again when he put an arm around her.

"Horse Runner," she gasped.

He tried to support her as best he could. Her weight, along with the current, almost pulled him down into the water. He had to plan each step and brace himself before he took it. At times he could feel the river almost winning, but at last he managed to climb onto the bank. He set Looking Glass down and fell to his knees, panting. "Woman, why did you do that foolish thing? I should cut a willow switch and beat you."

She began to sob. "It is Night Bird Woman!"

"Night Bird Woman? Is she all right? Is she hurt?"

"Men camp," she muttered, gulping back tears. "Hair-faces. She shouted for me to run. Two of them chased me, but I got away."

Without even realizing it, he was on his feet and running. It was a good four miles to the camp. His hands fumbled as he checked his knife and tomahawk and felt the caps on his Colts. He dimly wondered if the charges had gotten wet in the river. All he could think of was Night Bird Woman. Night Bird Woman in the hands of hair-faces, trappers. He heard her screaming long before he reached the camp, an ululating cry that seared through him and left him in a rage.

He stopped at the edge of the trees. Three bearded white men in fur caps and leather hunting shirts were tying his horses to a lead line. Another, with a red coat, stood looking at the sluice box, while two more with rifles watched the trees. They seemed more interested in listening to the screams coming from the lodge. McCabe shut them out of his mind. There were nine saddled horses. That meant there were three men he couldn't see. The other rifles were leaning against the lodge. He pulled back the hammer on his Hawken and raised it to his shoulder.

"Hey, Ef," one of the trappers called. "Where's the woman's buck, you reckon?

"Here!" McCabe shouted, and shot him through the head.

While the body was still falling, he dropped the rifle and pulled his pistols. The other guard whipped around to fire, and McCabe felt something smash into his side. He took a backward step, then braced and fired. The trapper who had fired dropped to one knee to reload, but a ball took him in the head. The three men who had been standing with the horses scrambled for the guns by the lodge door. McCabe followed them with the Colts, firing as fast as he could. One dropped short of the lodge. Another fell in the doorway, sprawling half in and half out. The third man whipped around in his tracks and raced for the woods. McCabe's shot caught him between the shoulders.

Suddenly McCabe screamed. There was a piercing pain in his side, and a weight forced him to the ground. He realized that the man in the red coat had jumped him while he was concentrating on the others, and that a knife had found his flesh. Ignoring the pain, McCabe smashed his elbow back into his attacker's mouth. The pistols had been dropped when he fell, but his hand gripped his tomahawk as he struggled to turn in the man's grasp.

He found himself staring into surprised brown eyes. "You're white," the man gasped. Then McCabe's hatchet sank into his skull.

Desperately, McCabe grabbed up the pistols and scrambled back to the shelter of a tree. The three inside the lodge still hadn't joined the fight, but the screaming had stopped. He felt his ribs for the bullet wound, and his hand came up with blood. Then, gingerly, he touched the knife, which was still sticking into his side. Bone grated when he pressed on the handle, and he clamped his jaws shut to stifle another yell. It had lodged in a rib. That had saved his life, for the time being, but he couldn't leave it there long. Gritting his teeth, he grasped the handle and gave a tremendous pull. The blade slipped out. He groaned in relief. If he didn't start bleeding too much inside, he would survive.

All the trappers lay still where they had fallen except for the man in the door, who was being pulled into the lodge. Grabbing his rifle, McCabe quickly reloaded, then started to do the same with the Colts.

"Ef!" someone shouted from the lodge. "Jacob! Henry! Where are you? How many are there?"

There was silence. McCabe rested the Hawken against the tree trunk.

"Goddamn it!" another shout went up. "There can't be but one or two of them! There was only two women!"

"There must have been twenty damn shots!" someone shouted back. "Ain't no two Injuns that could have fired all of them."

McCabe grinned wolfishly. He could see the muzzle of a rifle showing at the lodge door, and he tried to imagine how the man holding it was standing. Carefully he aimed at the wall a foot to the right of the door.

"Injuns! We got one of your women in here. Listen!" McCabe heard a woman shriek. "Hear that? You let us out of here with our goods and traps, or we'll peel every inch of hide off her."

McCabe pulled the trigger. There was a shout from inside, and the rifle dropped in the door.

"They killed Zack!" one of them shouted. "Right through the wall! They don't care about the woman! Kill her and let's go!"

"Goddamn you Injuns!" another voice screamed. Suddenly there were two trappers at the door, rushing out with rifles in their hands. "Goddamn you! Goddamn you!"

McCabe picked up the Colts as the men cleared the door and began to fire. The first man staggered, then came on. The other, who had a long mustache, went down with a cry, rolled to his feet, and went down again. Then the first man fell and didn't rise, but McCabe kept firing, aiming every shot carefully, until both guns were empty.

McCabe picked up the Hawken wearily and started toward the lodge.

Suddenly the man who had been with the horses rolled over and leaned against the front of the lodge. McCabe saw him and quickly blew down the barrel of the Hawken and reached for his powder horn.

"You shot me good, Injun," the man growled. His fur cap was off, revealing a shaven head above his beard. "What kind of gun was you. . . ." His eyes widened as he regarded McCabe. "You ain't no Injun. You're a white man."

McCabe seated a ball on a patch on the muzzle while the man continued to speak.

"Well, damn it, if we'd knowed you was a white man, we wouldn't have messed with your woman."

McCabe thrust the ball down atop the powder with the ramrod and replaced it beneath the barrel.

"Still, you surely played hell with us. It was only an Injun woman, after all. Damn it, we'd have gave you a few pelts to pay you back for our mistake. I . . . ." He licked his lips as McCabe raised the rifle to his shoulder, taking careful aim. "Hey, mister. I'll still give you them pelts. Hell, you can have the whole bunch! It wasn't such a good year anyway! Take the horses if you. . . ."

McCabe shot him between the eyes.

He slowly lowered the rifle, then dropped it and rushed past the body into the lodge. He realized he was crying. Night Bird Woman lay naked on the packed dirt floor, her delicate breasts and thighs covered with bruises. A trickle of blood ran down her face. Sobs shook him as he fell to his knees and took her into his arms.

She moaned and stirred, then her eyes fluttered open. "You came, my husband," she said faintly. "I knew that you would." Suddenly she turned her face away. "I am ashamed, my husband."

"No," he insisted. "No. You have nothing to be ashamed of."

"They raped me, my husband. I do not even know how many of them."

"No, no no." He began to rock back and forth, holding her to him tightly. "There is no shame in this. You were only one woman against many men. How is there shame in that?"

"But. . . ."

"No. There is no shame.

She sighed and settled against him. "You will not put me off, divorce me?"

"I will not. Not ever," he murmured into her ear. "Not ever."

Looking Glass appeared suddenly at the door. She was out of breath. "Are you hurt?' she asked Night Bird Woman, and fell to her knees beside them to stroke the other woman's hair. "He has killed them all, Night Bird Woman. You have gained vengeance. Horse Runner will take their hair."

"They are carrion," McCabe grunted. "Scalps are not taken from carrion. Leave them where they lie for the badgers and the crows. We are leaving this place. We are going home."

17

The Cheyenne were camped fifty miles north of the Arrowpoint River when McCabe finally found them. All of the bands were assembled in a great circle, which stretched for miles. Spotted Fox and Otter Belt rode out to meet the little group as they approached the camp.

"Ho, Horse Runner!" Otter Belt called. "You return with many new horses from trapping."

"And guns," Spotted Fox added. "I see many guns in your packs."

"We were attacked," he said simply. "You may have them if you wish. I brought them to give them to the men who have none. They are rifles, not muskets." Eagerly they rode close to the pack horses to pull out the rifles.

Otter Belt shook his rifle above his head. "With this I can kill many enemies from a great distance."

"Then the decision has been made," McCabe declared resignedly. "War."

Spotted Fox shook his head. "No decision has been made. That is why the bands have come together. The Council of Chiefs meets now."

"What do the warriors say?" McCabe asked.

"Some say one thing," Spotted Fox replied, "and some another. No one is sure what is best. They wait for the chiefs to speak."

"And you?"

"I, too, wait," Spotted Fox laughed. "Only a shaman could know the right way this time."

"The chiefs will tell us the right way," Otter Belt said. "Don't your chiefs choose the right way for your people, Horse Runner?"

"Sometimes even chiefs make mistakes," McCabe replied.

"When that happens," Spotted Fox said, "a new man becomes chief."

McCabe nodded. "Among my people also. But by then it is too late, isn't it?"

Otter Belt and Spotted Fox had left a space between their tepees at the south of the circle where McCabe's lodge would be raised. As soon as it was up, McCabe settled the women inside.

"You will be all right?" he asked Night Bird Woman.

She laughed. "I am just sore, my husband, and a little stiff."

"I must go to see Raven," he informed.

"Why must you see a shaman?" Looking Glass queried. "We have offended no spirits."

"No, but I may soon need the help of the spirits."

The camp was in a bustle as distant relatives exchanged gossip, and trade items changed hands. McCabe saw blankets from the Navaho, coiled Pima storage baskets and pine-pitch-coated Paiute water baskets, wooden flutes from the Dakota, beaded belts from the Utes, pottery from the Kansa, turquoise from the Zuñi. There were knives and axe heads from white traders, and seashells and oil from tribes on the coast of the great ocean to the west. Over great distances and by circuitous routes, even items made by tribes who were deadly enemies were traded.

In front of his lodge, Raven was doing a brisk business in herbal cures and magic charms. During the gatherings of the bands, many took the opportunity to try the magic of another band's shaman. Raven saw McCabe and gestured for him to sit, but he waited until the last of the shaman's patients were gone.

"Your business is important," Raven said when he sat at last.

"How did you know?" McCabe asked.

"Because you would not sit while the others were here. You did not want to speak where the others could listen. This makes what you seek important." He smiled complacently while McCabe chuckled.

"You are right, Raven, what I seek is important. Do you know how the chiefs will decide at their council?"

Raven's wrinkled face puckered into a frown. "The talk of the council is not the knowledge of the camp. It is not to be spoken of casually." He paused. "But I think they lean toward war."

McCabe breathed heavily. "I do not know why I thought it might be different. When I found out no decision had been made yet, I hoped there was still a chance for peace."

"Until the first battle begins, there is always a chance for peace. But many of the chiefs favor war."

"And you, Raven, what do you favor?"

"I am an old man, Horse Runner. I have seen enough of war. I favor peace."

"Then will you help me get to speak to the council?

"Speak to the council!"

"Aren't ordinary warriors sometimes asked to speak to the council? I ask you to get me such an invitation. It is not a great deal to ask."

"You want to stand before council," Raven grumbled. "What kind of speaker are you? I do not know. I must go to High-backed Wolf, who will ask you to speak, but if you cannot speak well, he will be embarrassed, and I will be embarrassed. You do not ask for a great deal, Horse Runner. Why do you not ask for Wihio's wonderful sack that let a buffalo out every time he opened it?"

"I will speak of the visions we had when we danced the Sun Dance. I will do you no shame, Raven."

The old shaman regarded him for a moment, then sighed and nodded. "I will do what I can. Return to your lodge. I will come to you there."

At his lodge Looking Glass had started the cooking fires, and a rack of buffalo ribs was turning on a thong over one while a stew pot boiled over the other. Spotted Fox and Otter Belt sat watching her, and from the color in her cheeks McCabe knew they had been teasing her.

"Night Bird Woman is well?" he asked her.

Looking Glass nodded. "She sleeps. Will you eat?"

He dropped to the ground beside his friends. "Later." He felt too agitated to eat.

"Horse Runner," Otter Belt said, "this is a fine woman you have, this Looking Glass."

Looking Glass turned to look at them suspiciously.

"She is a fine woman," McCabe agreed absently.

"Perhaps you will sell her to me."

Looking Glass made a sharp noise, and McCabe realized what Otter Belt had asked. If that was the sort of teasing that had been going on, no wonder her cheeks were red.

"How much would you pay?" McCabe asked. He smiled at Looking Glass' sudden look of indignation.

"Six horses," Otter Belt offered.

McCabe looked at his friend in astonishment. From Otter Belt's tone of voice, he couldn't judge whether he was serious or not, but the offer was a respectable bride price, let alone payment for a captive. He regarded Looking Glass out of the corner of his eye. Her mouth was hanging open. "I could not sell her without her consent."

"Consent!" Otter Belt exclaimed. "You need no consent. Simply sell her to me."

McCabe ignored him. "Looking Glass, do you want me to sell you to Otter Belt?"

Fury began to mount in her face. "Sell me to that ragged piece of buffalo hide? To that skinny bird that preens like an eagle and makes noises like a crow? I would rather belong to a field mouse."

"I am sorry, Otter Belt," he maintained. "She does not want to be sold to you."

Otter Belt scowled at her. "If you belonged to me, I would beat you every day."

She shook her ladle at him. "I would prefer being beaten every day to belonging to you."

"Your woman is very rude. She is not worth a single horse." Otter Belt scrambled to his feet and stalked away.

McCabe stared after him in surprise. "What is that matter with him?"

"He is not used to being bested at words," Spotted Fox explained. "Especially by a woman. What is this? Raven comes to your lodge."

The old shaman entered and squatted in front of McCabe, frowning worriedly. "You will speak to the council tomorrow morning."

"The council!" Spotted Fox exclaimed.

McCabe didn't take his eyes off Raven. "There is more, isn't there?"

Raven smiled sourly. "It is too bad I did not get you when you were ten. You would have made a good shaman. Yes, there is more. When I went to High-backed Wolf, two other chiefs were there. Walks on Mountains and Stone Bull. High-backed Wolf acts always with the perfect honor of a chief."

"What does that mean?"

"It means, Horse Runner, that he hides nothing from the other chiefs. They were very much interested in the Sun Dance and the visions. Since there was a vision for war as well as one for peace, they want to hear from a man who supports war as well as one who speaks for peace."

Suddenly McCabe understood. "Three Hatchets will speak to the council also."

Raven nodded. "He danced when you danced. He had the vision for war when you had the vision for peace. It seemed obvious to them that if you speak for peace, he should speak for war."

"The chiefs seem determined to have their war."

"They want what is best. Now, as I do not know what kind of speaker you are, I will instruct you in how to address the council. Keep your words few. . . ."

As the sun rose toward its zenith, McCabe started for the huge yellow ceremonial lodge in the center of the camp, where the Council of Chiefs waited. Raven had done his best to see that he was dressed properly for the occasion. His moccasins came almost to the knee, and two blue heron feathers hung down the outside of each. His leggings were fringed with strips of leather and tufts of elk hair. His shirt, also fringed along the sleeves, was quilled in red and black. He wore the bear-claw necklace, and a red wool sash into which he had thrust his pistols, his knife and his tomahawk. Otter Belt decorated his Hawken by making a five-pointed star on the stock with brass tacks, and hanging an eagle feather from the barrel. A cap of wolf fur held his coup feathers.

When he reached the entrance to the council lodge, the first person McCabe became aware of was Three Hatchets. The crooked-nosed warrior, even more resplendent in his dress than McCabe, wore a war bonnet, which fell almost to the ground behind him, and a lance, which was fringed with scalps. Three Hatchets sneered in McCabe's direction, then drove the butt of his lance into the ground and began placing his weapons at its base.

Carefully McCabe laid his own weapons on the ground before approaching the lodge. "I am Horse Runner," he called. "I have come to speak to the council."

Three Hatchets glared at him for speaking first, and shouted at the top of his lungs. "I am Three Hatchets! I have come to tell the Council of Chiefs of my vision of war!"

"Enter the council lodge, Horse Runner! Enter the council lodge, Three Hatchets!"

McCabe and Three Hatchets moved at the same time. For a moment they stared at one another, eye to eye. It was important, he knew from Raven's instructions, not to give way. The chiefs, aware of every nuance, would watch to see whose message was most powerful. McCabe suddenly put one leg through the entrance. A startled Three Hatchets did the same, then they ducked through the entrance together.

The chiefs sat cross-legged in a circle, as opulently garbed as the men who had come to address them. Every man wore his war bonnet and his most colorful clothing. High-backed Wolf sat in the place of honor facing the entrance, flanked by Walks on Mountains and Stone Bull.

"Horse Runner and Three Hatchets," High-backed Wolf said, "you have been asked to speak to the council because you have danced the Sun Dance, and you have had visions. Horse Runner, you had a vision of peace. Three Hatchets, you had a vision of war. Three Hatchets, speak to us of war."

Three Hatchets puffed his chest and strode into the center of the council circle. "I am Three Hatchets," he announced. "I have counted coup on Watchful Bull, a chief of the Pawnee, and taken his scalp. I have killed a white buffalo bull."

There was a murmur among the chiefs as he paused. The last act in particular was noteworthy. A great white buffalo was thought to be a crea-ture of great spiritual power, which was passed on to its slayer. "Speak, Three Hatchets," High-backed Wolf commanded.

"I am Three Hatchets, and I speak to the Council of Chiefs of the Cheyenne nation. In times past, the Cheyenne were not a great people. Once we grubbed in the dirt to plant corn. Then we fled from our enemies to keep from being killed. We were driven from our old land, then driven from the land we fled to. But then we became warriors. Great warriors. We fought every tribe, and we defeated every nation. Now we have gone against the Kiowa to avenge the deaths of forty-eight Bow String warriors. But we did not avenge those deaths. We were driven back. Many peoples now look at us and say that the Cheyenne were driven back by the Kiowa, that the Cheyenne's power fades. We come to be known as a people who once were mighty and now are prey. But I have danced the Sun Dance. I have danced the Sun Dance, and I have seen three visions. Three times I saw the spirit of the Cheyenne attack the spirit of the Kiowa, and three times the spirit of the Cheyenne was driven back. This is what was, so the spirits told me. But three times the spirit of the Cheyenne fought again, and three times the spirit of the Cheyenne defeated the spirit of the Kiowa. This is what will be, so the spirits told me. Heammawihio has reached down to tell the Cheyenne to make war. I have spoken."

He stepped back from the circle. For a moment there was silence as the chiefs were given time to consider his words. Finally High-backed Wolf spoke again. "Horse Runner, speak to us of peace."

McCabe took a deep breath as he walked into the council circle. Raven had told him what he must say, and how he must say it, but he kept re-membering that this was probably the final meeting of the council. From what he said could come peace, or failure.

"I am Horse Runner," he began. "I have, in the time a man might hold his breath, counted coup on three fully armed Utes, and left all three alive. I killed the great bear in single combat, using only my knife."

He made the ritual pause. The murmur was louder than it had been for Three Hatchets. To have counted coup on three men and left all alive was considered greater than to have counted coup on even a chief who was then killed. And for all the power gained in killing a white buffalo bull, more men had slain one than had killed a great bear with a knife.

"Speak, Horse Runner," High-backed Wolf said finally.

"I am Horse Runner, and I speak to the Council of Chiefs of the Cheyenne nation. Three Hatchets danced the Sun Dance, and a vision was sent to him. But there are many spirits, and even evil spirits may send visions along the pole that connects this world with theirs. When Three Hatchets danced the Sun Dance, I danced the Sun Dance. When Three Hatchets was given a vision, I was given a vision. His vision was of war. Mine was of peace. I saw four men clasp arms. A Cheyenne, an Arapaho, a Kiowa, and a Comanche. It was a true vision. Spirits did not show me strange things that must be interpreted. I saw what will happen. Another man danced the Sun Dance with us and had a vision that touches this. His name is Spotted Fox. He saw a spirit with two heads. A human head drank the blood of humans, while a buffalo head warned him of it. The vision was interpreted to mean that there were two paths before the Cheyenne, one good and one bad. The human head drinking human blood was the bad path, the path of war. The buffalo, which warned Spotted Fox, was the good path, for the buffalo gives us food and clothes and shelter and a thousand things of life. The chiefs now see that two warriors have had visions of peace, so the Cheyenne must follow the path of peace. I have spoken."

He walked to the entrance while the chiefs mulled his words. At last High-backed Wolf said, "These men have given their words to the council. Will any of the council question them?"

Walks on Mountains got to his feet. He was a heavy man whose face was marred by a scar that cut across his cheeks and nose. His war bonnet touched the ground behind him. "I ask Three Hatchets why he thinks Horse Runner believes a vision of peace is the true vision."

There was a moment of silence. If Three Hatchets displayed his usual rage toward McCabe, it would be considered a personal attack having nothing to do with the matter at hand, and the bias of the council would shift in McCabe's favor.

"Horse Runner," Three Hatchets answered, "is not truly of the Cheyenne." McCabe looked at him warily. That was the first time he could remember that the man had not called him Mack Cabe. "He has come to learn our ways. Soon he will return to his chief and his people. He will not remain here to see the fate his vision would bring to us. Every man wants to believe his vision, but Horse Runner is not Cheyenne. He cannot feel with the Cheyenne heart."

When he finished, he glanced at McCabe and smiled tightly. McCabe sighed. Obviously the other man had also been well instructed.

"Horse Runner," Walks on Mountains asked, "how do you answer Three Hatchets?"

"I came here to learn the ways of the Cheyenne," McCabe replied. "But as I have learned them, they have become part of me. I have married a Cheyenne wife." He took a deep breath. "Whatever fate the Cheyenne meet, I will meet with them."

Three Hatchets' tight smile faded into a glare as the chiefs murmured over McCabe's words.

"Horse Runner," Walks on Mountains said, "why does Three Hatchets believe his vision is the true one?"

"Because every man wants to believe his vision," McCabe said simply.

Walks on Mountains sat down, and High-backed Wolf said, "Wait outside while the council speaks of your words."

This time Three Hatchets ducked through the entrance before Mc-Cabe reached it. When McCabe got outside the other man was stalking up and down in front of his weapons. He whirled when McCabe appeared.

"You will not stay among the Cheyenne, Mack Cabe."

McCabe walked to his own weapons without answering, but he left them lying there, in case he was called back into the council lodge.

"I say to you, Mack Cabe, you will not remain among the Cheyenne. You will die."

"Has Three Hatchets become a shaman?" McCabe grumbled, still not looking at him. "Will he call down spirits to carry me away?"

"You have taken my woman," Three Hatchets returned, but for once his tone was calm. "Because of you, my brother was scalped by the Kiowa." He held up his hands. His fingers were curled into tight claws. "I could easily kill you myself, but High-backed Wolf has said that so long as you are among the Cheyenne, to kill you would be murder. So I must find another way, Mack Cabe. I will find a way, and you will die."

"I will not die as easily as you think," McCabe countered. Three Hatchets merely sneered, and for a long time they sat in uncomfortable silence.

At last the two men were called back into the council lodge.

"We have spoken of your words," High-backed Wolf imparted when they stood inside the council circle. "There is power in what both of you have said. If we go to war first, we cannot then start over and make peace. But if we try to make peace first, and that does not work, we can always go to war. Horse Runner, you may try to prove that your vision was true. The moon is full. When it has dwindled to half its size, you must have by then arranged a powwow with the Kiowa. If you have not, we will go to war."

McCabe left the council lodge in a daze. Two weeks, give or take a day, and he had to arrange a peace meeting between tribes that had been enemies for generations. It was a matter requiring months, not weeks. He said as much to Raven when he found him at his lodge.

"Do not complain," the old man said. "They have given you your chance."

"But it's so short a time! And why did they choose me as their agent?"

"If war had been chosen, Three Hatchets would be expected to be always in the front of the fighting. What is more natural or more just?"

"Perhaps," McCabe conceded reluctantly. "But how do I begin? I suppose I could ask the Arapaho to approach the Kiowa. The Arapaho trade with everyone."

"That would be the normal way," Raven said, "but now there is no time. There is among the Kiowa a band called the Kiowa-Apache. They are known to be friendly with everyone. Almost as friendly as the Arapaho. You must go alone to them, and speak of the meeting for peace."

"If I go to them alone," McCabe fretted, "my scalp will decorate a Kiowa lodgepole."

"The Kiowa-Apache are very friendly, as I have said. If you go alone, they will respect your courage. They will listen to you."

"If you're wrong, I'll be the one to pay."

"You must decide," Raven insisted. "If you want peace, you must trust me. If you do not ride alone to the Kiowa-Apache, before summer we will ride to war again. If this happens, I do not think there will ever be peace."

McCabe realized he had no choice. Raven was right. He had spoken for peace to the council, and it had become his responsibility. "I will go," he agreed.

That night he told Night Bird Woman and Looking Glass what he had to do. They listened gravely until he was finished.

When he fell silent, Night Bird Woman shook her head. "Do not go. If you do not want to go to war, we will go to the mountains again and trap until it is over." Her voice was strained as she made the suggestion.

He touched her cheek gently. "I will not take you to the mountains again. Not until you truly want to go there."

"I truly want to go there now," she insisted.

"Listen to her," Looking Glass urged. "The Kiowa will kill you, and there will still be no peace. But you will be dead."

"Do you believe that Raven lied to me, then?"

Looking Glass bowed her head sullenly and did not answer.

"I am Spotted Fox," came a call from outside. "I want to speak with you."

"I am Otter Belt. I want to speak with you."

"Enter my lodge, my friends," he answered. The women retreated into the shadows and sat with their legs drawn up as the men came in. McCabe motioned his friends to sit at his left.

"We have heard what has been said in council," Otter Belt revealed.

"It is said you must arrange a meeting for peace before the moon dwindles," Spotted Fox said. "I do not think this thing can be done."

"It can be done," McCabe replied with more confidence than he felt.

"He rides to the Kiowa-Apache alone," Looking Glass burst out.

Spotted Fox looked at him incredulously. "This is true?"

"It is true."

"It is madness!" Otter Belt exclaimed. "Even the Kiowa-Apache will kill a lone stranger very quickly."

"You do not think they will honor my courage in coming into their camp and listen to me?"

"Perhaps," Otter Belt said grudgingly. "Who knows what manners Kiowa will have? Even Kiowa-Apache. At least let me ride with you. If they attack us, we will make it a fight to remember. We will count many coups in their village before they kill us."

"No," Spotted Fox said suddenly. "I will go with you, not Otter Belt. I know the way of my death, and it is from the Pawnee, not the Kiowa."

"We will all go," Otter Belt laughed. "Let them come against us. We will show them that three Cheyenne are a match for a hundred Kiowa."

"Neither of you will go with me," McCabe said slowly. The temptation to bring company on that ride was nearly overwhelming, but he had to stave it off. "If I go alone, perhaps they will not kill me right away. They will see me and wonder at my bravery or my foolishness. Perhaps they will listen to my words. But if there are two of us, or three, they will think we are hunters, or scouts from a raiding party. They will attack us immediately. And I am not going there to die in battle. I go to make peace."

Finally Spotted Fox nodded. "Each man must meet his own fate."

"If you must go alone, then go alone," Otter Belt concurred. "But if they kill you, we will take a hundred scalps to avenge you!"

"You will have to take no scalps," McCabe said gently. "I will return safely."

After the two men were gone, he lay for a long time staring at the top of his lodge and tried to believe his own words.

18

◇

Tall cottonwoods grew along the banks of the Arrowpoint where Mc-Cabe crossed, but a hundred yards south of the river they gave way to scattered sagebrush and Spanish daggers. He rode over the rolling hills, making no effort to hide. Only at night, when anyone drawn to a fire might not wait to ask questions, did he conceal himself by making a cold camp and eating dried buffalo.

On his second day south of the Arrowpoint, the fourth since he had left the Cheyenne encampment, he began to get the feeling he was being watched. For as far as he could see, nothing moved except a single hawk circling lazily to the south. But men were there, he knew, watching to see what he was up to. He began to sing at the top of his lungs.

"'Yankee Doodle came to town, riding on a pony. He stuck a feather in his hat and called it macaroni.'"

Half a dozen squat men, clinging to the backs of shaggy horses, burst out of a ravine ahead. They couched their long lances and galloped at him, yelling in shrill voices.

"'Yankee Doodle, keep it up. Yankee Doodle dandy. Mind the music and the step, and with the girls be handy.'"

The charge slowed as he sat there signing, and the Indians came to a halt in a semicircle less than twenty feet from him. He sang on, but with a sinking feeling now. These short, bowlegged men weren't Kiowa. They were Comanche.

Something prodded him gently in the back—a lance point, it felt like—and he stopped singing.

A warrior, whose hair was tied up in the back with strung beads like a plume, rode closer, eyeing him with caution. "I am Red Blanket," he announced. "I am chief of the Comanche nation."

"I know," McCabe said.

"You know me?" Red Blanket didn't seem to know whether to be pleased or not. "I have never seen you before. How can you know me? You are not a shaman."

"I know you," McCabe repeated. I've got to put the other man off balance, McCabe thought.

"That is good. At least you will know who kills you."

"I am not going to be killed," McCabe said with as much confidence as he could muster.

Red Blanket seemed taken aback. "You are possessed by a spirit?" he asked suddenly. "Or perhaps your mind has been taken?"

"My mind has not been taken," McCabe replied.

"I have heard this song you sing before—at the white trading post on the Arrowpoint. And from your eyes I know you are white. But you dress as a Cheyenne." The warrior shook his head. "We kill Cheyenne. We kill whites too. How are you called?"

"Among the whites I am called Thomas McCabe. Among the Cheyenne I am called Horse Runner."

The Comanche's eyes narrowed, and there was muttering among the others. "I have heard of Horse Runner. Why does he ride to his death singing a song of the whites?"

"I do not ride to my death. I ride to talk with your friends, the Kiowa-Apache."

"This means nothing to us," one of the other warriors said suddenly. "Let us kill him and take his guns and his horse."

"What do you want to talk to them about?"

"Peace," McCabe answered. "I want to talk to them of peace."

"The chief looked him over curiously for a moment. "Come with me." Red Blanket galloped off.

McCabe had no choice but to mount up and follow, for the other Comanche closed in around him as he kicked his horse into a run. At least he was still alive, he thought. And they hadn't taken his weapons. For the moment his luck seemed to be holding.

The Comanche camp was sprawling. It was set up in a haphazard fashion. To McCabe, it compared unfavorably with the neat Cheyenne camps, especially the way in which the tepees were divided into two groups.

Red Blanket jumped down in front of a red-painted lodge and went in. The others, sitting their horses in a circle around McCabe, fingered their lances. A crowd began to gather and stare at him.

Red Blanket abruptly poked his head out of the flap. "Come into my lodge, Horse Runner." He disappeared back inside.

McCabe blinked. It was a change from Cheyenne formality. He slipped from the saddle and ducked into the lodge.

There was another man in the lodge with Red Blanket, a taller, broad-faced man, with his hair plaited on his forehead and a metal armband around each of his upper arms. McCabe became even more cautious. This was a Kiowa. The reason for the second group of tepees was revealed, and it brought a reason for worry. The Kiowa and Comanche had always been allies, but they seldom camped together unless they were going to war together. The Comanche were noted for the extreme cruelty of their practical jokes. He wondered if his being kept alive was just part of a Comanche joke.

"I am Little Mountain," the Kiowa said, "chief of the Kiowa. I would hear what Horse Runner has to say of peace."

"I have come from High-backed Wolf and the Council of Chiefs of the Cheyenne nation." The two men listened impassively. Not by so much as the flicker of an eye could he tell what they thought. "I come to speak of a meeting of peace between the Kiowa and the Cheyenne."

"Why should there be such a meeting?" Little Mountain asked.

"To save the Kiowa and the Cheyenne from destruction. Both are strong peoples. Neither can defeat the other. If they continue to fight, the day will come when only the coyote will roam where now the Kiowa and Cheyenne make their camps."

Little Mountain nodded. "We will consider your words."

"I will take you to a lodge to rest," Red Blanket told him.

McCabe followed him to a lodge near the middle of the camp, from which, he noted, it would be hard to escape. "How long will it take to consider this?" he inquired.

"You will wait here," Red Blanket instructed. "Food will be brought to you." Without another word, the Indian walked away, leaving McCabe standing alone in front of the tepee.

When he looked around, he noticed that a dozen Comanche warriors, who hadn't been there before, were now lounging about in view of the lodge. He smiled grimly and ducked inside.

An hour later a wrinkled old woman pushed open the door flap and set a bowl, a horn ladle and a steaming pot inside.

"How do the chiefs consider my words?" he asked her as respectfully as he could.

She stared at him for a moment with expressionless black eyes, then scurried away. He stuck his head out of the lodge to look after her, and three of the lounging Comanche immediately stood up and stared at him. He pulled his head back in.

For three days he stayed in the lodge, going out only to relieve himself, and then only under the watchful eyes of a group of smirking Comanche. None of them would speak to him, or even acknowledge that he had spoken. Every day he asked to be taken to Red Blanket or to Little Mountain, but nothing happened. When he tried to find them on his own, the warriors would suddenly form into a solid knot in front of him, blocking his way.

While he waited, all the tales he had ever been told of the Comanche came back to him. They were infamous for their cruelty. They would sometimes ransom a captive back to the Mexicans or the Texans, but if they decided the ransom was not enough, the captive was often delivered mutilated. No woman captive was ever ransomed until she had been raped. Sometimes, after a captive had been told he was being set free, he would be put down with no water in the desert. The Comanche would follow, watching his hope turn to desperation, and desperation to exhaustion and surrender. If the captive asked to be helped, the Comanche would bring him back to camp. Otherwise he was often left to die. By the third day, the thought of these stories was beginning to wear on him.

When the door flap was thrown back on the fourth morning, he grabbed up his rifle.

"Come," a bowlegged warrior commanded, gesturing with his hand. "You are wanted by the chiefs."

He followed the man almost gratefully. At least something was happening.

Red Blanket and Little Mountain were sitting cross-legged before the Comanche chief's lodge, smoking. When he appeared, they set their pipes aside without any offering to him.

"Horse Runner," Red Blanket said, "you are a brave man. I admire men of courage, even when they are my enemies. As a man of courage, accept these gifts." Braves came forward leading four horses, and they pressed the leads into McCabe's hand.

"I thank Red Blanket," McCabe stated carefully. "But I would like to know if Little Mountain has considered my words."

"I have given you gifts," Red Blanket said. "Take the gifts and go."

McCabe let the leads fall to the ground. "I must know if Little Mountain has considered my words."

Red Blanket stared at him, his eyes cold. "Take the horses and go."

"Has Little Mountain considered my words?"

"This means much to you," Little Mountain said suddenly.

"It means much to all of us," McCabe replied.

Little Mountain nodded. "I have considered your words. Tell High-backed Wolf that I will send my answer to the village of the Arapaho chief who is called Bull."

"Will you accept the meeting?" McCabe asked.

"That must be decided among the chiefs of the six bands," Little Mountain answered. "I have spoken."

"Take your gifts, now," Red Blanket said firmly, "and go. *I* have spoken."

McCabe took the horses and left.

—◇—

The bands had separated when McCabe reached the Cheyenne camping place. If they spent too much time together, their horses would quickly eat all the grass around their camp, and they would be vulnerable to their enemies.

The first people he saw as he rode into camp, trailing the Comanche horses, were Spotted Fox and Otter Belt, mounted and riding out.

"Horse Runner!" Spotted Fox cried. "You are alive!"

Otter Belt shifted awkwardly on his saddle. "It is good to see you, Horse Runner," he mumbled.

"It is good to see both of you. For a time in the Comanche camp I thought I would see no one again."

"Comanche!" Spotted Fox exclaimed. "What did you do among the Comanche? How did you escape?"

"I was the guest of Red Blanket," McCabe explained. "When I left, I was given these horses. I must put them with the herd and go to see High-backed Wolf."

"I will put them with the herd," Otter Belt barked. He snatched the leads from McCabe and galloped away toward the horse herds in a cloud of dust.

McCabe stared after him in surprise. "Is something the matter with him?"

"Nothing, except that he is young," Spotted Fox replied. "I suspect that, like many men of his age, his trouble is a woman."

"I hope that is all it is," McCabe laughed. "I must speak to High-backed Wolf. Come with me. After, I will tell you of how I visited the Comanche."

"You will not go to your lodge first, to tell Night Bird Woman and Looking Glass that you have returned?"

"They can wait. My message cannot. I have perhaps as few as three or four days before the moon dwindles. I must tell High-backed Wolf of the message of Little Mountain, the Kiowa chief."

"Kiowa!" Spotted Fox blared. "You said you were in the camp of the Comanche."

"I will explain after I have seen High-backed Wolf." He refused to say more.

High-backed Wolf was in his lodge, eating. "Sit," he directed McCabe once he was inside. "Will you eat after your journey?"

"I thank you," McCabe answered, accepting a bowl from one of the chief's wives. "My journey has been a long and difficult one."

"Has it been fruitful as well, Horse Runner?"

"I believe that it has. I have spoken to Little Mountain, the principal chief of the Kiowa."

"Little Mountain." High-backed Wolf was visibly impressed. "I did not expect that you would speak with him."

"Nor did I," McCabe admitted. "I was met by a Comanche party under Red Blanket as I rode south. They took me to their camp. The Kiowa band of Little Mountain was camped there also."

"And what message did Little Mountain send? Will the Kiowa come to a meeting of peace?"

"He said that it must be considered by the chiefs of the six bands of the Kiowa. His answer will be sent to the village of Bull, the Arapaho chief."

"I will send men to that village," High-backed Wolf said, "to bring me the message that comes. But the moon dwindles, Horse Runner. There are few days left, and no assurance that the message Little Mountain sends will be one of peace."

"It will be," he promised. "It must be."

As McCabe was walking back toward his own lodge, telling Spotted Fox what had happened to him on his journey, Three Hatchets suddenly growled from behind them. "Have you brought back peace, Mack Cabe?"

McCabe and Spotted Fox turned. The burly warrior sat his horse with a smug grin. He pointed contemptuously at McCabe with his lance.

"I have watched the moon wane, Mack Cabe, and hoped that your scalp was hanging from a Kiowa lodgepole. Instead you have come slinking back. It would have been better to hear of your death."

"I brought back peace," McCabe said coolly. He was pleased to see the smile slip from Three Hatchets' face.

"You lie," the big man spat. "No one could make peace so soon."

"I have not made the whole peace," McCabe said. "I have arranged a meeting between the Kiowa and the Cheyenne. But peace will be made. You will have no great war against the Kiowa, Three Hatchets."

Three Hatchets shook with rage. "You would put the spirit of the Cheyenne in a bottle, white man, but I will see you dead before you can destroy us!" Whipping his horse around, he galloped out of the camp, almost running down those who didn't leap aside fast enough.

"You must watch him," Spotted Fox warned. "He will kill you if he can."

"If he was going to murder me, he would have tried it by now."

Spotted Fox shook his head. "His spirit becomes more twisted every day. He must hunt alone, because no one will hunt with him. There is something in him now that makes him more akin to the savage bear than to a man. You must be careful."

"I do not intend to die easily. And Three Hatchets doesn't want to be called a murderer."

"What if you are found with an arrow in your back? Who will be named as your murderer then?"

It suddenly struck McCabe how much he had come to think like a Cheyenne. To the Cheyenne, murder meant killing a member of your own tribe without the acknowledged justification of revenge. Among the Cheyenne, such acts were almost always done in anger, face to face. In two years he had never heard of a single Cheyenne killing another from ambush or from behind.

"No," he said at last. "If Three Hatchets tries to kill me, his pride will make him face me. He will want me to see who is killing me."

"If he still thought as a man," Spotted Fox put in somberly. "His spirit is twisted, Horse Runner. No man can say what he will do."

McCabe nodded thoughtfully. "I will watch my back. But come, my friend. Three Hatchets is out of the camp, and I have not yet seen Night Bird Woman and Looking Glass. Come with me, and we will eat buffalo hump."

"I cannot. I must find Otter Belt. I have promised to hunt with him today. He is so befuddled of late that he will shoot himself if I am not there."

McCabe left his friend and went on to his tepee. Looking Glass and Night Bird Woman were cutting and sewing deerskins when he walked up. The moment they saw him, both women leaped to their feet with squeals. But then, as Night Bird Woman ran to throw her arms around him, Looking Glass stared at him, eyes wide, then turned and ran.

He stared after her in amazement even as he was hugging Night Bird Woman. "What is the matter with her?" he exclaimed.

"She . . . she is overcome with emotion at seeing you. We feared for you, my husband."

"Overcome with emotion! She looked terrified."

"Nonsense, my husband. She is frightened, true. She has had many bad dreams since you went away. Perhaps she is afraid you are only a spirit, or a vision that has come to taunt her."

"Then I will go show her I am not a spirit," he laughed, but she caught his arm as he turned to follow the other woman.

"You will only frighten her again, my husband. Let me talk to her when she has had time to calm herself."

"This is not the welcome I had hoped for," he grumbled. "Otter Belt is in a daze for some reason, Spotted Fox prefers hunting to my company, and Looking Glass runs away from me."

Night Bird Woman's smile became strained. "I am sure all will be as it should, now that you have returned, my husband." Suddenly she giggled and began drawing him toward the lodge. "And if Looking Glass is not here, I am."

Her coquettish smile and the twinkle in her eyes put everything else out of his mind. With a laugh of delight he followed her into the lodge.

19

For four more nights, as the moon slowly dwindled, no word came from the camp of the Arapaho. But when McCabe stepped out of his lodge on the fifth day, he knew there would be no more waiting. The crescent of the moon had not been very fat the night before. On the fifth night it would certainly be judged to be less than half the size of the full moon. If the message did not come before then. . . .

"Mack Cabe!" Three Hatchets pulled his horse up to a rearing stop before McCabe's lodge. He wore a satisfied smile. "This is the last day of peace, Mack Cabe. Tonight your time will be at an end, and my time will begin." With a malicious laugh he pulled his horse around in a tight circle and galloped across the camp.

Raven slowly walked up, with a disapproving eye following Three Hatchets' retreating figure. "He will kill someone," he grumbled. "Or someone will kill him. There will be murder done for that man."

"I have heard others say it too," McCabe nodded. "Like the spirit of Spotted Fox's dream, he cannot wait to drink human blood. It seems he will get his chance."

"There is yet time," the shaman remonstrated. "Not until the moon rises tonight and has been judged to have dwindled to half is the time gone."

McCabe shook his head. "Whether hours are left, or days, I do not think the message will come. No doubt it is an elaborate Comanche joke. We all sit waiting for a message that will never come."

"It will come," Raven insisted.

"You have had a vision?"

"No," the shaman admitted. "But it will come." He cleared his throat and looked at McCabe out of the corner of his eye. "I do not see you often with your friends since your return. Do you have trouble with them?"

"Otter Belt walks about in a daze all the time, and he will not stand still long enough for me to ask him what is the matter. And Spotted Fox always runs after him. It is just as well. Otter Belt needs someone to look after him until he gets over this woman, or he will hurt himself."

"A woman?" Raven asked sharply. "Why do you think the problem is a woman?"

"It is Spotted Fox who thinks so. And Otter Belt does like to catch a woman's eye. Perhaps one has refused to be caught."

"Perhaps. Perhaps. But you are well, Horse Runner? And those of your lodge?"

"I am well, as is Night Bird Woman. As for Looking Glass . . . here she comes. See for yourself."

Looking Glass strode toward the tepee, carrying a hide bucket filled with water in each hand. Her head was cast down.

"Looking Glass," McCabe called.

Startled, she jumped violently, and half the water slopped over her legs. Her eyes darted from McCabe to Raven and back to the ground.

"You see?" McCabe demanded. "She has acted this way since I returned, but she says she does not feel sick."

"How do you feel, child?" Raven asked.

"I am well," she mumbled.

The shaman shook his head. "You do not act well, child. Why do you act this way? Do you not know the suffering you bring to this man who cares for you?"

"I cannot help it." Abruptly she began to sob. "I cannot help it."

"She does not make me suffer," McCabe told him. "It is her suffering I am worried about."

"I have known this sickness to be cured by a few good beatings with a stout willow switch," Raven said grimly.

McCabe shook his head. "There must be some other way to cure her illness, for I have no wish to beat her."

She looked at the shaman piteously and the old man sighed. "I do not think it would bring a cure in this case anyway. A demon spirit follows her, Horse Runner. Perhaps if she ignores it, pretends very hard that it is not there, it will go away."

"You mean that she will get better with time," McCabe concluded. "I hope you are right."

"Girl!" Raven thundered. Looking Glass jumped again, spilling more water. "Girl, you must try hard. Very hard."

"I . . . I will try," she wailed. She dropped the buckets and fled.

She does not seem to be trying very hard," McCabe grumbled.

"She tries, Horse Runner."

At the entrance to the camp a half dozen young braves, covered with dust, galloped on lathering horses into the circle of lodges behind Dull Knife. They slowed to a trot and rode toward the chief's lodge.

"It is the men who were sent to Bull's village," McCabe exclaimed. He began to run toward the chief's lodge. The old shaman hurried behind him as fast as he could.

The braves were already dismounted when McCabe arrived and High-backed Wolf was coming out of the tepee. He glanced briefly at McCabe, then turned his attention to the waiting braves. "What word have you brought?"

A crowd of Cheyenne had gathered, and they now stood milling and murmuring as they waited for Dull Knife to speak.

"We have ridden all yesterday and all last night and all today to bring the word," he said. "The Kiowa and the Comanche will send their chiefs to meet with ours in two moons where the Arrowpoint marks the boundary between our peoples." He preened at the stir his words caused among the onlookers.

"The Comanche," High-backed Wolf said flatly. His face was expressionless.

Dull Knife seemed to realize something was amiss. "That is what the messenger said," he responded slowly. "But he was of the Kiowa-Apache, who are not very smart. He could have been adding things to make himself seem more important."

High-backed Wolf gave the young man an angry look. "A stupid man would not be sent with this message. Nor one who would add to it. Horse Runner, when you spoke to the Comanche chief, Red Blanket, did he speak of the Comanche coming to the peace meeting?"

"No," McCabe said, "Little Mountain spoke only of sending this message to the camp of Bull, and Red Blanket almost did not speak at all."

"Why do the Comanche want to come?" the chief asked quietly, but it was clear he didn't expect an answer. The Comanche had almost ten times as many men as the Cheyenne.

"It is a trick!" Three Hatchets shouted from the back of the crowd.

McCabe felt the hair rise on the back of his neck and turned to see where Three Hatchets was. "I saw the riders returning from the camp of the Arapaho, and I knew they brought a message with a trick in it," Three Hatchets continued.

"What is the trick?" McCabe asked him.

Three Hatchets ignored him. "No one makes peace without cause. Are we to believe that the Comanche have suddenly decided they no longer want to be the enemies of the Cheyenne?" Some of the crowd turned to listen to him.

"What is the trick, Three Hatchets?" the chief asked.

The heavyset warrior couldn't ignore his chief the way he had McCabe. His mouth opened and closed several times. Then he said, "I do not know. But it must be a trick." He seemed to sense that he had lost his hold on the crowd. "Mack Cabe will lead us to our deaths," he cried.

"We will send messages to the other bands," High-backed Wolf stated. "We must also send messages through the Arapaho that we accept the time and place of the meeting." With a roar Three Hatchets stormed away. "Horse Runner," the chief went on as if nothing had occurred, "you will come with me to this meeting."

"I will come," McCabe agreed.

◇

For two weeks the messages traveled back and forth. Finally, an exact spot was agreed upon for the first meeting: the Arrowpoint River, seventy miles east of the trading post at Bent's Fort.

The file of Cheyenne and Arapaho paused among the tall cottonwoods along the Arrowpoint to watch the southern bank intently. High-backed Wolf led them, as well as a half dozen Cheyenne and Arapaho chiefs and a score of warriors. McCabe wished more braves had come, but High-backed Wolf had insisted that the party be small. Ten pack horses bore gifts for the other side.

"There!" Spotted Fox called excitedly, pointing.

Across the river another file of Indians suddenly rode into view, wading across the waters that were chest-deep on their horses. McCabe recognized Little Mountain and Red Blanket. Spotted Fox named some others: Sitting Bear and Eagle Feather, who were also Kiowa chiefs, and Shaved Head, a Comanche chief, who had the left side of his head shaved and wore many brass rings in his let ear. The hair on his right side fell to his waist. There were also twenty warriors, both Comanche and Kiowa, and a boy riding with the chiefs.

No words were spoken as the two parties moved to a clearing near the river. The warriors hung back in two groups while the chiefs dismounted and walked into the clearing. The boy followed the Kiowa and Comanche chiefs. Eagle Feather carried a bundle wrapped in a Navaho blanket. They sat in two rows, facing one another. Eagle Feather produced a pipe, lit it, and passed it down the line. Each man took one puff, Red Blanket passing the pipe across the line of Cheyenne and Arapaho chiefs. The last person to receive it was High-backed Wolf, who solemnly puffed, then passed the pipe back to Eagle Feather. McCabe felt the tension draining out of the Indians. An accord had been reached.

"We are of one mind," Eagle Feather proclaimed, "and of one heart."

"We come to speak of peace," High-backed Wolf told him.

Eagle Feather nodded. "Our intentions are one." He laid the Navaho blanket in front of him, gently pushing it toward High-backed Wolf. "These things were taken from some warriors of the Bow Strings. We give them back to you."

McCabe realized with a jolt that the blanket contained the scalps of the forty-eight Bow Strings. He was happy that Three Hatchets was not there to see this.

High-backed Wolf considered the blanket gravely. Finally he shook his head. "If shown and talked about, these things will only make bad feelings. Do not let us see them or hear of them."

Eagle Feather nodded and put the blanket behind him. Sitting Bear, the chief who had led the ambush on the Bow Strings, sat without expression.

"The boy," High-backed Wolf said, pointing to a Comanche among the chiefs. "Is he the son of one of you?"

"He is my son," Eagle Feather replied. "Bull Calf."

"We have also brought gifts," High-backed Wolf announced. "Let the boy stand away from us."

Eagle Feather motioned his son to walk away from the lines of chiefs. He was perhaps ten or twelve, McCabe thought, and skinny. Cheyenne warriors began to take blankets from the pack horses and pile them around the boy. He stared fearlessly ahead while the piles mounded up around him. At last only his head could be seen.

"These are our gifts," High-backed Wolf presented.

Eagle Feather nodded. "We accept them." Some of the Kiowa warriors hastened to clear the blankets from around the boy.

"Before we speak of other things," High-backed Wolf went on, "I must ask a question of the Comanche chiefs. It is a question my people will ask me, and I must be able to answer them."

"What is this question?" Shaved Head asked.

"Why do the Comanche make peace? The lands of the Cheyenne and the Kiowa are close together. Without peace we will kill each other. But it is said the Comanche make no new peace with old enemies. Why do you wish to make peace with the Cheyenne?"

"There is a tribe of the whites," Shaved Head replied, "who are called Texans. They are an arrogant people. Many Comanche chiefs went to a parley at the place they call San Antonio. The Texans demanded that we return all our white captives to them. Few of our men wished to do so, but a girl whose nose had been cut off was sent, and a Mexican boy. The Texans said it was not enough, and attacked our people. Twelve chiefs were killed, and twenty warriors. We will teach these Texans a lesson. But we do not want to fight the Texans if we must worry about the Cheyenne. So we will make peace."

"It is a good reason," High-backed Wolf agreed. "We will make this peace."

"We must have a larger council for a final peacemaking," Eagle Feather claimed. "All the chiefs of the Kiowa must be there, and all the chiefs of the Cheyenne and the Arapaho."

"And the Comanche?" High-backed Wolf asked.

"We will send some chiefs," Shaved Head said, "but we must prepare for the war with the Texans. So that no one will believe that we have slighted the peace, we will send many horses as gifts for our new friends."

"That will be good," High-backed Wolf said. "Now we must decide when to meet, and where."

For the first time Little Mountain spoke. "As a sign of our good intentions, we ask that you choose the site. Let it be a wide place for the big camps we will make, and with much grass for the horses."

"Upstream from us is the white trading post called Bent's Fort," High-backed Wolf said. "Close to it the trees have all been cut down for firewood, and the grass is grazed to the ground. But two hours' walk down from the trading post, where the cottonwoods stand tall and cool with shade, there is a broad plain between two hills. There the grass stands tall. Let us meet there."

"When?" Little Mountain inquired.

High-backed Wolf pondered. "If our peoples begin to gather now, the council cannot be held until the year is cooling. So close to winter there will not be enough food for all our people, or enough grazing for the horses. We must wait until after the winter, until next year. When the grass grows again, there must be time for the horses and the people to fatten. We will gather at the Arrowpoint in *Hiviutsishi*, the month when the buffalo bulls are rutting."

"It is done," Little Mountain said.

"It is done," Eagle Feather repeated.

Pray God it is done, McCabe thought. July of 1840 was a long way away.

20

With the peace meeting arranged and winter coming, life returned to normal for McCabe. He hunted, raced horses and wrote in his journal. And while Looking Glass still went about with her eyes on the ground, Night Bird Woman had regained the sparkle that she had had before the time of the trappers.

In early October, when the winds across the rolling prairie from the north carried the first hints of snow, McCabe was returning to camp with an antelope across his horse. He saw a movement on a low hill nearby.

"Spotted Fox, there is a man on that hill. I think he is naked," he remarked incredulously.

"It is Otter Belt," replied Spotted Fox, who also had an antelope across his saddle, and a brace of sage hens hanging by a thong. "He does a *wuwun*."

"A starving!" McCabe exclaimed. To gain good fortune, sometimes a young man would go alone to a hilltop from which he could look across the prairie, and he would lie on a bed of white sage for four days *wuwun*. Go to him and bring him to me. Perhaps he will come for a shaman."

"I will go," Raven allowed, "but I will not bring him unless he wants to come." The old man's face was determined as he got to his feet. "Wait at your lodge, Horse Runner. Alone," he added as Spotted Fox rose too. Despite his years, the shaman vaulted spryly onto his horse.

McCabe watched him ride away and shook his head. "This thing must be serious, Spotted Fox. I had better do as Raven asks."

McCabe led his horse back to his lodge. He was very worried about Otter Belt. The antelope hung by their front feet from two tripods. One animal had already been skinned. Looking Glass worked at the other with a short knife.

"Where is Night Bird Woman?" he asked, tethering his horse.

"She has staked the other skin in the sun and is scraping it," she replied without looking up from her work. The blade flew in short strokes, slicing the hide away.

"Go help her."

"But I am not finished with this hide."

"You can finish it when you come back. Raven is bringing Otter Belt to me, and he says we must talk alone. Go to Night Bird Woman." He went into the lodge without waiting for her to answer.

To his surprise she followed him inside. "Horse Runner," she said hesitantly.

"What is it?" His tone was terse, impatient. He pulled out his quilled pipe pouch. If this matter was as serious as Raven seemed to think, smoking would be required before they spoke of it.

"Horse Runner, you must beat me."

He turned slowly to stare at her. "Beat you!" he exclaimed.

"Beat me!" She snatched up a willow withe from a pile of basketing and grimly held it out to him.

"I do not want to beat you. Raven said you would in time get well without my beating you."

"It does not work," she sobbed. Tears began to roll down her face. "I want to stop, but I do not want to stop. I cannot stop. If you beat me, perhaps I will stop. You must beat me hard, every day."

"For the last time, I am not going to beat you."

The willow switch fell from her hand, and she dropped to her knees. Sobs shook her. "Then I will never stop," she wept.

Gently he stroked her hair. "Stop your crying. Whatever it is, I will help you to stop, and without beating you."

Her weeping increased in intensity. "We did not mean to do it. He played his flute and teased me, but we did not mean to do it."

His hand faltered in its stroking, then continued. "What are you trying to tell me?" he asked quietly.

Her words came in pants. "He would steal berries from my basket and tell me stories. Then, one day, when I went to gather cherries. . . ." She trailed off into a wail of tears.

"You are trying to tell me you have been with another man," he whispered.

She pulled back from him, covering her nose with her hands. "You will cut my nose?" she murmured. Among the Cheyenne, an adulterous woman sometimes had the side of her nose cut so that a thin scar would mark her for all time.

"I will not cut your nose."

"Then beat me!" she cried. "I cannot stop if you do not beat me!"

"The only thing I will beat your for," he said irritably, "Is hurting my ears. Be quiet." Her sobs faded again, but her body still shook. "Who is the man?

Looking Glass' eyes widened slowly. "You did not know? Aiee! Then I have killed him!" She clutched at his arms. "You must not kill him, Horse Runner. Otter Belt is your friend. You must not!"

The name hit him like a hammer blow. "Otter Belt," he breathed. "So that is why he has avoided me."

"You must not kill him," she pleaded desperately. "He is your friend. You are brothers. You have fought side by side. Kill me, Horse Runner. If someone must die, kill me."

"Be quiet," he said harshly. "I must think." He pushed her away. "Stay here."

Ducking out of the lodge, he drew a deep breath. He should have known; he should have guessed from the way they were acting.

Cheyenne women were the property of their men. Oh, they had some rights, he knew: they could not be killed or robbed; a father would not force his daughter into a marriage; a woman could divorce her husband and take her children and property with her. But for all other purposes, they belonged to their men. And a captive like Looking Glass had no rights at all. She could be beaten or sold or given away or killed, and it would be of no more consequence than if it had happened to a dog.

When Raven arrived with Otter Belt, McCabe was seated cross-legged before the fire, poking at it with a stick. The young warrior had dressed himself in his finest—quills, beads, and fringed buckskins. McCabe didn't look up from the fire.

"You have brought him, Raven," he said.

"I have brought him," Raven replied.

Otter Belt took a deep breath. "Horse Runner, I must tell you something. I. . . ."

"I know," McCabe said quietly.

Raven and Otter Belt looked at each other with consternation.

"He came to tell you what he has done," Raven said.

"I will pay you damages," Otter Belt offered. "Whatever you ask."

"I do not want damages," McCabe grumbled.

Otter Belt straightened. "I have no weapon. You have saved my life. If you want to kill me, I will not fight you."

Looking Glass burst out of the lodge and hurled herself at McCabe's feet. "Do not kill him," she begged. "Do not kill him."

McCabe looked at her, then raised his eyes to Otter Belt. "Do you love this woman?"

"I do," the young man replied. He looked startled.

"Her bride price is ten horses."

Otter Belt's mouth fell open. "You will sell her to me?"

"Only as a wife, not as a captive. If you do not value her enough to marry her, I will keep her and beat her until she does not want you anymore."

"I will marry her," Otter Belt said hastily. "I love her."

Looking Glass had been staring at McCabe in amazement. "You value me so much? I am only a captive, a Dakota, the people you call the cutthroats."

"Otter Belt values you so much," McCabe replied.

Otter Belt nodded vigorously. "I do. I would give twice that many horses for you. Three times as many."

A mischievous twinkle appeared in her eyes. "Ask him for them, Horse Runner. Set my bride price at thirty horses."

McCabe laughed at the dismay that suddenly appeared on Otter Belt's face. "Be quiet, Looking Glass, or I will set your bride price at one gopher. Tomorrow," he announced, getting to his feet, "we will have the wedding."

On Otter Belt's behalf, Spotted Fox led the string of ten horses past McCabe's lodge and tethered them. McCabe nodded. Otter Belt had sent his best: two war horses and two buffalo horses, among others.

"He is eager," Spotted Fox noted. "He has been standing outside his lodge since dawn."

McCabe smiled. "It is good for him to be eager. Were you able to hang the elk skull in his lodge without him seeing?"

"I hung two," the other man laughed. "Looking Glass will think that he is boasting."

"Horse Runner," Looking Glass called. She stepped out of the lodge onto the blanket that would carry her to her new husband's lodge. She walked to the edge, but was careful not to step off. "The horses have arrived from Otter Belt?"

"They have, eager bride."

She blushed, but went on firmly. "According to custom, I accept them. Since you are acting as my father, will you send them to the herds?"

"I will do better," McCabe answered. "Dull Knife! Pulls His Horse!" The two young men came out from behind his lodge, each leading a string of ten horses. At McCabe's nod, Pulls His Horse started off toward Otter Belt's lodge with his string. "According to custom, I return Otter Belt's bride price. Two are stallions. Of the rest, four are good war horses, four buffalo horses."

"You do me proud," she said shyly.

"These others are for you," he went on.

She gave a squeal and almost stepped off the blanket. "You give me ten horses for my own?" she cried.

"I give you ten mares. The stallions will provide you with much increase." He smiled at her gently. "I would not send you to your new husband a poor woman. Tell him if he treats you badly you will leave him and find another."

"Thank you, Horse Runner. I love Otter Belt, but I will always love you too."

Elk Antler's wives and their sisters stepped in to act as Looking Glass' female relatives. As she sat down on the blanket, they gathered in around her, crowding until their hands touched all the way around the edge of the blanket. As they lifted, they began to chant. Blue Sky Woman, Night Bird Woman's mother, led the way, beating a hide drum with her palm as the procession started toward Otter Belt's lodge. Dull Knife followed with the horses. Looking Glass looked back one time.

McCabe went inside and found Night Bird Woman sewing. "I thought you would come out to see Looking Glass on her way."

"It would not be good luck," she replied.

"Are you not happy to see her married?"

"I am of two minds." She sighed and put down her sewing. "I am happy to see her marry a man she loves, but now I must do all the work. And there will soon be more than ever."

He sat before the fire and began loading his pipe. "Why would it be bad luck for you to see her go? Many women watch the weddings."

"Not when they are with child, my husband."

"I know the custom, but. . . ." The impact of what she had said suddenly hit him. "You are with child, my wife?" She nodded, and he whooped with joy. "You must not be working," he said suddenly. "I will buy women to do your work. You must rest, and. . . ."

"Shoot your bow, my husband," she laughed, "and leave having babies to women. I can do my work. If you must, you can buy one woman, so that I may have someone to share my work and talk to."

"I will do it. I. . . ." A sober thought struck him. "Your time will be near the time of the peace council next summer. That will be a hard journey for you to bear."

"I will be all right, my husband. Why do you act as if no woman ever had a baby before? I will be all right."

"I know you will," he said softly, putting his arm around her. "We all will."

21

◇

The winter was hard, with numerous snows. Many of the very young and the very old died from sickness and from the cold. There was always food, however, for McCabe led hunting parties in snow or sleet or hail. And when the last of the dried meat had gone into the cooking pots, he found a small herd of buffalo sheltered in a gully. He was determined that Night Bird Woman and her baby would survive the winter, even if he had to perform miracles to make that happen.

Spring came slowly, patches of snow lingering on the ground until April. By the end of that month, buffalo hunting parties mustered out in full force.

It was on one of these hunting forays that McCabe watched with interest as Spotted Fox stepped down from his horse and caught a cricket beneath the sharp leaves of a Spanish dagger. Dull Knife and a dozen others also watched.

Cupping his hands around the insect, Spotted Fox whispered, "Brother cricket, where are the buffalo?" He carefully looked through a crack between his fingers. "He shows the way," he declared, tossing the cricket aside. "He points to the east."

McCabe laughed as Spotted Fox scrambled back onto his horse. "The last time we followed the cricket, all we found was a badger."

"But the badger was near a buffalo skull," Spotted Fox reminded. "The cricket knows. That time he was simply confused."

McCabe still thought the idea humorous, but he followed Spotted Fox and the others when they rode east. Buffalo were as likely to be in that direction as any other.

For an hour they rode, fanning out to search for fresh droppings or tracks. Nothing appeared but dried out buffalo chips.

"Will you agree your cricket has led us. . . ." McCabe began, when Dull Knife suddenly shouted.

"Look! It is one of the white man's boxes on wheels."

Across the prairie a single roofed-in wagon, with a step at the back, rolled along, pulled by six horses.

"Perhaps this is what the cricket pointed to," Spotted Fox speculated.

"Horses are not buffalo," McCabe said drily as he looked the wagon over. There didn't seem to be any markings to tell if it belonged to the Army or to some trader.

Spotted Fox refused to back down. "Perhaps the white men will be able to tell us where the buffalo are. Perhaps they have seen them. Perhaps that is what the cricket meant."

"Perhaps there's a badger in the wagon," McCabe teased. "Oh, very well. We can ask."

As they rode closer, he could make out the driver, a man wearing a black frock coat and broad-brimmed hat who sported a long, neatly trimmed beard. To McCabe's amazement there was a woman beside the driver. He'd never heard of anyone bringing a white woman into the Unorganized Territory.

The wagon stopped when they were no more than a hundred feet away, and from the way the driver jerked the reins, it was obvious he hadn't seen McCabe's party until now. He was a large man, weathered by the years, with a sharp nose and small grey eyes. The woman raised her head, pushing back the sunbonnet that shaded her face, and McCabe got the worst shock he'd had in years. It was Isobel Grantham.

"My red brothers," the bearded man began. He handed the reins to Isobel, picked up a book clearly marked as a Bible, and stood with one hand upraised. "My red brothers, I come in peace."

"Isobel?" McCabe asked. He pulled in by the lead team. "Isobel, is that really you?"

The bearded man's mouth worked with astonishment and he looked back and forth from McCabe to the woman. "You sound like a white man." He sounded flabbergasted. "Isobel, do you know this man?"

"Where would I meet such a man, Henry? I've never seen him before in my life." She was still pretty, but a sharp, biting expression marred the corners of her mouth.

"I'm Thomas McCabe, Isobel."

She blinked in disbelief. "That's imposs— Oh, my God. It is." She began to shake with laughter. "I knew you loved Indians, Thomas, but I never thought you would become one. Oh, my God."

"Do not take the Lord's name in vain, my dear," the driver instructed primly. "It ill-befits a minister's wife."

"Yes, dear," Isobel consented, and the lines at the corners of her mouth tightened.

"Then you're married," McCabe beamed. "Congratulations, Isobel. Or should I call you Mrs. Campbell, now?"

"Campbell?" the bearded man grouched. "My name is Elkins, sir. The Reverend Henry Elkins, of the Presbyterian Church. Who is this Campbell fellow?"

"No one, dear," Isobel soothed. Her eyes shot daggers at McCabe. "Just a young man I knew in Boston at the same time I knew Mr. McCabe, here."

"But why would he think I was this Campbell? Why, sir?"

"He looked something like you," McCabe lied. "And it's been a long time since I've seen him. We weren't close friends." He cut off, fuming at Isobel's amused grin.

"Those, ah, those men," Elkins said, peering past him. "Are they, ah, safe?"

McCabe looked back at his friends. The hunting party had grouped together, wondering who the strangers were, and were watching, blank-faced, to see what would happen. With their muskets and bows slung across their backs, and their lances in hand, they did seem menacing.

"They're perfectly, ah, safe," McCabe answered, playfully mimicking Elkins. "So long as you're with me."

Elkins accepted that with a nod. "But you, sir. If you will pardon me, I mistook you at first for one of the heathen. Your mode of dress, sir. Do you mind if I ask what you're doing out here?"

"I came to write a report for the Office of Indian Affairs," McCabe explained. "Perhaps I'll finish it one day. But what are you doing out here, Reverend Elkins? Few men travel this land alone, and fewer still with a wife."

"I am on my way to the trading post of Bent's Fort, Mr. McCabe, to bring God to the heathen," Elkins replied, ending with an upraised finger.

McCabe suppressed a smile. "You mean the white traders?"

"I meant the Indians, our red brothers. Though I have no doubt that the traders are also in dire need of my teachings."

"Reverend Elkins, do you have any idea exactly where you are?"

"Certainly. I have a good map, the instructions of a godly man in Independence, and the guidance of the Lord. Any day now I shall reach the Arkansas River, which I will follow to Bent's Fort."

McCabe shook his head. "Reverend, I'm afraid either that map is no good or your godly man wasn't. You've been riding parallel to the Arkansas for some time now. You keep heading the way you're going, and you'll hit nothing but mountains till you reach the Pacific. You're north of Bent's Fort, and west of it, by perhaps seventy-five miles."

"But the map," Elkins protested.

"Even if you had managed to keep on the trail, you'd have had to pass through Osage country, then along the edge of the Kiowa lands. Easy to get yourself killed in that country. The supply trains to Bent's Fort and Sante Fe travel under heavy guard for good reason."

"I would have preached the word of God to them," Elkins stated simply.

"You'd have ended with your hair on an Osage lodgepole." McCabe realized he was growing angry at the man's foolishness. He tried to calm himself. "Isobel, Mrs. Elkins, might have been lucky. She might have ended up chewing buckskin to soften it for Osage or Kiowa moccasins."

Isobel gasped and flushed. "I told you we should have waited for those supply wagons to leave."

"It would have been another month," her husband muttered. He heaved a sigh. "I fear you were right, though. The Indian is childlike, often senselessly violent, and destroying what he does not understand."

McCabe stared at the man in amazement. "Reverend, one thing these people are not is childlike. That idea might get you killed by the friendliest of them. You'd better realize that if you're going to preach to them."

Elkins' back straightened like a ramrod. "I thank you for your advice, Mr. McCabe," he said coolly. "If I understand you, heading south will bring us to the Arkansas, and we must then head downstream to Bent's Fort."

"Reverend, you and your wife look like you've been on the move for a good while." He blinked; it had seemed that Isobel had slumped more in her seat just as her husband glanced at her, as though to appear more tired than she really was. "Not far from here is the village of High-backed Wolf. That's where I live. Why don't you come there and rest for a while?"

Elkins hesitated, glancing at his wife again. This time McCabe was certain Isobel had made herself appear limp just as her husband looked. "Very well, Mr. McCabe. My wife does seem a bit weary from our journey. I accept your invitation."

"Just follow me." McCabe rejoined his friends, and the wagon fell in behind as he headed west.

"Horse Runner," Spotted Fox said, "how can this hair-face say there are buffalo to the west? With my own eyes I have seen him come from the east."

"He does not claim to have seen buffalo," McCabe replied. "I am taking them back to the camp."

"Is that a woman of your people?" Dull Knife asked abruptly. "Why is she covered when the winter is over?"

McCabe looked over his shoulder. In addition to her high-collared dress, Isobel wore gloves, a long shawl, and a bonnet, which covered most of her head and hid her face in shadow. After three years, the clothing looked awkward to him too. "Custom, Dull Knife. It is custom."

"But why are we taking them to camp?" Spotted Fox queried. "We are hunting buffalo, not strangers."

"I know them," McCabe said. At least, he thought he knew one of them, and he needed the other.

When the camp circle was in sight, the other braves galloped away to their own lodges. McCabe motioned for Elkins to follow him with the wagon.

"Mr. McCabe," Elkins called. "I thought you said you were taking us to a village."

"This is the village," McCabe returned. He swung down off his horse behind his lodge. "Just stop your wagon anywhere along there."

"I expected houses of some sort, Mr. McCabe. Or at least huts. When you said a village . . . why this is no more than a savage campsite."

"These savages," McCabe grumbled, "bathe more often than the people of Boston or New York, share their food, clothes and shelter with anyone in need, and if they kill their enemies, at least they do not murder, rape, or rob their own. All in all, I think they come off well against the white man."

Elkins sat with his mouth open, but Isobel seemed amused. "You always were a romantic, Thomas," she giggled. "I'm not at all surprised to find you defending the Indians and aping their ways. I wouldn't even have been surprised if I found you had taken an Indian wife."

At that moment Night Bird Woman came around the tepee, walking with her back arched and a hand on her hip to ease her swollen stomach. Sparrow, the fat Ponca woman McCabe had bought to work for her, waddled behind with a basket.

"This is my wife," McCabe presented, holding out his hand to her. "Night Bird Woman." He put his arm around her and kissed her.

Isobel's face darkened momentarily, then she said sweetly, "She is a pretty thing, Thomas. Is the child yours?"

"Isobel!" Elkins gasped.

McCabe felt Night Bird Woman stiffen. "Are not your children your husband's?" she said in English, then immediately switched to Cheyenne. "My husband, must I stay near this woman? If I must, I may pull her sharp tongue from her head."

"No," McCabe answered hastily in the same language. "No, my wife. You may go if you wish."

Night Bird Woman shot a dark look at Isobel, then walked away in her awkward gait. The silent Sparrow followed like a shadow.

"Isobel," Elkins scolded, "I am shocked at you. I never dreamed that you could say such a thing. Mr. McCabe, I must apologize for my wife. I am glad that you have married this woman, though in general I do not approve of marriages between whites and Indians, for I have heard many disturbing stories of men who simply live with an Indian woman for a year or two after a so-called wedding at one of their heathen ceremonies. It is a pleasure to meet an upright man, sir, and I apologize again for my wife's words."

"Think nothing of it," McCabe said. "Come. I'll take you to High-backed Wolf. He's a principal chief of the Cheyenne. You'll need his permission to remain in the camp."

"High-backed Wolf," Elkins mused. "A quaint name, don't you agree my dear?"

"Reverend," McCabe sighed, "the chief speaks English. Please remember that when you're around him. I doubt he'd like to hear you call anything about him quaint."

He wondered, as he led them to the chief's lodge, if what he wanted made sense anymore. From the first he had dreamed of marrying Night Bird Woman in what he was now embarrassed to think of as a "real marriage." The appearance of Elkins had seemed too good to be true. Now all he had to do was keep Elkins from offending any of his friends, endure the man's overbearing ways for a while, keep Isobel from offending Night Bird Woman any more than she already had, and find a way to admit that he had yet to be married in a Christian ceremony to a woman who was seven months pregnant with his child.

"All these men," Isobel murmured demurely. "Many of them aren't wearing shirts. Or anything except for that. . . ."

"Avert your eyes," Elkins said hastily. "Can't they cover up, McCabe? My God!" he exclaimed as a horde of boys whooped past on stick horses. "Some of those boys are naked!"

"They're no more than five or six years old, Reverend. Anyway, the Cheyenne figure they have to worry about clothes enough in the winter. Be quiet, now," he advised as they arrived at the chief's tepee. "And remember what I said." In Cheyenne he announced, "I am Horse Runner. I want to speak with High-backed Wolf. Two people of my tribe visit this camp."

High-backed Wolf, in breechcloth and moccasins, stepped out of the lodge. Isobel gasped. He looked first at her, and then at her husband.

"These are people of your tribe?" he asked in Cheyenne.

"They are," McCabe replied.

"I am the Reverend Henry Elkins," Elkins said suddenly and loudly. McCabe opened his mouth, then shut it without saying anything. Elkins wore a wooden smile, which he probably thought was friendly, and continued to speak in a booming voice as if the chief were hard of hearing. "I am very pleased to be in your village. It is a very nice village. I am sure that the Great White Father in Washington would be pleased with the peaceful and friendly way his red children have greeted me."

"Horse Runner," the chief said, still speaking Cheyenne, "who is this Great White Father he speaks of? Washington is the place where your chiefs camp, is it not? And who are these red children?"

McCabe took a deep breath. He surely couldn't tell the truth. High-backed Wolf was too proud to let Elkins remain after that. "Some of my people," he explained in Cheyenne, "believe that one great chief of our people fathered all men. They believe that the chief's spirit lives in Washington, where our other chiefs are."

High-backed Wolf nodded. "Your people have many strange beliefs, Horse Runner. But is this man deaf? He talks very loudly."

"I believe he is a little deaf," McCabe nodded.

"You are welcome here, Reverend Henry Elk!" High-backed Wolf shouted in English. Elkins took a step back in amazement. "You are the guest of Horse Runner, and you may remain as long as he wants you. I have spoken." With that the chief went back into his lodge.

Elkins stared after him, and his mouth closed with a snap. "Mr. McCabe, what is the matter with that man? He was shouting at me."

"He's a little hard of hearing," McCabe said, taking them both by the arm. "We'll go back to my lodge now."

Elkins let himself be pulled along. "I'll talk louder to him next time, so he can hear me better."

"No," McCabe said quickly. "He doesn't like people to do that. You should try to talk to him in as normal a tone as you can. Even more softly than you did today."

"He was very rude, walking away like that, Mr. McCabe."

"Reverend, he said what we wanted to hear, and he left. It's the Cheyenne way not to waste words."

"Nonetheless," Elkins maintained pompously, "it was rude."

McCabe sighed and hurried them across the camp.

That night was a sleepless one for him. He stared at the top of the lodge, blackened by the smoke of hundreds of cooking fires, until the grey dawn could be seen at the entrance. When Night Bird Woman and Sparrow went out to get water, he mounted his horse and rode out of camp. He had no purpose in mind except to be alone with his thoughts. With the birth of his baby looming closer, the need for a marriage by a minister was becoming more important in his mind. But he didn't like the idea of revealing to Elkins, or to Isobel, that Night Bird Woman wasn't his wife according to the Church or the law.

When he finally returned to camp, he found Isobel sitting on the step at the rear of the wagon holding a parasol over her head as she read a book. Elkins' horses, hobbled, cropped grass nearby.

"Isobel," he greeted, nodding. "I'd like to talk to your husband."

"Do you know," she said folding the book and squinting up into the sun at him, "you look splendidly barbaric. Or perhaps it's barbarically splendid."

"If your husband's not here, Isobel, where can I find him?"

"Oh, he's inside," she replied, then waited until he had dismounted to add, "asleep. His back was hurting him last night." Her lips curled. "Old men have so many aches and pains. When his back hurts, it's always the same. He sits awake praying until almost daybreak before he finally goes to sleep. Then nothing can wake him till noon."

"I'll come back when he's awake."

"Don't go," she appealed. "I've been wanting a chance to talk to you. Stay awhile."

"For a few minutes," he said reluctantly.

She stretched, smiling, and looked around. "This land can be pretty at times. But don't you find it a dull life with no books, no theater, no conversation?"

"I brought the Bible, Shakespeare, Montaigne, and Montesquieu with me in my packs. I've no need for more books than that. The conversation of my Indian friends is at least as interesting as what passed for conversation in Boston, and if there is no theater, there are storytellers, dancing, and singing almost every night."

"I heard it last night," she said with a shiver. "A dreadful sound. I was afraid it might be a war dance, and that we would be murdered as we slept."

"But you managed to sleep anyway," he said drily.

"So I did," she laughed. "Perhaps I felt safe with you nearby. Do you ever think of returning to Boston? You'd create quit a stir, you know. Oh, I don't mean this fancy Indian dress. But there's something about you, a presence you didn't have three years ago. If you walked into a room of men from Boston, or New York, or Philadelphia, they'd seem to fade away in your presence."

"I don't know if I'll ever go back," he said slowly. "Perhaps for a visit, to show Night Bird Woman where I was born."

"Now she would certainly create quite a stir in Boston," she responded maliciously, then immediately became apologetic. "I'm sorry, Thomas. I really shouldn't have said that. It was unkind."

He was confused. This woman who was so quick to apologize, who seemed so sorry for her tongue's sniping, bore little resemblance to either the woman he had seen the day before, or to the Isobel he remembered from Boston. But perhaps she had just been tired the day before. Or perhaps marriage had changed her for the better.

"I'm sorry about the confusion I caused yesterday," he said. "When you called him Henry, I remembered your mentioning Henry Campbell the last time we met. I don't know why I said it. He doesn't look a thing like Campbell."

"Dear Henry," she mused. "I really did intend to marry him, but Mama pointed out to me that doctors have very little social status. And then Henry Elkins appeared. He was a bit old, but he was a Philadelphia Elkins. Banks and shipping, you know. And ministers are received well everywhere."

"And such matters are still important to you. I'm surprised you came out here."

"So am I," she admitted with a touch of sadness. "Although Henry is of the Philadelphia Elkinses—as he's willing to tell anyone who'll listen—and although he does like to entertain, he has very little money. It wasn't until after the wedding that I discovered poor Henry is just a poor relation of the Elkinses, with no income other than his church salary."

"That must have been a terrible disappointment to you, Isobel."

"Oh, it was," she said with a wide-eyed look. "I've regretted not marrying you every night since you left." She wetted her lips and leaned toward him. "I regret it even more, now that I've seen you again."

"Unfortunately," he answered drily, "we've both married since."

She smiled brightly. "That's true. But nothing stays the same forever."

"I think this conversation has gone on long enough. When your husband wakes up, tell him I'd like to speak to him." As he walked away, he could hear her laughing softly.

Once he was back in the lodge, he threw himself onto his bed. Night Bird Woman sat making quilled decorations on a cradleboard that Spotted Fox had built.

"Did you take your morning walk?" he asked.

"Of course."

"That's good. Walking is healthy for you."

She laughed. "You have many strange ideas, Horse Runner. It is not for myself that I walk. Babies grow in the mornings, and walking helps them to grow faster."

"So long as you take the walk," he said.

"The woman Isobel was here when I returned."

He lifted up on one elbow with a frown. "What did she want?"

"She asked many questions about you, my husband. She wanted to know all about you. All morning I had to tell her stories of how you trap beaver, of how you hunt buffalo. She would not see that I had work to do and that I had to go."

"Perhaps it was her way of being friendly."

She snorted and began to jerk the cradleboard about as she worked. "That woman wants to be *your* woman. She tries to discover how to make you want her. I saw you talking to her, and I could see it in her face."

"We are just talking," he comforted. "And besides, she already has a husband."

"Her husband is old, Horse Runner. She would like to have a young husband, like you. If you say to her, 'Come,' she will divorce her old husband."

"That is very difficult to do among my people. And even if she did, I would not take her. I do not want her."

"She is pretty," his wife went on. "I cannot be sure, for she wears many clothes, but I think her hips are broad enough to have many children. Would you not like to have a pretty second wife?"

"Night Bird Woman, I thought you did not like this woman."

"I do not like her tongue," she replied grimly. "But if she is second wife, I am still first wife. If she is rude, I will hit her with a stick until she learns manners." She smiled in pleasant anticipation, and it was more than he could take. He doubled over, laughing.

"I almost would marry her just so you could teach her manners, my wife, but I do not want her. I want only you."

Her smile became one of contentment. She patted her round belly. "Soon, my husband, our child will come, and I will make certain you do not want another woman even more."

He came to her and kissed her lightly on the lips. "Why would I want another woman when I have you?"

She stroked his hair. "I just want you to be happy."

"I am," he smiled, and returned to the bed to rest.

When he awoke, she was once more at work on the cradleboard. The murmur of voices came from outside, and the long shadows he could see through the open door flap told him the sun was low.

"Has the man Elkins sent a message to me?" he asked.

"He is outside," she said without looking up. "He talks with Spotted Fox."

Suspicion rose in McCabe, and he got up and stepped outside.

"And so," Spotted Fox was saying in English, "Horse Runner sold the woman Looking Glass to his good friend Otter Belt for ten horses. Was that not generous?"

"Very," Elkins remarked without enthusiasm. When he swiveled his eyes to McCabe, they were full of fire, like those of the bear he had killed. "It seems, Mr. McCabe, Horse Runner, that you have not told me all there is to tell about your life among these people."

"Ho, Horse Runner," Spotted Fox smiled. "I have been telling this man of your people how you have become a great warrior among us."

"And a great horse thief," Elkins spat.

"Oh, yes," Spotted Fox exclaimed. "In one raid, Horse Runner took more than a thousand horses from the Crow." He saw McCabe's expression, and shrugged. "Well, perhaps it was not quite so many. But it was very many."

"Spotted Fox," McCabe said calmly, but with a grimace, "could I speak to Reverend Elkins alone?"

Spotted Fox frowned at the two men. He seemed not to sense that he was making the hackles rise. "I will go to see Otter Belt," he said. "He has a new horse he wishes to show me."

After the young warrior had gone, McCabe and Elkins faced each other, Elkins with his head hunched low between his shoulders as if he were about to charge, McCabe with the wary eye of a man who faced a wild animal.

"You have dared to entice me into accepting your foul hospitality," Elkins breathed. "Your hands are red with blood, murderer!"

"I have murdered no one," McCabe said levelly.

"It's no use to lie! Your own savage friend has told me of the killings you've done."

"I've killed only when I had to: to defend myself, or my friends or family."

"You try to justify yourself!" Elkins squawked. "You have murdered men, and maybe women and children for all I know. You've stolen horses and the good Lord alone knows what else. You've taken another woman to your bed while you were married, and when your lust was sated, you sold her like the savage you are, for horses."

"I've killed only men who tried to kill me," McCabe fumed. "The Crow stole a winter's worth of furs from me, so I took horses from them in repayment. As for Looking Glass, she was given in marriage to the man he loved, not sold like a horse."

"Liar!" Elkins yelled. "Foul liar!" Veins stood out on his forehead. The shouting was beginning to attract some attention, but most people tried to ignore it out of good manners. "When I get to Bent's Fort, I will let them know what kind of man you are McCabe. I will see you arrested and convicted for your crimes."

Suddenly Isobel was between them. She looked at each man worriedly. "Henry, don't be hasty." Suddenly she darted past McCabe into the lodge.

There was the sound of a moment's commotion, and then she was outside again, followed by an angry Night Bird Woman.

"My husband, this woman roots in our lodge like a badger."

Isobel threw herself to her knees beside her husband and pushed a small pouch into his hands. McCabe recognized it with a sense of shock.

"It's gold!" Isobel said hoarsely. "Feel it, Henry. It's gold. And McCabe knows where it came from."

Elkins stared blankly at her, then at the pouch. He hefted it before opening the drawstrings. A slow smile appeared on his face. "It . . . it *is* gold. There must be a pound or more here."

"That's right. And McCabe is the man who found it. Henry, he dug it out by himself more than a year ago."

Elkins licked his lips. "Perhaps," he said hesitantly, "I was mistaken, Mr. McCabe. It . . . it is quite possible that things actually could have happened as you say."

"For the love of God." McCabe shook his head. "Elkins, that's all the gold there is. It's all the gold there ever was. I found a small pocket, and I've just never traded it for goods. Gold doesn't seem to have the same importance out here."

Elkins looked at him as if he were a fool. "Don't try to trick me, McCabe. No one leaves a pound of gold just lying around for—what was it— over a year?" He barked a laugh. "Since you don't have any tools for mining, it must be lying around on the ground."

"It took me most of a winter to get the gold you have in your hands. I sifted it one grain at a time, and at the end, it was one grain a day. That's all there is, Elkins."

"It's no use. You're just trying to keep it for yourself, McCabe." He bit his lower lip and laughed, his eyes drifting shut. "The things that gold can do. The things that gold can buy." His eyes snapped open suddenly. "For the church, of course. For . . . for the missions, McCabe. Gold to bring the word of God to the heathen." He sprang to his feet and caught McCabe's shirt in his grip. His eyes were half crazed. "Even you must want to help spread the word of God, McCabe."

He pried Elkins' hand loose. "For the last time, there's no gold."

"For the love of God, McCabe, I'm not asking for all of it. Not all of it.

Not even half. A third. No, a quarter. You'll never miss a quarter of it. Isn't it worth a miserable quarter to know I'll never tell the authorities about the murders you've committed?"

"Elkins, you disgust me."

"A fifth, McCabe. A mere fifth share to secure my silence."

"You want gold? Well, you have all the gold I know about in your hand this minute. And you can have it if you'll perform a marriage ceremony for me and Night Bird Woman."

Elkins backed away, his eyes darted from McCabe to Night Bird Woman. "You . . . you are not married to this woman?"

"We were married in a Cheyenne ceremony. I want a Christian ceremony as well."

"For a fifth share?" Elkins cast a crafty look at Night Bird Woman's swollen belly. "A fifth share to buy your child a name?"

"Done," McCabe growled. "Now get your book and perform the damned. . . ."

"Oh, no," Elkins said. "Once I've done the ceremony you'll cheat me. You'll refuse to show me the mine. Take me to the mine first. Show me the gold in the ground, and I'll perform your marriage."

"Goddamnit, there is no mine!"

"You just admitted there was!"

"I'd have said any damned thing to get you to perform the ceremony."

"You admit you tried to cheat me! You're trying to cheat me out of a share in the mine!"

"There is no mine."

"For the last time," Elkins panted, "take me to the mine, and I'll marry you and the woman."

"I can't take you to something that doesn't exist."

Elkins' finger rose toward the sky. He began to back away from them. "Whore of Babylon! Beware the sins of Sodom and Gomorrah! Your evil. . . ."

"Elkins," McCabe grunted, "leave the gold."

Elkins' mouth twitched, and his eye fell slowly to the pouch clutched against his chest. Abruptly he hurled it to the ground and ran toward the wagon.

McCabe had no regrets. He already felt married to Night Bird Woman, and any ceremony Elkins might perform would only cheapen that marriage.

Isobel still crouched where she had watched the argument. Hesitantly she put out a hand toward the pouch.

"Leave it!" McCabe strode over, snatched it from under her fingers and handed it to Night Bird Woman.

"I was just going to pick it up for you," Isobel laughed nervously. "I think he's finally gone completely . . . I want to talk to you, Thomas. Alone."

"No," McCabe replied.

"I will wait inside," Night Bird Woman said. "Talk to this woman." She went into the lodge.

"Thomas," Isobel began, then faltered. She got to her feet and moved to where she could put a hand on his arm. "Thomas, I think he really has gone insane. I've never seen him act like that before."

"If he has, Isobel, I pity you for the life you'll have with him."

"Thomas, do you know how good it could be for you and me, together? New York, London, Paris. Especially with a gold mine. . . ."

He cut her off with a harsh laugh. "You still don't believe me, do you?"

"Of course you didn't want to share your mine with a crazy old man, Thomas. But I'm not a crazy old man. You could leave this savage life, and. . . ." She broke off with a cry as he grabbed her arms.

"I don't care anymore if you think there's a mine or not, Isobel. I just want to tell you one thing. I don't want you. I have the only woman I want. Now you get away from me, or I'll show you how savage I can be." He abruptly pushed her back.

For a moment she stood rubbing her arms, glaring at him. "May God damn your soul to hell, Thomas McCabe," she said, and she ran after her husband.

22

The Cheyenne camp was quiet in the late afternoon. Henry and Isobel Elkins had left in their wagon. Only a few girls were kicking an antelope-hide ball back and forth, trying not to let it touch the ground. The boys, who usually would have been racing among the tepees, yelling and hunting imaginary buffalo from their stick horses, were all down at the stream in the willow brakes, hunting mice and dragonflies.

From somewhere across the camp, McCabe could hear a flute. Dropping an armful of firewood near the cooking pot, he wiped his hands and looked to see where he had left his journal.

"Ho, Horse Runner," Spotted Fox called. McCabe grinned as Spotted Fox and Otter Belt approached. Both stared at him in mock amazement. "What is this?" Spotted Fox cried. "Horse Runner carrying wood!"

"And water!" Otter Belt put in. "I have seen him carry water with my own eyes."

Spotted Fox shook his head gravely. "No more will Horse Runner hunt the buffalo."

"He will work with the women," Otter Belt muttered sadly, "and make quilled shirts."

"I can't wait until Looking Glass bears a child," McCabe grumbled. "I want to see how you enjoy a few weeks of hauling wood and water." He sat on the ground and found his journal and his book of pens and ink. "Now go away. I must write."

As if to be contrary, both men squatted on the other side of the fire.

"Why do you scratch little marks like that?" Otter Belt asked. "When first you came, you made them often. I thought they were part of your religion. But you have not made them in a long time."

"Do not be foolish," Spotted Fox carped. "I have seen the white trader at Bent's Fort make such marks whenever someone trades with him."

"I have seen this too," Otter Belt replied, "but it does not mean it is not part of a religion. Perhaps a prayer is offered when goods are traded."

"Horse Runner trades no goods."

"It is a record of my life here," McCabe explained. "There are men who can read these marks and understand them. So I am recording here all that I have learned of the Cheyenne people and all that I have done among you."

Sparrow popped out of the tepee and waddled away quickly. McCabe started to rise, but Spotted Fox spoke.

"It is not a time for you, Horse Runner. This is not a time for men. Sit."

McCabe nodded. "I suppose. . . ." He let himself drop back.

"This record," Spotted Fox mentioned. "When you came here, you said your chief had sent you to learn our ways. This record is for your chief? He can decipher these marks?"

"He can."

"Have you told him of the great bear?" Otter Belt asked excitedly. "And the great horse hunting against the Crow? Your chief will be pleased to learn you have become such a great warrior."

Spotted Fox frowned. "When I told the holy man Elk Ins of these things, he did not seem pleased. Perhaps you should not tell your chief these things, Horse Runner, if he is a man like this Elk Ins."

"I will be careful of what I say, my friends."

Sparrow reappeared, scurrying back across the camp followed by Looking Glass and Blue Sky Woman. They all ducked into the tepee without so much as a glance at the men.

"Let us talk," Spotted Fox urged, noting McCabe's worried look. "We will speak of the peace council."

"What?" McCabe said absently. "The council? In a few more days we will be at the Arrowpoint, and the council will be held. What else is there to say?"

"Do you not worry about treachery?" Otter Belt asked.

"Treachery? No, I do not." McCabe frowned as he looked at the lodge.

"What if we are being drawn to the Arrowpoint only to be attacked by the Kiowa and Comanche?" Otter Belt continued.

"I have heard many people say this," Spotted Fox agreed.

"It is a thing to worry about," Otter Belt went on. "What if this story of a war against the Texans is just a trick? There could be many Comanche and Kiowa warriors ready to attack us when we reach the river."

Spotted Fox nodded gravely. "I have heard it said that many Comanche bands have come together. Two or three thousand warriors."

That managed to pull McCabe out of his concentration on the tepee. "How could anyone know this?" he demanded.

"It is said, Horse Runner," Spotted Fox answered.

"It is stupid," McCabe replied. "Think of how fast grass and game disappear when all the bands of the Cheyenne are together. A camp with so many warriors would strip the ground bare in days."

Spotted Fox nodded thoughtfully. "That is true. I had not thought of that."

"But it is said," Otter Belt persisted.

McCabe cut him off. "Said by who? Has High-backed Wolf said this thing? Who says that he knows so much of a Comanche camp, and that they will attack us?"

"Many people say it," Spotted Fox replied, "but always they say that they heard it from someone else, who had in turn heard from someone else."

"So it is with rumors," McCabe concluded. "They come without foundation. If these things were true, there would be a man to say, 'I saw it.'"

There was a low moan from inside the lodge. McCabe whipped

around, his friends instantly forgotten. Another moan. He took a step toward the lodge. Then, pounding his fist into his hand, he began to pace.

"Sit," Otter Belt commanded. "Why do you walk back and forth?"

"He does not hear you," Spotted Fox said. "Let him walk. Perhaps it is another of his people's strange customs."

McCabe paid no mind to either of them. He paced in larger and larger arcs until he was traveling all the way around the lodge, his eyes on nothing and his ears cocked for the slightest sound from inside. Low groans flogged his fears. The other women's soft murmurs did not help.

Women often died giving birth. Children died. Even back East, with proper doctors, mother and child sometimes died together. A horrible thought came to him: if one of them had to die, let it be the child. He could not bear the thought of living without Night Bird Woman. He managed to push the thought to the back of his mind. Both would live. He would have both wife and child.

This time, as he rounded the back of the lodge, something burned past his cheek. He glanced to his left and saw an arrow quivering in a lodgepole on the side of the tepee. Astonished, he dropped as another arrow streaked past to strike a foot below the first.

"Stop that!" one of the women inside called. "This is no time for joking! Stop shaking the lodge!"

From his place on the ground, McCabe realized for the first time that the night had come. In the darkness there was no sign of his attacker.

He got to his feet cautiously, and with two quick yanks he pulled the arrows free of the lodgepole. What he saw in the dim, flickering light from the camp's cooking fires made him frown. Along with the owner's personal markings, the arrows bore a wavy line down each shaft, which identified the tribe of the maker. The People of the Snake. Comanche.

He walked around to the other side of the tepee, where his friends still lounged by the fire, and he dropped the arrows into the flames.

"Arrows!" Otter Belt exclaimed. He rushed to the fire and snatched one of them from the flames. "You cannot burn good. . . ." His eyes widened as he made out the markings. Slowly his hand opened and let the shaft fall back into the burning wood. He stood over the flames for a long time. Then, without looking up, he asked, "Why do you burn Comanche arrows, Horse Runner?"

"Comanche!" Spotted Fox exclaimed.

"They were shot at me," McCabe answered quietly. "Just a minute ago."

Both men leaped to their feet, snatching up muskets and peering into the night.

"I did not see who fired them," McCabe said.

"That much is obvious," Otter Belt retorted. "Comanche arrows are fired by Comanche."

McCabe shook his head. "Three days north of the Arrowpoint? One Comanche who fires two arrows and flees? Why?"

"I cannot read Comanche thoughts," Otter Belt griped. "Perhaps he wished to stop the peace. A Cheyenne warrior murdered in the night, in his own camp, by Comanche arrows."

"Either the Comanche are going to betray us at the Arrowpoint," McCabe said, "or they want peace. They would not stop us here. But there is someone much closer who does not want peace. One who would also like to see me dead."

"Three Hatchets," Spotted Fox whispered.

McCabe nodded.

"Let us go to him," Otter Belt said angrily, "and confront him with this thing he has done. Let us tell the people of his deed."

"And what will we tell them?" McCabe asked.

Otter Belt wrinkled his brow, but Spotted Fox explained. "Will we tell them that a man tried to kill Horse Runner? Or will we tell them we did not see the man, and the arrows had Comanche markings, so therefore we suspect Three Hatchets?"

"We cannot let him get away," Otter Belt exclaimed.

"We must watch him," McCabe decided. "Sooner or later he will try again. Then we will have proof. Until then, say nothing of this to Night Bird Woman. She will only worry."

"Nor to Looking Glass," Spotted Fox added to Otter Belt. "She will tell Night Bird Woman as soon as she hears."

"I do not tell everything to my wife," Otter Belt said defensively.

Suddenly a baby's wail drifted out of the lodge.

"A child!" Spotted Fox and Otter Belt shouted together. They raised their muskets to their shoulders, aimed at the heavens and fired. "A child!"

"A child!" McCabe shouted along with them, and fired his Hawken into the air. People began to rush out of nearby lodges, babbling happily.

"Spotted Fox," McCabe went on loudly, "go to Raven. Offer him two horses for prayers for my child. Otter Belt, take two of my horses from the herd and give them to the first two poor men you find. I call a feast! Everyone, come tomorrow night and I will have buffalo and deer and antelope. I call a feast for my child!"

Through the crowd went an approving murmur. Then the people grew silent as Blue Sky Woman appeared at the lodge entrance with a wrapped bundle in her arms. She held it out to McCabe.

"Horse Runner, I give you your son."

Whoops and shouts of joy broke out as McCabe took the infant gingerly into his arms. He moved the edge of the blanket aside to look at the infant. The baby's skin had been greased with buffalo fat and dusted with the spores of the star puffball. He let out a thin wail as McCabe held him overhead.

"My son!" he roared. At the back of the crowd a few young men began an impromptu song and dance of thanks to the gods for sending the tribe a healthy child. "I give him the name Charles William McCabe, the name of my father's father."

Raven appeared out of the crowd in his ceremonial garb—a wolfskin robe and a headdress made of buffalo horns and heron feathers. He shook a gourd rattle and broke into a thin chant as McCabe lowered the child. Raven's rattle sung around the baby, first from the head to the feet, then from the feet to the head. He fumbled some powder from his pouch with his free hand and paused in his chant long enough to blow it off his fingertips into the baby's face. Young Charles coughed and broke into loud wails.

Raven nodded. "You have good luck, Horse Runner. No evil spirits follow this child. Take him to his mother."

McCabe grinned and ducked into the tepee with his son.

Looking Glass and Sparrow had just finished tucking robes around Night Bird Woman. He saw at one side the hay-covered buffalo robe where she had knelt to give birth, and also the stout pole fixed in the ground that she had grasped during her pains. The women bustled out as soon as he appeared.

"I have brought you our son," he beamed, kneeling by her side.

She smiled as he unwrapped the blanket and slipped the naked infant beneath the buffalo robes beside her. *"Moksois,"* she murmured affectionately. "Little potbelly. You have named him, my husband?"

"Charles William McCabe. It was my grandfather's name."

She grimaced. "It is a difficult name to say, and it has no meaning. Why do you name your son so? You are no longer called Mack Cabe. Let your son have a real name."

He hesitated. "His real name is Charles William McCabe. But he can have a nickname, if you want."

"Morning Eyes," she smiled. "Because his eyes are like yours, like the sky in the morning." Suddenly she yawned. "I am tired, my husband. Forgive me."

"Sleep," he whispered. Her eyes drifted shut, and he lay down beside her, their child between them. Peace, he thought. We must make peace.

23

The Cheyenne riding into the valley of the Arrowpoint were as grand a sight as McCabe had ever seen. All the bands had joined the march, along with several of the Arapaho, and now the great nation streamed down onto the broad flood plain. Verdant grass covered the prairie on both sides of the river, which was no more than knee-deep now that the run-offs of the spring melt had subsided. Lofty cottonwoods grew in groves near the banks, with clumps of willows between. A light breeze whispered down the valley, carrying the scent of fresh water and flowers.

Excited murmurs ran through the people as the huge circle of a camp began to form near a small stream on the north bank. High-backed Wolf rode to a low hill where McCabe sat his horse with Otter Belt and Spotted Fox.

"Horse Runner," the chief began, "we should send someone to Bent's Fort, to tell William Bent that we are here. He is a good man, married to

Owl Woman, the daughter of White Thunder, and I do not want him to worry when he hears that many of us are camped here waiting for the Kiowa and the Comanche."

"I will ride to the fort," McCabe agreed. He noticed the worried looks the other men kept casting across the river. "They will come," he added.

"I know they will come," the chief replied. "It is how they will come that I do not know."

Bent's Fort was half an hour upstream by horse, a huge adobe structure with walls thirty feet high. At the northeast and southwest corners were hexagonal towers armed with cannons, and on the east wall, over a broad gateway of heavy timers sheathed in iron, was a square watchtower topped with a belfry and a flagpole. From the pole flew an American flag. McCabe could make out a man in the tower with a huge spyglass. The man was constantly swinging it about to look in all directions.

When McCabe and his friends rode up, the gates were standing open. Indians and white traders passed in and out without a second glance at one another. The courtyard was a mass of men and horses, chickens running loose, and pigeons cooing on the eaves.

McCabe leaned from his saddle as a buckskin-clad trader walked by. "Can you tell me where to find William Bent?"

"He's in the store," he began, pointing, but his words trailed off, and he blinked as he got a good look at McCabe.

"Spotted Fox," McCabe said. "Otter Belt, we will go into the store and speak to William Bent." He ignored the trader's unbelieving stare as he tied his horse in front of the store. Cradling his rifle in the crook of his arm, he strode in.

Men crowded the large room. Four clerks were perched on ladders to reach goods on the high shelves behind the counters, while another was showing a musket to an Indian, and a sixth extolled the virtues of a huge bear trap to a white man in fringed leather. A dozen Indians of various tribes stood in small knots, examining the tall piles of multicolored blankets that dotted the tightly packed dirt floor, discussing the pots and pans hanging from the ceiling, or standing idly and smoking.

McCabe made his way to one of the counters as a redheaded man got down from a ladder. "Excuse me, I'm looking for William Bent."

"He's in the . . ." The redhead's eyes widened. "Well, I'll be damned. I thought you talked English mighty good. You must be Cheyenne Mc-Cabe."

"My name is McCabe. I don't know anything about the rest."

"Well, I surely do. I've heard a lot about you. Name's Charlie Hammer-smith."

"Mr. Hammersmith," McCabe acknowledged, shaking hands. "I need to see Mr. Bent. I have a message from High-backed Wolf."

"He ought to be out any . . . there he is. Mr. Bent! Sir, there's someone to see you."

William Bent was a tall man, about thirty-five, with a weathered face and a sharp eye. Everyone, Indian and white, treated him respectfully as he made his way from the back of the store, and he had a friendly word in return for each. When he saw McCabe, his eyebrows went up.

"Since there's only one white man living with the Indians out here that I've ever heard of," he said, "that must make you Cheyenne McCabe. I'm William Bent, Mr. McCabe. Welcome to Bent's Fort."

"Thank you, Mr. Bent," McCabe replied. "But my name is Thomas Mc-Cabe. I live among the Cheyenne, but I've never been called by that name."

"I know. My wife, Owl Woman, is Cheyenne. She tells me your name in Horse Runner. It seems every time a trader stops at a Cheyenne village, there's some new tale about Horse Runner, the white Cheyenne warrior. I'll admit you'd have to be eighty years old to have done everything folks say you have, but you are a much talked about man."

"There's no reason for it," McCabe grumbled, shaking his head. "I've done no differently than any Cheyenne warrior would. I've managed to stay alive."

Bent looked at him quizzically. "Mr. McCabe, you are an unusual man. What can I do for you?"

"I came to deliver a message from High-backed Wolf. Much of the Cheyenne nation is camped about six miles downstream from here. The chief wanted to make sure you knew about it and weren't worried."

"Why should I worry? The Cheyenne have traded at Bent's Fort since it was built."

"They're not here to trade, Mr. Bent. They're waiting for the Kiowa and the Comanche."

Bent's mouth tensed. "A battle?"

"I hope not. It's supposed to be a peace council. The tribes want to put a stop to the fighting."

"Admirable, if it comes to pass. But you'll have to excuse me, Mr. McCabe. Peace council or no, with so many lifelong enemies and only the Arkansas River to divide them, I must see to special precautions."

Bent hurried off, calling to the men who followed after him.

McCabe wandered about the store to find a gift for Night Bird Woman. He decided on a box of molasses candy and a Mexican shawl and took them to the counter. Spotted Fox and Otter Belt were watching Hammersmith serve a short, slender man whose ramrod-straight back contrasted sharply with his sloped shoulders and soft voice.

"I'll want a hundred pounds of cornmeal, Mr. Hammersmith," the man said. "And be sure there aren't any weevils in it this time."

"There are never weevils in our cornmeal, Mr. Carson," Hammersmith replied patiently.

Kit Carson snorted. "Last year, by the time I got to Brown's Hole, there was more meat than cornmeal in my sacks."

Hammersmith noticed that McCabe was watching, and an eager smile appeared on his face. "Mr. Carson, this is somebody you ought to meet. This here is Cheyenne McCabe. Mr. McCabe, meet Christopher Carson."

"Kit," Carson corrected, extending a hand. "Folks call me Kit."

McCabe returned the handshake. "Thomas McCabe. You're a trapper, Mr. Carson?"

"Trapper, hunter, guide, teamster. I'm whatever it takes to skin the bear. I understand you trap too."

"Not anymore. The first year I tried it, the Crow took all my pelts, and the second, I didn't take enough skins to make it worthwhile. My friends here, Spotted Fox and Otter Belt, tell me the beaver aren't there anymore."

Carson nodded to the two Indians. "I reckon you two are likely right. The beaver are getting mighty scarce. I aim to try one more winter, but if it doesn't improve, I'll give it over." He gave Hammersmith a half-amused, half-angry look. "'Course, if the prices for furs don't improve, I'm not sure as there's a reason to go again even this year."

Hammersmith looked pained. "Mr. Carson, I've been telling you for two years now that the market for beaver was going under. Look here. I'll show you what's killed off the trade." He scrambled up the ladder behind him and came back down with a box under his arm. "God knows why, but this was on the last supply train from St. Louis." He opened the box and took out a top hat. he thumped the black side with a finger. "Made out of silk. Folks don't want beaver hats back East no more. They want silk."

Carson shook his head. "We trap the damn beaver till there aren't no more, and now they go and make hats out of worm guts. McCabe, you want to come up to the long room with me and have a drink to the end of the beaver trade?"

"I haven't had a drink in close to three years," McCabe mused. "But I don't suppose one will hurt. Spotted Fox, Otter Belt, you want to come along?"

"No," Otter Belt said. "I will trade for a gift for Looking glass and return to the camp."

"Spotted Fox?"

Spotted Fox, who had been staring quietly straight ahead, shook his head. "No, Horse Runner. I must trade, too. I will see you again in the camp."

McCabe followed Carson across the courtyard. A chest-high wooden balustrade fronted a porch, from which steps led up to a room above the west wall of the fort. Inside, two men were bent over a large billiard table that took up the center of the floor. A few others sat at tables scattered wherever there was room. A skinny, bald man wearing a long apron stood behind a small bar.

"Two whiskies," Carson called, sitting at a table beneath the rack of billiard cues.

"We can't serve Injuns, Mr. Carson," the balk man answered. "I'm sorry, but it's Mr. Bent's orders. Says he's scared to have liquor in the camps, what with there going to be all them Kiowa and Comanche and Cheyenne downriver at the same time. Say. Did you hear about that? Seems they're . . ."

"Frenchie," Carson drawled, "in the first place, this isn't the camps. And in the second place, this isn't no Indian. This is Cheyenne McCabe. Only, don't call him that, 'cause I've got a feeling he don't like it."

The men at the billiard table straightened and stared.

Frenchie hurried out from behind the bar with a bottle and two glasses. "I'm powerful sorry, Mr. Carson. Dreadful sorry, Mr. McCabe. I didn't know. And it being Mr. Bent's orders and all . . ."

"That's all right," McCabe soothed. he propped his Hawken against the wall while Carson filled the glasses.

Frenchie wiped his hands on his apron. "I'll be getting on back to the bar, Mr. Carson. Pleased to make your acquaintance, Mr. McCabe. I . . . well . . . I . . ." He ducked his head and scurried back to the bar.

"An awful lot of people seem to know my name," McCabe commented. He took a sip. It burned on the way down and exploded in his stomach. "Whew! I'll have to go slow with this. It seems strange—people knowing my name, I mean."

Carson laughed. "There've been a lot of tales the last few years about a white man living with the Cheyenne. To tell the truth, I'm not sure how much folks believed, but then a couple of months back some crazy Bible thumper showed up, and you became purely famous."

"Elkins," McCabe grimaced. "I was glad when I didn't see his wagon here. What did he say about me?"

"I believe you're right. his name was Elkins. Well, sir, according to him, you're either the devil himself, or his right-hand man. He told more tales about you than we'd heard from traders and the Indians in a year. Crazy stuff. He ranted on about gold mines, and claimed you had a bevy of girls as slaves."

"Lord! And people believed him?"

"Hardly a word of it. But according to that little wife of his, they really had seen you living with the Cheyenne. And alongside what he was telling, the tales we'd been hearing were downright mild. Some folks even began to believe some of the nonsense they'd heard about you. Hammersmith believes you regularly go hunting grizzly bears with a hunting knife."

"My God!" McCabe laughed. He briefly told Carson what had happened with the bear.

Carson nodded. "I figured it for something like that in the beginning. Don't try explaining it to Hammersmith, though. He'll likely figure you're just being modest. And if he did believe you, he'd be so disappointed he wouldn't be worth being around for days."

McCabe gave a wry laugh. "When Elkins left me, he was ranting about my Indian wife and calling me a murderer. I halfway expected to be arrested if he was still here. I surely never expected him to make me famous."

"Nobody believed that guff he was handing out, or leastways, nobody who counts. He was acting plumb crazy, buttonholing folks in the courtyard to preach to them, even grabbing hold of them right in the store. After he come up here and ranted and raved awhile about the evils of strong spirits, Mr. Bent said he couldn't preach inside the fort no more, so he started standing on the steps of his wagon by the gate, waving his Bible and shouting fire and brimstone at everybody going in or out."

"What happened to him? Did he go on back East?"

"No, McCabe, he didn't. It was the strangest thing I've ever seen. A lot of men passing through here started paying court to Mrs. Elkins. Not serious, mind you, but all the women around here are Mexican or Indian, and fat as you please. Being a white woman, she kind of stood out so a man wanted to talk to her, or just to sit in the same room with her. She started taking to all the attention, but her husband never even seemed to notice. Finally she up and run off down to Santa Fe with a Texas horse rancher. Elkins kept right on preaching like nothing had happened. A few days later some drifter came in claiming there was gold discovered around Taos. Damned foolest thing I ever heard, but Elkins' ears stood straight up."

"He was crazy for gold, all right," McCabe agreed.

"That he was. For two days he forgot all about preaching. He ran around asking everybody he could corner about that gold. Wouldn't believe anyone who said they never heard of gold around Taos. Finally climbed in his wagon one morning and took off down the same road his wife had taken with the Texan."

"Stone crazy," McCabe commented. "I could almost pity him."

"Out here, sometimes being crazy helps. He'll likely find gold before either you or me." Carson pushed back his chair with a regretful sigh. "McCabe, I'd like to talk to you some more, but I've got to see the blacksmith about my traps."

"It's been a pleasure to meet you," McCabe said, shaking the trapper's hand.

After Carson left, McCabe sat over his drink, which was still only smaller by one sip. Isobel had been dragged West by a husband she didn't love and had found what she wanted: a rich man who didn't care that she was already married. Henry Elkins had come to set the heathens' feet on the path to righteousness and had put his own on the path to a gold mine. And Carson, who seemed a good enough sort, was going to struggle through another winter at Brown's Hole trying to trap scarce beaver that nobody wanted to buy. It seemed that only the wicked and the foolish prospered in the West.

"Frenchie!" a harsh voice shouted. "Ain't you heard there's no liquor to be sold to Injuns?"

McCabe looked up to find a big, bearded man in a red hunting shirt and fringed moccasins glaring down at him.

"But Mr. Godine," Frenchie began.

"Ain't no buts," Godine snapped. "Come on, Injun. You're getting out of here."

McCabe snatched the whiskey bottle from the table as the man reached to grab him, and smashed it against the side of his head. Godine staggered back and fell, overturning a table. All around the room, men leaped to their feet.

Struggling to his feet, his face bleeding, Godine snaked out his knife with a snarl. "Injun, I'm going to . . ." He cut off at the sharp click of the hammer on a Paterson Colt.

"Godine," came a familiar voice from the far end of the room, "I'd just lay it there if I was you." Phillips Russell walked by without looking at either man and leaned on the bar. "Frenchie, how about letting me have about three fingers of the good whiskey. Not the rotgut you usually sell." He waited till he had his glass before speaking again. He still did not look at them. "If I was you, Godine, I'd think real hard about whether I really wanted to pull a knife on Cheyenne McCabe. Especially when he's got a gun in his hand."

"McCabe!" Godine spat. "He don't look so tough to me."

Russell shook his head gently. "Then you ain't looking right. He's the man sitting at the table with a gun, and you're the one bleeding on your shirt. Now, I'm hungry, and a killing is likely to spoil my dinner, so you take your time and try to figure it out before you get yourself killed."

Godine hefted the knife in his hand and shifted unsteadily on his feet, as if calculating his chances of reaching McCabe. McCabe never let the muzzle of the Colt waver from the big man's chest. Snarling, Godine jammed the knife back into its sheath and, with a last glare at McCabe, he stalked out.

McCabe eased the hammer down and set the pistol on the table close to his hand. "It's good to see you again, Russell."

Russell eyed the pistol as he sat across from McCabe. "Pilgrim, how did you and the Cheyenne ever get on with that corn?"

McCabe began laughing. "I ate it."

"It does thicken the soup up," Russell laughed. His laughter faded into a cough. "How are you getting on, McCabe?"

"Well, I have a wife now. Night Bird Woman, Elk Antler's daughter. And a son. It's a good life, Russell."

"Pilgrim, you ain't a pilgrim anymore. You've changed a lot."

"Not that much," McCabe insisted.

Russell snorted. "Three years ago, Godine would've had your liver for breakfast. Today I reckon you could grease his ears and swallow him whole."

"Maybe I'm a little tougher," McCabe admitted.

"A little tougher, hell! If Carson hadn't told me he left you up here, I'd have figured you for one fine figure of a Cheyenne warrior. And it ain't just the clothes. Speaking of which," he said with sudden interest, "does that bear-claw necklace come off that grizzly you killed?"

McCabe stuffed the necklace into his shirt. "It does."

"Figured as much. Heard about that from some Shoshone up in the Wind River country. When I left you downriver, that bear would've tore your meat house down."

"All right," he said grudgingly, "so I've changed. Any man changes in three years."

Russell nodded. "That's the thing about this land. It changes you, kills you, or it chases you back home with your tail between your legs. But whatever, you're not the same after. The old places don't fit anymore. They don't look right, or smell right, or feel right. And if you try to force yourself to stay, your feet start itching for the next hilltop, and your eyes ache for whatever's over the horizon." He caught himself and looked sheepish. "Hell, I do ramble on sometimes. Must be getting old."

"It has nothing to do with age," McCabe replied. "I can feel some of what you say too."

"Yes, well." Russell rubbed the side of his nose with one finger and peered at McCabe with one eye shut. "I hear the Cheyenne and the Comanche are coming together downriver to make peace. That the truth of it?"

"It's the truth. Them and the Kiowa and the Arapaho."

"I'll be damned. Never figured to see it. You reckon they'll keep it?"

"They'll keep it. I know High-backed Wolf, and I've met Little Mountain and Red Blanket. They all just realized there's no profit in killing each other off."

"Yes," Russell sighed. "I guess the whites will do that fast enough for them."

McCabe looked at him gravely. "What's that supposed to mean?"

"Country's changing, McCabe. And I don't mean just the end of the beaver. People are coming West. Farmers mainly, but where the farmers go, there have to be storekeepers and blacksmiths and schoolteachers."

"Russell, the sun's been getting to you. There aren't any farmers coming out here."

"Not here, no. They're going to Oregon, to all that good farmland that's up there free for the taking . . . if you forget about a few Indians who were there first."

"So some farmers are going to Oregon. That makes them the problem of the Indians out there, not the Cheyenne."

"That'd be true, McCabe, if they was all going by ship like they have in the past. But now I hear talk about them crossing the country in wagon caravans."

"Talk," McCabe snorted. "A bunch of farmers would be lost out here in two days, starved to death or killed by Indians in a week."

"May be just talk, but Tom Fitzpatrick has allowed as how he'll guide a party, if he can find one big enough to make it safely. He aims to take them up through South Pass. You're right about one thing, though. Some of them are going to get killed by Indians, sure as hell's hot."

"There are plenty of Cheyenne around South Pass," McCabe mused. "And Utes and Shoshone on the other side."

"That's what I'm talking about. A few trappers get killed, the rest just figure it's the Indians' country and they'd better be more careful next time. But them farmers ain't going to see it that way. Some Cheyenne or Shoshone will steal a horse, 'cause that's what he figures another fellow's horses are for, and some farmer will rush after him to get his horse back and get himself killed instead. Then the other farmers will start screaming that they're not safe like they was back in Ohio, and they'll yell for the Army, and those idiots in Washington will send soldiers."

McCabe was suddenly chilled by a memory. "I met some of them a couple of years back. An Army captain named—what was it—Early, that's it. He was mapping a wagon road, he said."

"I know about the Early party. Nearly starved to death trying to find a pass through the mountains. Didn't have enough sense to talk to the local trappers, even though they met a party or two. Had most of their horses run off. By Utes, I reckon. They finally made a couple of rafts, and them as were left floated down the Arkansas to right here."

"Do you remember a professor among them? A redheaded man names Chalmers?"

Russell shook his head. "Sorry, I don't rightly remember any of them except Early himself."

"No matter. Chalmers was no friend. You know, Early did tell me troops would be sent along to protect people using the road he was mapping. Damn! You really think the government will send them? I mean, hell, people in the territories can't even vote."

"But they have brothers and cousins back East who can. It may take ten years, or it may take twenty, but the soldiers will follow the emigrants. And once that happens, there'll be fighting with the Indians for sure."

"The Indians won't just be pushed aside. And man for man they're better fighters than any soldiers. If it comes to fighting, the Indians might win."

"Yes, sir," Russell said quietly, "you have changed a sight." He cleared his throat and shifted in his chair. "Now, then. You put whatever brains you got into using a little common sense. Man for man, you're right, the Indians are better fighters. But there's a hundred whites for every Indian. Look at what happened to the tribes back East, to those that fought and those that didn't. Seneca, Shawnee, Cherokee, Creek, Seminole, Choctaw,

Chickasaw. You want to travel downriver a spell and talk to the ones who lived long enough to be resettled?"

"Lord," McCabe muttered. "I was going to see that didn't happen to the Cheyenne. I was going to teach them agriculture, and how to build houses." He held up his arm and looked at the fringed and quilled sleeve. "I surely haven't done much, have I?"

"You've held on to your hair for three winters now. That's something right there. Hell, McCabe, if you'd walked on water, and got the Cheyenne living in houses and going to Sunday school, it still wouldn't change a thing. The Cherokee learned to live like whites. Some of the Creek bought slaves in Alabama and planted cotton. It didn't do them any good."

"But they had land people wanted. The Cheyenne have nothing for anyone to steal."

"You've lived with them awhile now, McCabe. You want to see them shut up inside walls to make imitation whites out of them? You want to take away the life they know, and love?"

"No," McCabe sighed.

"Then stop browbeating yourself. Hell, I could be wrong. There might never be any soldiers. The Cheyenne and the rest might keep on hunting buffalo for another couple of hundred years."

"Maybe you're right," McCabe said. But he could see that Russell didn't believe it any more than he did.

When he rode out of the fort, it was almost twilight, and the setting sun cast the flagpole's shadow eastward. He paused a moment to gaze downriver. This peace council had to be successful. Only then might the Cheyenne be able to find a way to deal with the whites. A way that wouldn't mean war.

A rifle cracked in the hills, and the iron gate above his head clanged with the bullet's impact. He dropped low in his saddle. He could see smoke dissipating on a hilltop five hundred yards away.

"You all right?" a man on the wall called.

"I see him!" the lookout in the watchtower shouted. "He's an Indian, a big man, riding hell-bent for creation. You down there. You need any help?"

"No," McCabe answered. "I'm all right. It's a personal matter." Three Hatchets, he thought. It couldn't be anyone else.

"Well, keep your personal shooting matters away from the fort," the lookout called down.

McCabe rode on without answering. He kept a careful eye out for spots where an ambush was likely. When he reached the Cheyenne camp, women were fetching wood from the trees along the river, and a group of young men raced horses outside the camp circle. Night Bird Woman was kneeling in front of their lodge, grinding corn with a stone mortar and pestle. Charles hung in his cradleboard not far from his mother.

"I have gifts for you, my wife," McCabe smiled as he dismounted. He opened the box of candy and set it before her, then spread the shawl around her shoulders.

She smiled as she fingered the embroidery of the shawl. "My husband is kind." She tasted a piece of the candy and immediately put it back in the box. "This must be saved for special occasions."

"I will buy more for special occasions. This is for you. I should have brought you beads as well. When I return to the fort, I will buy you pretty beads, and a comb made from the shell of the tortoise."

"You will make me vain, my husband," she laughed. "All I want is to have you near me."

He touched her cheek gently, but his face darkened. "Have you seen Three Hatchets come into the camp?"

"No, my husband. I have been busy working, except for a little play with Morning Eyes."

McCabe tickled his son's nose. The boy grinned. "I must speak with Otter Belt and Spotted Fox. I will return shortly."

His two friends were outside the camp watching the horse races. A boy on a spotted horse had just beat another on a roan.

Otter Belt grimaced. "He did not run as he should have," he cried. "How can I win a bet if the horse will not run as he should? Ho, Horse Runner. You have to come to watch the races?"

"I have come to talk to you and Spotted Fox," McCabe said. "Let us step to one side so our words will not be overheard."

Otter Belt gave him a puzzled look, but he followed along.

"There is trouble in your eyes," Spotted Fox noted. His face was sober and distant.

"As I left the fort, I was shot at. By Three Hatchets. I did not see him, but it could only have been him."

"This is indeed trouble, my friend," Spotted Fox declared. "Perhaps it is time to kill him before he kills you."

"I am not ready for murder yet," McCabe answered. "A worse thought has come to my mind. Think what would happen if, during the council, he were to shoot one of the Kiowa or Comanche chiefs."

"They would fall on us immediately," Spotted Fox gasped.

"It cannot be," Otter Belt protested. "Pledges have been given. he would not break the peace of the council."

"He has twice tried to murder me from ambush," McCabe replied. "Between me and the peace, I do not know which he hates worse. What would he not do to stop it?"

Otter Belt shook his head. "That he would murder, I know. But that he would break the peace of the council?"

"Yes," Spotted Fox said gravely. "He would do this thing. To commit murder or to break the peace of the council, what is the difference?"

"It is too bad he did not try to kill you inside the fort, Horse Runner," Otter Belt said.

"At least I would have had witnesses," McCabe sighed. "I could have accused him."

"I did not mean that," Otter Belt replied. "Five winters ago I was at the fort when a man of the Utes attacked a trapper with his knife. The man called William Bent said he could not come again to the fort, but many of his friends camped nearby to trade, and they asked that he not be sent away. William Bent asked what the greatest oath of the Utes was, and he said the man could remain only if he swore upon that oath that he would hurt no man while he was in the fort or near it."

"Spotted Fox," McCabe fretted, "do you really believe that an oath would stop Three Hatchets?"

Spotted Fox thought for a moment, then nodded. "He does not want to die, or he would not try to kill you from ambush. If he swears an oath by his life, he will not break it, for the spirits will know, even if no man does, and he will die. But how can he be made to swear the oath, Horse Runner?"

"Do you know someone who will tell something to Three Hatchets even if it is not true?" McCabe asked. "Someone that Three Hatchets will not be suspicious of?"

"Half Horse," Otter Belt concluded. "He likes to play jokes. But how will this help?"

"You will see," McCabe answered. "Ask Half Horse to tell Three Hatchets that there is a man at the fort named Godine, and that this man has heard stories of the great bravery of the warrior Three Hatchets and wants to give him whiskey."

"I will do it," Otter Belt assured him, "but I still do not see how it will help."

McCabe only smiled.

Early the next morning McCabe saw a rider gallop into the camp, a trader from the fort. He rode straight to High-backed Wolf's lodge. In a few minutes the chief and the trader came out together. The trader rode out again, but High-backed Wolf went to Raven's lodge. When the two of them came out together, the shaman carried a bundle wrapped in buckskin.

When they mounted to ride out, McCabe rode to meet them. "I saw the messenger, High-backed Wolf. Is there trouble?"

"There is trouble," the chief admitted. "Three Hatchets has fought with a man of the fort. William Bent has locked him in a room until we come."

"I met some of the men of the fort yesterday," McCabe told him. "Perhaps I can help."

"Come with us, then," High-backed Wolf said.

As they rode out of the camp, Raven pulled his horse closer to McCabe's. The old shaman cast an eye at the chief, riding in front of them, and spoke quietly. "I did not know that you cared for Three Hatchets."

"I do not," he replied.

"Why, then, do you come to help at the fort?"

"I want to see peace," McCabe said soberly.

Raven frowned, but he said no more.

At the fort the gates were still open, but now there were many men with guns on the walls and the towers. The first thing McCabe noticed when they rode in was that there were no Indians among the people crowding the courtyard.

William Bent strode out to meet them. "High-backed Wolf," he greeted, offering his hand. "I regret that you must come to me under these circumstances."

"I regret this too, William Bent." The chief dismounted, and one of the traders took his reins with a respectful bow. "How did this thing happen?"

"The man Three Hatchets came to the fort this morning," Bent explained, "and demanded whiskey of a man named Godine. Because there will soon be many former tribal enemies gathered here, I have ordered that no whiskey be sold."

"That is good," High-backed Wolf concurred. "It inflames young men and robs them of their sense."

"When Godine would not give him whiskey, Three Hatchets drew a knife and tried to stab him. I am afraid Godine was not very polite in his refusal, but I can't allow killings in my fort."

"I understand," High-backed Wolf nodded. "The man Godine. He is dead?"

Bent shook his head. "He suffered only a gash across his chest. Another man knocked Three Hatchets unconscious with a chair before he could do any more damage." He took a deep breath. "High-backed Wolf, I will accept your word that no other of your people will cause trouble, but I can't let Three Hatchets go free while he swears he will kill Godine and the man who knocked him out. And I can't post a man just to keep him out of the fort. Even if I could, there'd certainly be trouble if he tried to enter with friends and was stopped. For that reason, I cannot allow any of your people into the fort until Three Hatchets has sworn an oath that he will not raise a hand or use a weapon against any man in the vicinity of this fort except in defense of his life. I'm sorry."

There was dead silence in the courtyard. McCabe was aware of Raven's eyes studying him.

"I give my word for my people," High-backed Wolf declared. "No one will offer violence to the man Godine or to any other man of your fort. I know of the oaths you require, William Bent, and for this reason I have brought Raven. Bring Three Hatchets to this place." Bent signaled to a man, who then disappeared inside, and Raven, with his bundle, dismounted.

Everyone in the courtyard watched curiously as the shaman opened the buckskin. The first thing he removed was a buffalo skull. A black line had been painted from between its horns to its nose. Each eye socket was rimmed in red. On the right side of the skull was a large black dot, and on the left a red half-moon. Raven stuffed the nostrils and the eye sockets with green grass, then leaned four arrows against the skull. McCabe nodded to himself. The skull represented the medicine lodge; the arrows symbolized the four Sacred Arrows of the Cheyenne. This was to be the most powerful oath a Cheyenne could swear.

An excited murmur ran through the watching crowd as Three Hatchets was manhandled into the courtyard. He didn't see Raven and the skull, but when his eye fell on McCabe, he howled.

"He has done this to me! Mack Cabe has done this to me!"

High-backed Wolf looked at him contemptuously. "How has he done this to you?"

"I do not know, but he is my enemy, and I know he has caused this evil to befall me!"

"Do not blame on Horse Runner your own weakness for whiskey," High-backed Wolf commanded. "You have brought much trouble to our people. Now you must swear an oath." He gestured to the skull, and Three Hatchets' eyes went wide. "You must swear to neither raise your hand against any man, nor use a weapon against any man, so long as we camp here, except in defense of your life."

Three Hatchets' head swung like that of a bull looking for an escape. "Why must I swear? What have I done? I have only struck a man who cursed me."

"You must swear," High-backed Wolf said coldly. "If you do not, our people will be kept out of the fort like unworthy animals. You will be the cause of this shame on our people, and all will know of it. Who will hunt with you then, or give you food when your hunting is not good? Who will build his lodge next to yours? Who will even talk to you? Women and children will point at you and say, 'There is Three Hatchets, there is a man who caused our shame.' All people will know that it is Three Hatchets who has caused the shame of the Cheyenne."

"I have caused no shame!" Three Hatchets shouted. "I am a warrior! My enemy Mack Cabe has caused this thing."

"You will take the oath," the chief repeated.

Slowly, deliberately forcing himself to take each step, Three Hatchets made his way to the skull. Raven began chanting and shaking a gourd rattle. The big warrior sank to his knees, and his hands jerked as they touched the skull.

"Spiritual powers, listen to me," he said hoarsely. "I swear . . . I swear that I will harm no man of this fort . . ."

"Say it as I told you," High-backed Wolf ordered. "I will have no troubles among us during this peace council. I will not have you seeking revenge from Horse Runner because you wanted whiskey. Say the words I spoke."

Three Hatchets began to shake. His eyes locked malevolently on McCabe. "I swear that I will not raise my hand against any man." He stopped to swallow, then went on in a growl. "I swear that I will use no weapon against any man except in self-defense. These things I swear to be true so long as we camp here. If I lie, may I be shot far off." The breath rushed out of him, and he slumped where he was.

The crowd began to murmur. Bent stood forward again. "High-backed Wolf, I am sorry that this had to be done. I would have avoided it if I could have."

"I know that, William Bent," High-backed Wolf answered. Without looking at Three Hatchets he went on. "Three Hatchets may return to our camp when he wishes. I go now."

Three Hatchets was still slumped in the courtyard when McCabe rode out with the chief and Raven.

Raven motioned McCabe to let High-backed Wolf ride a little ahead, and when he did the shaman said, "Three Hatchets has always hated you. Now he hates you more than ever."

"You think that it was I who did this?" McCabe asked.
"My eyes are old," Raven retorted, "but they have seen many faces. No one else saw, but I did, when he accused you. Why did you do this thing?"

He does not hate only me, Raven. Now there will be nothing to disrupt the peace council."

The old man's mouth fell open, and slowly he nodded. "You are a strange man, Horse Runner. But perhaps a wise one."

McCabe rode forward at a gallop to join High-backed Wolf.

24

◇

"Aiee!" cried a boy in one of the tall cottonwoods. "I see dust to the south! They come!"

McCabe shaded his eyes. Far in the distance across the river, great plumes of dust stirred over the plains. For three days the Cheyenne had waited for the Kiowa and the Comanche. Earlier that morning scouts had been seen, lone riders cresting the ridges to the south. Now the main bodies were coming at last.

More boys scrambled into the tree to watch, and men began to gather on the riverbank. Three Hatchets sat his horse in front of his lodge, armed with bow, shield and lance.

"He waits for an attack," Spotted Fox noted.

"He may not be a fool," Otter Belt returned. He held his musket with elaborate casualness. More than one man in the camp did. Spotted Fox, though, carried only a knife at his belt.

"At least *you* do not seem to be worried," McCabe remarked.

"Today is not my day to die," Spotted Fox replied serenely. "I see you carry weapons, though, Horse Runner. Perhaps you are not as sure of this council as you say."

He touched the Colts in his belt. "Until I am sure how they come, I will be careful."

"Horses!" one of the boys cried. "I see many horses!"

"More horses than there are in the world!" another shouted.

And then horses began to spill over the hills and down into the far side of the river valley, thousands of them driven by boys and Mexican slaves, more than anyone in the Cheyenne camp had ever seen, all rolling into the valley in a milling mass of greys, blacks, tans and browns. The air came alive with the pounding of hooves and shrill neighs and the cries of the herders as the horses were brought to water. They lined the bank for miles as they crowded to drink.

"The boy was right," Otter Belt consented. "There are not so many horses in the whole world. I never dreamed to see such a herd."

"It is magnificent," McCabe agreed.

Young Comanche boys and slaves, captives taken on the many Comanche raids into Mexico, stared in wonder across the river at the Cheyenne as the horses were watered. Then, suddenly, they walked among the animals again, swinging their quirts and shouting. The herd swirled, then broke away from the river and back across the hills. A sigh went up in the Cheyenne camp.

Even as these horses went, a great mass of Indians appeared atop the far hills, warriors, women, children, pack horses, horses pulling travois. Now a human flood descended into the valley.

"They have all come," McCabe observed. "All six divisions of the Kiowa."

"And Comanche," Otter Belt added, pointing to some squat, bow-legged men with lances who clung to their mounts like monkeys. "I recognize at least two bands."

Night Bird Woman came out of the lodge with Charles on her back in his cradleboard. She squinted at the approaching Indians.

"Why do you carry Charles?" McCabe asked.

"If I must run," she said without taking her eyes off the spectacle across the river, "it is the easiest way to take him with me."

"You will not have to run, my wife."

As the Kiowa and Comanche reached the river, they immediately began making camp among the tall cottonwoods on their side. Kiowa women raised their teepees, and a few built brush arbors. Parties of them wandered along the banks searching for firewood. Others started up cooking fires. The men simply sat their horses, or squatted where they had dismounted, and stared across the river.

"Those women," Night Bird Woman said scornfully. "They have no order. See how they squabble to get places closest to the water, or in the best shade? Why do they not camp in a circle, as is proper?"

McCabe didn't answer, for High-backed Wolf had come out of his lodge, dressed in his finest. The tails of his war bonnet dragged on the ground, and his long coup stick was crowded with feathers. He vaulted into the saddle without touching his stirrups and trotted out of the camp. McCabe noted as he passed that he carried no weapon, not even a knife. The chief splashed across the river and into the other camp. Tension built among the people of the Cheyenne.

For a quarter of an hour there was no more sign of High-backed Wolf. When at last he appeared again, his horse was moving at a slow trot. Behind him came Little Mountain, wearing a necklace of silver dollars around his neck, and Sitting Bear, erect and slender, with his newly grown mustache drooping in the ancient Kiowa style. Behind them came the others, the rest of the Kiowa band chiefs and the Comanche chiefs. They rode across the river as had High-backed Wolf, resplendent in war bonnets and quilled shirts, and without weapons.

When they reached the special lodge in the middle of the Cheyenne circle, they dismounted and sat. High-backed Wolf lit a pipe and passed it. When Little Mountain took the first puff, some of the tension in the Cheyenne camp began to disappear.

Smells from the two camps permeated the air: boiling cooking pots, wood smoke, fat dropped on burning coals from broiling meat. Now that the chiefs were talking, men began to wander freely across the river from one camp to the other. Arrows, buffalo robes, horses, and tales were traded. Some braves began to play the wheel game, throwing hoops of stretched hide across the ground and then shooting at the rolling, bouncing targets with arrows. Courses were set up on both sides of the river, and soon the shouts of men urging on horses were heard.

For some reason, a young Cheyenne warrior wading into the river caught McCabe's eye. An Arapaho youth splashed out to join him. Both stopped as a young Comanche and a Kiowa entered the river from the other side. For a few minutes the men stared at each other without moving. Then, slowly, the Cheyenne took a step forward. With wary glances the Kiowa and the Comanche did the same. Abruptly they were face to face. Suddenly the Arapaho laughed and clasped the men from the other side of the river by the arm. Nodding and smiling, the Cheyenne did the same. Then the other two were also nodding and laughing. Behind them two dozen young men on horses galloped across the river to find a race.

McCabe felt a shiver go through him. "That was my vision," he murmured. "What I just saw in the river is what I saw in the Sun Dance."

"Of course," Spotted Fox said simply. He looked at McCabe in surprise. "Did you not believe your own vision? It was a true vision. Why is it strange that you should see it come to pass?"

McCabe only shook his head. He could think of nothing to say.

In the council lodge the chiefs talked for hours. Finally, as the shadows of the cottonwoods began to fall over the camp, Little Mountain walked out of the lodge and raised his voice. "My friends, tomorrow morning I invite each of you, even the women and the children, to cross over the river into our camp. Let all of you come afoot. All will return on horseback."

A pleased murmur ran through the camp as the visiting chiefs left.

"That is good," Otter Belt declared. "I thought that the horses we saw were the gifts they had promised, but I was not certain they had not forgotten."

"Listen to me!" Three Hatchets rode down the line of the camp circle, calling as he went. "Listen to me! This is the time of the trap! We are to go tomorrow, even the women and children! We are to sit in a long row in their camp! They will kill us there, my brothers! Listen to me!"

"He will not believe the truth," Spotted Fox grumbled, shaking his head.

"So long as he does not break his oath," McCabe replied, "I do not care what he believes."

From the far side of the camp came the rhythmic beating of drums. Chanting in deep voices, a few men began a dance, shuffling toward the center of the circle they formed, then moving back out again, turning to go around to the left, then back to the right. Women joined in, their chants coming at a higher pitch, and old men, their voices quavering, also began to chant. More people joined, and more, until almost everyone was dancing in a great circle that stretched all the way around the camp. Long after the only light remaining in the valley was the scattered glow of the cooking fires, the drums and the dancing continued, celebrating the peace that was to come.

In the morning, as the sun began to climb, the Cheyenne and Arapaho waded across the Arrowpoint.

"I do not like coming without weapons," Otter Belt complained, a pained expression on his face.

"You sound like Three Hatchets," Spotted Fox said.

McCabe looked for the big warrior. He couldn't see him anywhere, but that wasn't surprising. There were thousands of people crossing to the Kiowa camp, and the bands were mixed together. he kept a close eye on Night Bird Woman and young Charles.

"High-backed Wolf went among them unarmed," he asserted. "And their chiefs came into the camp circle unarmed and remained all day. What more do you need, Otter Belt?"

Otter Belt was still frowning, but he followed the others into the Kiowa camp with Looking Glass close behind.

The Cheyenne settled into long rows, waiting, men in front, women behind, and children farthest to the rear. The Kiowa and Comanche men appeared suddenly, bearing in their arms great bundles of sticks. They moved among the rows, handing the sticks out, sometimes giving more than one. With each stick the man would say. "This represents a horse. For each stick you may take a horse from the herd." Everyone, even the smallest child, was given at least one stick. A stick was even placed in each cradleboard so the infant's parents might claim the horse for it.

Sitting Bear, wearing the broad black elkskin sash that marked him as leader of the *Kaitsenki*, the Society of the Ten Bravest, walked before the rows of Cheyenne with as many sticks as his arms could carry. When he reached McCabe there were ten left. He stopped.

"You are Horse Runner," he said. "The man the Comanche call Man Alone, the man who rode into the camp of Red Blanket and talked with Little Mountain."

"I am Horse Runner," McCabe replied.

Sitting Bear handed him the remainder of his sticks. "You are a brave man, Horse Runner. We would have been good enemies. Now let us be good friends."

"We will be good friends," McCabe agreed, offering his hand.

Sitting Bear grasped it. Then, turning to a nearby bush, he broke off another armful of branches. He handed two to Otter Belt. "Each stick represents a horse. For each stick you may take a horse from the herd." He passed the new sticks on down the line.

When the sticks had all been handed out, the gift horses were driven into the camp and presented to their new owners. Among the horses Sitting Bear gave to McCabe were two stallions and a great bay gelding that he promised was a fine war horse. McCabe, in return, promised that this horse would never be used in war against the Kiowa or the Comanche.

As Cheyenne boys drove the horses back across the river, High-backed Wolf announced, "My friends, now it is time for us to give you gifts. Come across to our camp. Feast and receive our gifts. Do not be afraid if our people fire the guns before they are given. It is our custom."

The great mass of people waded back across the river to the Cheyenne camp. Women scurried to their cooking fires, and soon the huge kettles, filled with delicacies that had been traded for at the fort, were brought out: huge pots of cooked rice, kettles of stewed apples, and stews of fresh meat and bone marrow, thickened with cornmeal. There were even hard candy and sugar and molasses from New Orleans. It was a feast the likes of which had not been seen before by most of the Indians.

While everyone was still eating, High-backed Wolf called out again. "The gifts, my people. Bring out the gifts."

After a few moments of scurrying about, the Cheyenne produced great stacks of blankets, strings of beads, mirrors, bolts of calico, knives, axes. Despite the chief's warning, there were some startled shouts as men brought out their guns and fired them into the sky before handing them, still smoking, to their guests.

McCabe brought two brass kettles and three rifles. He wandered amidst the excited gathering, watching the Kiowa and Comanche fill with joy as their gifts piled up. He discharged a gun in the air, then handed it to a smiling Kiowa brave. He gave a kettle to a Comanche woman. The other kettle and a gun were also quickly disposed of, but he had a particular man in mind for the third rifle. He found Sitting Bear surrounded by a stack of blankets and piles of other gifts.

"Sitting Bear, I give this rifle to you. It is a new Hawken rifle, which I got at the fort. The Hawken rifle is the best in the world. It is the fittest rifle for the leader of the Ten Bravest."

The Kiowa war chief took the gun gravely. He ran his fingers over the brasswork. "It is a fine gun, Horse Runner. I will use it long, but never against the Cheyenne."

"I know that," McCabe replied. "We will keep this peace."

"Horse runner," the chief said, pointing into the distance, "who is that man? He did not cross the river to receive horses, and he has not come here to eat with us, or give us gifts."

McCabe looked to where Sitting Bear pointed. Three Hatchets sat his horse atop a low hill overlooking the village. Even at that distance, Mc-Cabe could make out the scowl on the man's face.

"He is a man who is left in the past," He answered. "He has no place here. Come, Sitting Bear. My woman has prepared a mush of fine corn-meal sweetened with molasses. We will not let this man spoil our enjoyment."

25

In the weeks after the peace council, High-backed Wolf's band moved north along the mountains, where they hunted buffalo so they could stock dried meat and robes for the winter. During those weeks, Three Hatchets became more and more belligerent toward McCabe. Finally, one day late in August, he rode up before McCabe's lodge and cried out, "Mack Cabe! White man! I go to find the spirit of your death. The white will never live with the Cheyenne. You must die, or we must, Mack Cabe!" And he galloped out of camp.

"I must go see High-backed Wolf," McCabe told Night Bird Woman the following morning. He tickled Charles' nose with a piece of straw as the child hung against the wall of the lodge in his cradleboard. The boy grinned at him, and he grinned back.

"Why must you go to see him?" Night Bird Woman asked.

"Do not worry," he replied. "I will return soon."

Three Hatchets' words had haunted him all night. Perhaps the man was right. Indians might never be able to live with white, so long as there were white armies with guns and artillery. Russell had thought so. But maybe there was a chance, if the Indians could only unite all their nations . . .

As he stepped out of the lodge, he saw Otter Belt and his hunting party ride in, but he didn't see Spotted Fox.

"Ho. Otter Belt. Where is Spotted Fox? Does he dally at some maiden's tepee?"

"Spotted Fox is dead," Otter Belt replied, his jaw set hard as granite.

McCabe felt as if he'd been struck. "Dead? How?"

"We found a camp of the Pawnee, Horse Runner. And Spotted Fox fulfilled his vision of the Sun Dance."

"His vision?" McCabe answered blankly.

"When he saw the Pawnee camp, Spotted Fox said, 'It is a good day to die.' He took each of us by the hand, and he gave us his possessions, all except his coup stick and the black hat he had traded for at Bent's Fort."

"Black hat? What black hat?"

"You were there," Otter Belt recalled. "The red-haired man showed it to you and the man Carson. Spotted Fox put the hat on his head, and singing his death song, he rode into the Pawnee camp. I myself saw him count ten coups before he died."

"And you just let him go?" McCabe exclaimed. "You let him ride alone into a Pawnee camp without weapons?"

Otter Belt nodded, frowning. "Yes, Horse Runner. It was his vision. How could I interfere?"

"Yes, my husband," Night Bird Woman said behind him. She stood in the entrance of the lodge and touched his shoulder comfortingly. "We will mourn our friend, but Spotted Fox had to fulfill the vision of the Sun Dance. A true vision cannot be avoided."

"I am sorry," McCabe murmured. "I am sorry, but I cannot accept the death of my friend so easily."

They stared after him worriedly as he hurried across the camp.

Something seemed to have gone out of him when he heard the news. Spotted Fox has been his friend, the very first Cheyenne he had seen, his teacher and companion. The thought that he had died because of a black hat and a dream made McCabe sick.

It took McCabe a long time to realize he was standing in front of High-backed Wolf's lodge. When he did, he shook himself. His friend was dead, but now he had to try to see that no more of his friends died senselessly.

"High-backed Wolf! I am Horse Runner! I need to speak with you!"

"Enter my lodge, Horse Runner."

He took a seat next to the chief but couldn't go straight to the subject he had planned to discuss. Instead he said, "Spotted Fox is dead."

"How did he die?" the chief asked.

"He rode into a camp of the Pawnee, alone and without weapons. It was senseless."

"I remember the vision he had in the Sun Dance," High-backed Wolf said. "But his death was not senseless, Horse Runner. It was his fate."

"That is what Otter Belt said. But that is not what I have come to talk to you about. Or perhaps it is, in a way. I want to talk to you about stopping the people of the Cheyenne from dying without a purpose. I want to suggest a way in which no more Cheyenne would die because they had to war with their neighbors."

"I do not understand your words, Horse Runner. They are without sense."

McCabe tried to slow the whirl in his head, the feeling of being dragged down, sucked under by spinning confusion. "The Cheyenne have made a peace with the Kiowa and the Comanche. These people will not kill each other anymore. That is good."

"Yes, Horse Runner, but I do not see what it has to do with what you say."

"What if there were no wars between the Cheyenne and anyone? What if the Cheyenne lived in peace with the Dakota and the Crow and the Blackfoot? Yes, and even the Pawnee. Let the Cheyenne make a peace with every tribe, as they have with the Kiowa and the Comanche. Soon there would be no war at all among the peoples of the plains."

"No war!" High-backed Wolf sounded shocked. "How would our young men test themselves and prove their courage?"

"Let them test themselves against buffalo, or wolves, or the great bears. But let us stop Indian from killing Indian."

"I do not know this word Indian. I am Cheyenne. Pawnee is Pawnee. Still, there is something in what you say," the chief mused. "I have heard thought of making a peace with the Dakota. They are powerful, and war with them would be bloody. Many men would die."

"That is what I have said. Let us stop the killing."

"You ask for very much, Horse Runner. We have just made a peace with the Kiowa and Comanche. Let us wait a little while before we make another."

"There may be no time for waiting. Peace must be made quickly."

"Why do you seek to hurry, Horse Runner? Why must this thing be done now?"

McCabe took a deep breath, and chose his words carefully. "There is a country called Oregon, where many of my people want to settle. To reach this country they must cross the lands of the Cheyenne and the Arapaho, the Shoshone, the Utes, and others. If there are many wars among these people, many raids, they will cause fear among the whites. My people will ask our chiefs in Washington to send soldiers to build forts to protect them. If there are no wars, the soldiers will not come."

"Why should your soldiers come to our land? And why should we worry if they do? Remember that I have seen your people's fort called Bent's Fort. The men there cause no trouble, and in that place are good things to trade."

"These forts will not be the same," McCabe insisted. "There will be many soldiers. If an Indian steals a horse from a white man, the soldiers will come to get it back. There will be trouble."

"If these soldiers of your people cause trouble" High-backed Wolf said, "we will fight them."

"That is what you must not do. If you fight them, many more will come. More soldiers than there were warriors of the Cheyenne and Kiowa together will come, and they will bring many guns. Big guns that shoot far off."

"If they come against us, we will fight them, Horse Runner."

"Would it not be better if they did not come? If there was peace, and the people who crossed the land were not afraid, the soldiers would not come."

"Perhaps," the chief replied slowly. "I must think on what you have said. Let us speak again some other time."

When McCabe left High-backed Wolf's lodge, the sky was dark. Cooking fires dotted the camp like fireflies, Suddenly there was a scream and a shot from the far end of the camp. McCabe began to walk faster as another shot sounded and men began to yell. Abruptly he realized the shooting and the cries were from the area of his lodge. He broke into a run, stumbling on rough ground in the dark, falling, scrambling to his feet without slowing.

Along the whole south end of the camp circle, men ran shooting and waving muskets and bows. Women screamed and wailed. McCabe threw himself at his lodge He froze in the entrance.

A long slash had been cut down the back of the tepee, toward the outside of the camp. Night Bird Woman lay dead by the fire in the center of the lodge. Her bloodied shinning knife was still clutched in her hand. A pool of blood had gathered beneath her head, which had almost been severed by a savage gash across her throat. Young Charles hung in his cradleboard, his skull split by the single blow of a tomahawk. McCabe herd someone screaming, and realized dimly that it was himself.

Otter Belt wrestled him back from the lodge. "Come away, my friend. Come away. You can do no good there now."

"Who?" McCabe breathed. He shook uncontrollably. Tell me who!"

"Crow," Otter Belt told him. "We have killed two of them we will kill the rest, Horse Runner. Everyone is after them."

McCabe stifled a whine deep in his throat and took a step toward the lodge against Otter Belt's pull.

Suddenly a Crow horseman appeared out of the night stopping short of the camp circle and casting his eyes about wildly for an escape route. From behind him in the night came the shouts and hoofbeats of pursuing Cheyenne. He turned to the left and galloped a few paces. The sound of horses came from that way also, and he turned back.

With a shriek McCabe tore free from Otter Belt. The Crow watched with a confused expression as McCabe rushed at him. He freed his toma-hawk and slowed to kill the lone man without gun or bow.

Just as he was nearing the Crow, he heard an arrow whir over his head. It drove right through the Crow's chest, and he tumbled from his horse onto the ground in a deep heap.

McCabe looked back, but could not find the Cheyenne who had launched the arrow at the warrior. Still frenzied with rage, he scrambled over to the dead Crow, clawing out his knife as he did. His anger drove everything else from him. With unnatural calmness he grasped the warrior's long hair and inserted the tip of his knife just above the left ear. McCabe smoothly completed the circular cut. He had to tug three times before the scalp came free. At last, though, he rose with the bloody trophy gripped in his hand.

McCabe stared at the mass of hair and blood in his fist and felt his gorge rising. Tears rolled down his face. With a shout he hurled the scalp into the night. "Night Bird Woman! Charles! Oh, God, Night Bird Woman!"

Otter Belt grabbed him by the shoulders. "Come my friend," he said quietly. "The rest have been taken. Come." He took the knife from McCabe's hand, cleaned it on the ground and returned it to its sheath.

McCabe let himself be pulled to the center of the camp circle, where four huge fires had been built to illuminate the crowd of men and women gathered around High-backed Wolf and the three Crow who were standing there, their hands bound. McCabe stared at them dully as Otter Belt pushed him to sit. People around him murmured sympathetically, but he didn't hear them.

"You will die," High-backed Wolf told the three men, "but first you may say why you have done this thing. If you do not want to say, you will die and no one will remember your names."

The three Crow looked at one another, and one with a crooked nose stepped forward. "I am Black Elk. I will say why we have done this so that our people may one day hear of it, and know how and why we died."

"Speak," the chief commanded.

"We came to kill the man called Horse Runner."

An angry mutter ran around the fires, but McCabe sat silent. He felt as if he were wrapped in cotton, as if all the words he heard came from the other end of a long tunnel.

"Speak," the chief ordered again. "Why have you done this thing?"

"Long have we known of Horse Runner," Black Elk continued. "It is our shame how he got his name, stealing Crow horses to buy the daughter of a Crow princess, the granddaughter of a Crow chief as his slave. Long has it been thought that any warriors who had the chance would kill this Horse Runner and gain much honor."

"The woman called Night Bird Woman," High-backed Wolf replied, "was bought as a bride. She was Horse Runner's wife. It was she you killed. She was a Cheyenne, not a Crow. Whoever has told you this story has lied to you."

The Crow seemed shaken, but went on. "He still deserved death for the stealing of our horses. And we have heard from his own people what he thinks of the Crow. He says that counting coup on a Crow warrior means no more than counting coup on a dog. He says that he defecates on the Crow, that he shows the Crow his naked rump-end." He said the last in a scandalized tone. It was one of the worst insults that could be offered to an Indian of the Plains.

"I have never heard him say these things," High-backed Wolf asserted. "How is it that you have heard these things?"

"Saying that we wanted to trade, we came to a village of the Arapaho near this place. We have been to many Arapaho villages searching for word of Horse Runner. There was a Cheyenne warrior in the village. He told us these things, taunting us with them. In his taunting he even told us exactly where Horse Runner's lodge would be in the camp circle, and that it was painted with black horses. He told us we were not men enough to kill Horse Runner, whom he called Mack Cabe. He said this Mack Cabe would cut off our manhoods."

"Three Hatchets!" McCabe screamed. He was shaking again, and couldn't stop. He is the only one who calls me Mack Cabe!"

"And he said he would go to the Arapaho village," Otter Belt exclaimed. I heard him say this yesterday."

"Three Hatchets!" High-backed Wolf called. "Stand out and speak against those who accuse you." People in the crowd looked at each other, but no one moved. "Three Hatchets, stand out!"

Slowly, arrogantly, Three Hatchets moved out of the crowd into the firelight. He ignored the chief and the Crow and stared at McCabe.

"That is the man," Black Elk declared. But Three Hatchets didn't take his eyes off McCabe.

"At last I know what the spirits have meant for me, Mack Cabe. You are the means of my death. When you first came, I thought you were just a white man. But my brother died because you inflamed his heart, and you took the woman I wanted. You gained honor that no white man should have. The council listened to your vision and not mine. But still I thought you were just a man. For a time I thought you would leave to go back to your own people. Then I would follow and kill you. But you remained. I tried to murder you. Twice I tried. My arrows would not hit their mark. My rifle would not shoot true. In some manner you tricked me into swearing the oath while we camped on the Arrowpoint, and I knew at last you were no ordinary man. I knew that I would never be able to kill you myself, for you had set the evil spirits that protect you to watch me. Then at the Arapaho camp I saw these Crow, and I heard how they looked for you to kill you. I rejoiced. Your evil spirits did not watch for the Crow, but only for me. Pretending to taunt them, I told them where our camp was, and how your lodge could be found, but your evil spirits must have been watching and listening, for once more you have escaped me. Now I know I will never kill you. I will never see you die, Mack Cabe, because you cannot die. You are a spirit yourself, and you have sealed my death. I have spoken."

"Now I will speak," High-backed Wolf began. "This man has acted with the Crow against us. He has aided the Crow to raid a camp of the Cheyenne. Does any man speak for him?" He paused, but there was only silence. Three Hatchets stood with his arms folded as if he did not care whether anyone spoke for him or not. "Very well. Three Hatchets is not of the Cheyenne. He is a traitor and enemy to his people. Let him suffer the same fate as the other Crow enemies. Let him die the slow death."

With a roar, the men of the band rushed onto the prisoners, seizing and stripping them. Three Hatchets was seized at the same time, and handled even more rougly. In minutes the four men were staked, spread-eagled and naked, on the ground.

McCabe still had not moved. He watched, as if the scene were something far off that was only of passing interest.

Dry twigs were piled on Black Elk's hand. A burning coal was dropped on them. As they burst into a flame, he wriggled his hand enough to knock most of the twigs away, but men with sticks scraped the burning pieces back into his hand. He did not cry out. Sweat beaded on his forehead.

McCabe frowned.

Around the foot of another man a small fire was started. Coals were piled on Three Hatchets' stomach. Someone held a torch to the greased hair of the third Crow. He grunted and shook his head wildly as it became a ball of flame, but he did not scream. The flame was doused before he could die. Splinters of wood were driven into the arms and legs of all the captives and set afire.

McCabe looked around at the people watching, at his friends. Otter Belt was laughing and lighting the splinters in Black Elk's thighs. Looking Glass cheered him on, shouting wildly, her eyes gleaming brightly. Even High-backed Wolf wore a small, satisfied smile. This was more than justice or revenge, McCabe knew. The Cheyenne were enjoying themselves. And what about him? He wanted to kill these Crow butcherers. Fiery rage burned in him at the thought. But then he looked at the fires built around the hands and feet of the men, smelled the burning flesh, and his blood-thirstiness seemed to evaporate within him.

From one of the big fires, Otter Belt grabbed a heavy brand that blazed at one end. Almost gently he laid it in Three Hatchets' crotch. A long breath heaved out of the man, and then a scream that shivered its way into McCabe's bones. Otter Belt took another brand and started for Black Elk.

Bolting upright from his place, McCabe dashed away from the fire. Another scream tore at his ears, and he doubled over to vomit. Desperately he ran on. He saw his lodge ahead, and the thought of what he would find inside started a growl in his throat. He veered and ran out onto the prairie. He wanted to keep running until he couldn't hear the screams anymore, but they followed him. They followed, and finally he dropped to the ground in a hollow, his knees curled against his chest, his hands clamped over his ears. But the screams kept knifing into him as he kept running in the bitter darkness of his own mind.

When McCabe finally realized the screams had stopped, it was late morning. He wasn't sure how long he had been there, only that he had been in blackness, and he had hidden there until the horrible screaming had ended. Stiffly he got to his feet and started back to the camp.

Halfway there he came upon a platform supported by four poles. He wanted more tears to come, but they wouldn't. Night Bird Woman lay up there, he knew, along with Charles, dressed in their finest garb, their bodies facing the sky so their spirits might easily reach the Hanging Road that led to the world of the spirits. He had missed their funeral rites, but somehow he couldn't find any more emotion inside himself.

"I am sorry," he called. "Night Bird Woman, I am sorry. I should not have gone. I should have waited."

Head down, he trudged back into the camp. Few people were out of their lodges. In the center of the camp a knot of boys poked with sticks at four burned and lifeless hulks. When they saw him, they stared. Two made a sign against evil and fled.

Without a word to anyone, he mounted the horse that was still tethered outside his lodge, the black war horse Sitting Bear had given him, and rode out to the herds. It took only a short time to rope a good pack animal and bring it back into the camp.

Inside the lodge he rummaged among his belongings. He found a pair of pants to replace the breechcloth and leggings, and a shirt, but there was no coat, and no boots, so he had to keep his heavy Cheyenne hunting shirt and his high-topped moccasins. He removed the coup feathers from his wolfskin hat, and put his pistols, knife and tomahawk through the scarlet sash he wrapped around his waist.

He then went quickly through the rest of his belongings, choosing what and what not to keep. A few pots, his books, a few shirts and another pair of pants, the journals in their leather case, and food were all that would go with him, along with some spare powder and shot, and the few furs he had left. In an hour he had everything loaded on the pack horse. He was just cradling his Hawken to mount when Raven appeared.

"So, Thomas Mack Cabe," the shaman said, "you will leave us."

With a sense of shock, McCabe realized that that was the first time in years that anyone of the tribe except Three Hatchets had failed to call him Horse Runner. "I'm going, Raven."

"Why?"

McCabe looked at the old man sharply. "My wife is dead. My child is dead. What is there for me to stay for? I am not a Cheyenne, Raven. I found that out yesterday. I am not a Cheyenne. I took no pleasure in the deaths of my enemies."

"Where will you go?"

"Back to my people," McCabe said slowly. He frowned. "Back to Washington or Boston."

"You think so, Thomas Mack Cabe? I will tell you something. No man can fight his gods. Three Hatchets' gods said he would be destroyed by you, and he was."

"I saw some boys this morning, Raven. Some of them made the sign against evil at me.

Raven sighed. "Boys. Some believe what they heard Three Hatchets say: that you are a spirit who can never die. They remember the great bear, and the fight at Wolf Creek, and they believe."

McCabe nodded and swung up onto his horse. "One third of my horses are yours, Raven. The rest of all my horses and possessions are to be divided between Otter Belt and Looking Glass. Perhaps one day I will see you again."

"A man cannot fight his gods," Raven repeated.

McCabe gathered up the pack horse's lead and rode out of the camp.

Four days after leaving the Cheyenne camp, a few miles south of the Platte River, McCabe came upon a cairn. Rocks were piled to a height of eight feet, and four buffalo skulls topped the whole. Here and there among the rocks he could see sacks and high-wrapped bundles, none too old. It was another post office, like the one Russell had shown him on the Arkansas. He was getting closer to civilization. In seven days he would be at Independence. From there he could take a steamboat down to St. Louis, another down the Mississippi, then a third up the Ohio until he reached the Cumberland Road, and the stage for Washington or Boston. The prospect left him feeling empty. What awaited him in Boston? His father's law office. A practice of his own. In Washington was the Office of Indian Affairs. There would be another assignment, another people he would learn to love, knowing that the government he represented would push them aside if it decided it wanted their land.

A plume of dust in the distance caught his eye. Fascinated, he watched as it resolved into six wagons, each pulled by four horses. Three of the wagons had a cow tied on behind. Men walked beside the wagons, guiding the teams with long lines. A dozen boys of various sizes walked alongside the wagons as well. On every driver's seat was a woman and two or three girls. Fifty yards from him the wagons halted. The man driving the lead wagon took off his hat long enough to wipe his brow, then called, "Pardon me. Are you an Indian, or a trapper?"

"Just a fellow passing through. Where do you think you're going?" McCabe asked.

"We're on our way to Oregon," the man said proudly. 'My name is Jepson and this . . ."

"You're on your way to hell, Jepson." McCabe grumbled.

Jepson blinked. The woman on his wagon, probably his wife, McCabe thought, covered the ears of the girls sitting with her. "I have perfect instructions, Mr.—ah, I didn't get your name."

"McCabe."

"Mr. McCabe I have perfect instructions, and a good map drawn by a trapper. All I have to do is follow this river. That will lead me almost into South Pass, which takes me across the Rocky Mountains, and from there it's downhill all the way to Oregon."

McCabe shook his head. "This river takes you through the country of the Cheyenne and the Arapaho, not to mention a few Crow wandering about. Besides, it's late in the year, Mr. Jepson. You spend too long trying to find South Pass, and you and the rest of these folks will freeze to death right in the middle of it. And if you do get to the other side, it surely is not all downhill. There's Shoshone and Utes waiting for you. And there's more mountains than you can shake a stick at. My advice to you is to go back to Independence. Winter there, then next spring hire yourself a guide. Maybe you'll make it."

"We can't turn back," Jepson insisted. He looked at the other men gathered around him. "We're farmers, Mr. McCabe, and we sold everything we have to make this trip. If we winter in Independence, we won't have the money to buy fresh supplies in the spring, and we won't have any money to stay on or turn back either."

"What about you?" a grizzled old man asked McCabe. "You surely look like you know this country."

"Talks like it too," a younger man put in.

Jepson looked up. "What about it, Mr. McCabe? Would you guide us to Oregon? We've got about a hundred dollars among us."

McCabe looked over all the eager faces, the hopeful men, the smiling women, the giggling children. They were going to have trouble for sure. If they didn't make it through Indian country, they might even be just the excuse the government needed to bring in the Army. If he could keep them alive, keep them from killing any Indians and keep the Indians from stealing too much of their stock . . .

He dug the journal out of his packs and tore a page from the back. Quickly he dipped a pen and wrote:

To whoever finds this,
The gold is for you. I would appreciate it if you saw that the contents
got to Mr. Charles Madden, Chief Clerk, Office of Indian Affairs, the
War Department, Washington, D.C.

> *Yours sincerely,*
> *Cheyenne McCabe*

The note and an ounce of gold went into the case, and the case was laid on the postal cairn. McCabe turned his horse to the west.

"We'll camp about an hour before dark," he said. "I know a spring where you can fill your canteens and water your horses."

Jepson and some of the others shouted their thanks to him as they whipped up their teams, but he didn't hear. His eyes were searching for the mountains that lay just over the far horizon.